CW00339562

Beneficial Effects

Beneficial Effects

Janet Kelly

A Bobaloo Books Original

Beneficial Effects

Published in 2020 by Bobaloo Books
www.bobaloobooks.co.uk

Printed and bound in Great Britain

ISBN: 978-1-8381510-0-3
E Book: ISBN 978-1-8381510-1-0

Dedicated to
Sylvia Lichfield

CHAPTER ONE

Pussy the parrot had been behaving particularly badly the day Buke came to talk to me about teaching at the Outreach Centre. It had already taken a little bit of explaining to the cleaning lady, Ada, that the parrot didn't really mean to call her a 'dirty whore' and that she was just a bird with some very bad habits.

The telephone thing had always been a bit more difficult to clarify and after weeks of trying to explain that a parrot can mimic most things, including the ring of a phone, I just left Ada to continue picking up the receiver, even though there was never anyone to talk to.

I thought she'd get fed up with it but even after fifteen calls she didn't believe it was another one of Pussy's 'tricks'.

'Whoever is making dem calls needs to git some manners,' she said on more than one occasion. 'They got summat to say den say it. Stop wastin' me time.'

Pussy usually made a belching noise when Ada got cross, followed by a lot of scratching around in the bottom of her cage, and she even copied the same muttering noise that Ada made in response to answering a call with no-one at the other end. It was a constant activity for the two of them, with neither giving in to the tedium. I couldn't help but find it quite amusing.

I'd been living with Darius for over a month and was getting restless. Not because of any desire to go back home but I needed to do something. He was increasingly busy at Forensix, particularly after all the publicity about our kidnap, and often working late or in other countries. It couldn't be helped and of course I understood that he needed to develop his career.

One of the disadvantages of having/being involved with a younger man is reliving ambitions and goals – all those things that consumed Colin before his "get up and go" took the last train to Inertia, never to return. Darius, quite rightly, was getting noticed for his skills at flushing out scammers, terrorists and the basically undesirable. It has to be said he played a rather magnificent part in rescuing Tracey and me after our particular adventure. In a country as rich with criminal activity as Nigeria, that means he was in constant demand. I couldn't help being very proud. I never felt quite the same about Colin whose job interested me about as much as watching a fly struggle to escape from a glass of wine.

Thankfully the advantages of being with such a vital man continue to constantly intrigue – and often surprise - me. Darius is a devoted and passionate partner whose interest in my needs, both physical and emotional, never seems to wane. He puts as much energy into our private life as he does to his business one. So, I certainly can't moan. Well, apart from those occasions when it can't be helped.

But there's no doubt that daytimes can be a tad boring. I do my best to entertain myself in the house but with little to buy in terms of food ingredients, coupled with the presence, and assistance, of a daily cleaner and a distinct lack of garden, television or bridge clubs, I often find myself struggling to get enthused about the general agenda of my day.

I was surprised at how much I missed programmes such as *Homes Under the Hammer* – a title that has an entirely different meaning in Africa to anything happening in leafy suburbia. I even thought about trying to get a satellite TV fitted so I could at least watch *The Chase* to keep up my general knowledge (and I do rather fancy that Bradley Walsh in a very basic and probably unsatisfactory sort of way). But I have been too embarrassed to admit to my desire for such basic entertainment. Darius still thinks very kindly of my mature intellect – I think it was something to do with knowing who wrote the book that was made into the film *Gone With The Wind* – and would like to keep it like that.

Tracey, my 'partner in crime' pops round every now and then but even that isn't always as beneficial as it might seem. As fond as I've become of her – it would be hard not to have a bond with someone you've shared open toilet facilities with on a regular basis — there's still only so much discussion I can have with her about make-up, shoes or what Baz likes to do with the end of a cricket bat and some coconut oil.

Buke's suggestion that I could get involved with one of her projects seemed the ideal solution and I was only too happy to have something useful to do.

'Wat we will av to do, is get dem girls sorted once and for all,' she told me, while trying to ignore Ada's feather duster as it flicked around the back of her chair.

Ada doesn't seem to like Lady Buke Osolase. She told me she found her 'unladylike' which is kind of ironic, I thought. Every time she visits, Ada makes her tea too strong — or whistles annoyingly while we try to speak. Buke ignores it mostly but will occasionally come out with a cutting remark – the sharpness of which is lost on my cleaner.

'Is it a wig?' Buke once asked of Ada, looking at her short, straightened bob while raising an eyebrow in my direction.

'No, it damn well is not!' said Ada as she huffed and puffed and followed her duster out into the hall, where the noise of a phone could be heard ringing – probably for the fifth time that day.

'Why you don't spik to me!' shouted Ada, to which Pussy responded: 'Aw shit. Wrong number,' and then cackled so loudly, Ada threw the bird's cover over the cage.

Buke made a face at her tea so I made a fresh pot, choosing to pick mint from the garden rather than risk the Nigerian brew that had a tendency to include surprise ingredients, such as spiders' legs, small beetles and twigs of indeterminate provenance. I'm sure I once found a toenail in the local market mix and have avoided it, as much as possible, ever since.

'Our girls need many, many things to help dem,' said Buke as she sipped the mint drink appreciatively.

She told me she wanted me to teach home skills such as cooking, home-management and basic financial facts.

'But isn't that putting stereotypes on these young women?' I asked, concerned that the next generation of women could be trapped into believing a life of domestic drudgery was their only choice. The whole process reminded me of my secondary modern education where, unless you were a maths genius or the daughter of the local business tycoon, it was likely you'd spend much of the later years of school learning how to make shepherd's pie and open a bank account – which according to the Suburban Surrey Mafia were the necessary skills for a successful marriage.

Strangely those activities used to be carried out separately – now everyone seems to 'multi-task' and do everything at once, which is why I found it quite ironic when one of my grand-daughters was chucked out of a lesson for using her mobile phone. She explained to the head teacher that she was 'Googling' some relevant information and seemed to get away with it. I doubt for the same reason she would have got away with it with me – i.e. for thinking that 'Googling' was a strange facial expression when staring at someone a little too long.

What the teacher probably didn't realise was that my grand-daughter was probably on some kind of 'app' to buy an unsuitably short skirt, or a ticket to a concert featuring a number of effeminate men wearing make-up and singing about sex. Never love, like The Beatles. Just very basic carnal instinct stuff that girls of fifteen-and-a-half seen to find immensely more interesting than the best method for fool proof mashed potato; and who can blame them?

'For many of da girls dis is their only chance of survival. Gitting dem to school and stay there is hard enough. Most don't stay beyond the age of twelve or thirteen,' she explained.

Buke showed me through a basic itinerary for the school, set up in the camp where Tracey and I were held by the kidnappers hoping to blackmail our families into handing over cash for our release. She explained that these young girls often have no education whatsoever. Even those showing particular promise can be trapped by the circumstances of their birth; poverty, lack of support and a continuing belief that women don't need schooling. I wanted to call up my grandchildren and tell them how lucky they were to be able to squander the education they can, so rightly, take for granted. But, as us older folk know only too well, youth is wasted on the young.

It is strange to think that only a few weeks ago Tracey and I weren't sure of our futures and we were reliant on the nature and also miscalculations of those keeping us hostage. Now the huts that served as our prison could be the place where many women could find their freedom. The irony didn't escape me.

Just as we were discussing the types of lessons I'd be scheduled to teach, Tracey barged through the front porch.

'Only me!' she shouted before throwing the door open and slamming it into Pussy's cage, waking her up and causing a stream of blasphemy.

'Shut yer mouth, yer foul-mouthed beast,' said Tracey to the parrot as she ran back outside to stub her cigarette out in a plant pot.

'Dirty bitch,' said Pussy, still under the cover of the cloth. 'Open the window, open the window.'

Tracey ran back in, clipping her high heels along the wooden floor of the hallway.

'That bird still ain't got no manners,' she said, slumping herself down in the only spare chair. 'Ooh, lovely,' she added, looking at the teapot.

She helped herself to a cup from a tray, not bothering with a saucer, and poured herself some of the mint tea. I knew what was coming from when we first had tea with Buke, when we only knew her as Lady Osolase.

'Ugh, what is it with Africans and their tea? It tastes like mouthwash,' and Tracey spat back what she'd sipped. 'You got anything else?'

I nodded to the cupboard and let her open my last packet of loose leaf tea from Waitrose, sent over by Mavis from the Bridge Club along with a tea towel featuring a variety of African violets and a box of stale Scottish Highland shortbread biscuits. The same ones I'd donated to the whist drive raffle over a year ago. She was nothing if not careful, my Mavis.

Sometimes I wondered where Tracey got the confidence to walk into other people's houses and feel so at home. I would always wait to be asked — which in Tracey's house is a mistake, because then you end up with nothing.

It's not that Tracey isn't generous. She'd give you her last false nail and leave herself without a full set; she just didn't come from the sort of background where everyone knew it was polite to offer someone a seat to sit on – and a drink. I've been to her house where I've stood for ages only to be reprimanded for 'cluttering the place up'. If only she knew I was also likely to wither to the floor and make even more of a mess thanks to my upbringing which would have a person collapse in a heap of dehydration rather than ask for even a cup of tea before it's offered.

'So, what's occurring?' said Tracey as she poured water from the just-boiled kettle into the cafetiere she'd liberated from the cupboard and filled with tea leaves. I knew she'd ask for a strainer at any moment.

'We is discussing da need to look after the girls in the Outreach Centre,' said Buke as she looked quizzically at Tracey's shoes. They were pink with high heels and a platform, with laces crossing over the top. Tracey leaned forward in them when she walked and little pockets of skin poked through the lacing.

'You got a strainer?' said Tracey, stirring round the leaves in the glass container of her make-shift teapot.

'You don't need one,' I said. 'It's a cafetiere. It has its own strainer.'

'Eh?' said Tracey, leaning forward further than her shoes really allowed, to have a look at the jug.

'Inside the lid,' I said, going over to help her. As I plunged the top into the tea infusion you'd think I'd discovered the meaning of life.

'That's bloody amazing!' said Tracey. 'Why aren't all teapots like this!'

Buke raised her eyebrows at me and I resisted the urge to be sarcastic. Tracey had her faults, and an incredibly bad taste in men, make-up and clothing, but had a heart of gold.

Tracey found herself another cup and some milk from the fridge. I wondered if she realised it was goat's milk and not the cow's version.

'Ugh, I can't get used to how the tea tastes here. It all tastes like... well, I won't say what it tastes like,' she carried on, sniffing a few times at her cup like a puppy might sniff at its own poo. 'Still, better than nothing.'

'Buke has asked me to help out with teaching at the centre,' I said to Tracey who was still screwing her nose up at her drink, simultaneously removing her shoes and rubbing her feet.

'That right, Cynth?'

I baulked at being called Cynth. It sounds so common, particularly coming from Tracey's mouth. But I've sort of got used to it. There were so many other things to worry about when you're stuck in a hut with a group of potentially murderous Africans waiting for a pay-out before they'll consider any kind of release.

'I wondered,' I said, looking questioningly at Buke, 'whether you might like to help me?'

Tracey was still rubbing the top of her feet where there were various lines etched from the tight lacing of her footwear when Buke nearly spat her tea out. She feigned a coughing fit, clutched at the table and rolled her eyes around until I thought they were going to fall out.

'Yeah, why not,' Tracey answered. 'Not sure what I'd be good at though.'

'Sex,' said Buke, having gained some composure and thought quickly about how she was going to deal with Tracey being part of a serious education establishment. I nearly choked on my own tea.

Tracey screeched with laughter.

'Well, you've got me there, Mum! Not sure it's what my mother-in-law should know about me though!'

'Sex education, it is very important to da girls. If dey get pregnant then their schooling stops and dey cannot progress. I'm sure you'll be very good at telling dem what they need to know.'

I could feel the colour rising in my cheeks as I imagined Tracey's initiation into teaching. I wasn't entirely sure that her take on the birds and the bees would exactly fit Buke's ideas on the subject.

'Don't look so worried, Cynthia. I'm sure dat Tracey will provide a very entertaining platform for da girls and they'll be intrigued by what she has to tell them.'

Buke looked at me with wide eyes as if challenging me not to say anything more. Perhaps she had a point. Tracey did have a way of making people listen to her. Sometimes it was intrigue, other times just pure fear.

'I'd better be going. I'll sort out da dates and an introduction session for you,' said Buke. 'I tink you will make a very good team.'

She turned to look at me with her eyebrows raised to acknowledge her lack of confidence in that last statement. She then flowed out and through the hallway, her billowy rainbow of colourful cloth following in her wake like a child keeping up with its mother.

Once she'd left, Ada reappeared in the kitchen with her duster.

'Upstairs done. What next Ms Cynthia?'

I suggested she clean the mirror in the hallway even though I'd done it myself that morning. It was hard thinking of jobs for her to do although without her around I'd have been busy doing them myself without any thought. I sometimes wondered why she didn't use her own initiative. It would be far easier on all of us.

'Have a good day,' said Pussy in a deep voice from underneath the covers on her cage. She was mimicking Darius. 'Ooh, that's lovely,' she added in a more throaty fashion that caused Tracey to look at me sideways.

'Don't say a thing,' I said to her, so she stuck her tongue in her cheek then smiled sarcastically. Ada busied herself noisily with the polishing and a rather untuneful African song about illicit love.

I regretted sometimes keeping Pussy in the bedroom and just hoped that she wouldn't drop some of the phrases she'd picked up; particularly the one about the banana.

CHAPTER TWO

'Intelligent Schooling Intervention Scheme,' I said. 'It's the name Tracey and I came up with for our programme. It involves bringing in teaching at the right time, to interrupt some of the accepted ways of behaviour.'

'Good name, innit?' said Tracey, puffing on an electronic cigarette – I got Darius to buy it for her last time he was out of the country. I hoped it would be our compromise on the matter of smoking in the house.

'We need to be careful how we put our views to these young girls who will be used to a certain way of life,' I said, sounding as knowledgeable as I could but recognising I was just repeating what I'd already been told.

Buke looked at the documents I'd created, now all spread over the kitchen table. There'd been hours of work and thought put in to how we were going to teach a lot of young African girls enough to give them some curiosity of the world, without presenting any unobtainable goals.

Tracey had 'helped' me through the process by making tea, cafetiere style, while talking me through her ideas for sex education. The 'Pin the Tail on the Celebrity' game we played while in captivity had reappeared as a potentially brilliant method of getting young girls to understand a little more about the male form.

It needed a bit of adjustment from Tracey's first, quite basic, thoughts but, I had to hand it to her, the woman has imagination. She'd devised a rather alluring full-sized cut out of Daniel Craig – the one when he was walking out of the sea as James Bond. It occurred to me that there would be little difficulty matching up Tracey's 'tail' with the position of Mr Craig's personal appendage. Even with his waist-high shorts, it wasn't exactly hidden and, despite my own recent experiences, was still something of an eye-catcher.

'Yes, I think that would work very well,' said Buke as she scanned through the headings and charts I'd put together with some careful advice from Darius. He was always sensitive to pointing out my inadequacies with technology, following the 'Dear Beneficiary' incident. Not that I'm embarrassed. If I hadn't fallen for that scam I would probably still be stuck in Surrey, re-arranging my underwear drawer and wondering how many geraniums is too many.

Buke raised an eyebrow at Tracey's 'model' but also looked amused and quietly impressed. I could tell by the way her eyes laughed but the rest of her didn't.

'You haf some very good ideas, well done,' said Buke, her top lip twitching. 'Everything is looking very professional.'

It was Chinaza – Darius's far too attractive colleague – who put the coloured bits in to all the documents and she'd also worked out some of the detail, using her own experiences of the African education system. She came from a totally different background to the girls we were going to meet but had some empathy with their situation.

'Don't under-estimate these young women,' she'd told me. 'They may be deprived of those things the Westerners take for granted but they have a lot of intuition. They absorb information even when it isn't presented to them formally.'

I wasn't quite sure what she meant by that but was very grateful for her assistance in putting together the material that Buke had asked of me. I did, at least, manage to work the printer by myself, something of a feat considering it took me over an hour to work out how to turn it on.

Darius, ever my supporter, had also given us some great ideas in terms of how we could integrate basic teaching of subjects such as domestic science with other, more academic, subjects such as geography. Although there would be other teachers responsible for a basic syllabus, he said he thought that Buke would appreciate us considering how our work would impact on the school as a whole. He made it sound like he willed my success which I could only think was a good thing. I hoped it meant he wanted me to stay.

'If you look at different foods you can show them where they come from, or where they are popular. Just think about the Irish and potatoes,' he said, laughing, one evening while I was at a loss for what more I could teach them about how to cook a chicken. I didn't think they'd be much interested in recipes for salmon mousse or learning the intricacies of boning a duck. He had a very good point.

Chinaza was proving to be something of an ally in the entire process of propelling me towards what would be my first career. I still felt slightly uncomfortable with her working in such close proximity to Darius and often amazed he didn't want to whisk her off and show her his special moves, rather than keep himself for me. Praise the Lord, I think to myself, with a sudden and (being an agnostic) quite irrational urge to go to church.

'Would you be able to start on Monday, do you think?'

There was a short silence and then Buke coughed.

'Cynthia!' shouts Tracey.

'Oh, sorry,' I said. I'd been distracted by Darius and the thought of his special moves, especially the one where he likes me to join him in the shower before he goes to work.

'Yes, Monday, of course,' I say, feeling myself blush a little and also wondering whether or not we'll have time for such activity with us both having to get to our jobs. He's more of a 'wash and go' person than I am. Maybe we'll just have to get up a bit earlier?

'Shall I bring Daniel with me, then?' says Tracey as she pulls a cigarette from a packet with her teeth and nods towards the cardboard cut-out of the James Bond film star.

I look at her – and to the cigarette — with what must have been an obvious warning.

'It's OK. I ain't gonna smoke it in here. I'll go outside,' said Tracey, throwing a contemptuous glance towards the electronic smoking device she'd demoted to the kitchen table.

'Those things just don't cut the mustard,' she added, and I sighed, knowing that the constant smoking habit would just interrupt our conversations. The nicotine is mightier than the sword, or in this case the vaping machine, so I might as well give in.

'It's OK. I'll open a window.'

Tracey is overcome by her addiction and so I am weakened by it too. If I don't allow her to smoke in the house, then I will have to spend my time going in and out of the garden every time she has a cigarette. She'd be out there during pestilence and plague rather than face the prospect of nicotine withdrawal.

The Intervention Scheme was taking on something of a shape of its own. The idea Darius had taken on of integrating other elements of teaching into the basics of domestic science had no bounds.

'What about music?' said Tracey. 'Kids love rap and stuff.'

I didn't know what she was talking about and couldn't help but revert to visions of the many but not so varied concerts I'd attended at the children's primary school. There was the one when Bobby was violently sick in the middle of a recorder recital. She hadn't taken the instrument out of her mouth, so the puke spurted out of all the holes, spraying the elderly music teacher who'd been accompanying the children on the piano. They were very nice about it, but Bobby wasn't asked to play the recorder, or any other instrument for that matter, again.

'Chiddy did his bit, didn't he, with his music and that. He was poor but he was passionate about his Chiddy Bang Bang.'

I recalled that his passion was significant enough to distract him from his job of keeping us under lock and key. It was Tracey's ability to engage him on the subject that helped lead to our eventual escape. I was suddenly grateful for 'rap' and all it could offer.

'I'll leave that to you then, it's more your sort of thing,' I said to Tracey as she started to sway her head and shoulders around in time to an imaginary song. I didn't like to think of what she was planning for these poor unsuspecting girls.

Once she came back from 'Planet Tracey', we looked at ways we could bring science into the cooking lessons. I did once go to the Fat Duck in Bray but got food poisoning, so couldn't vouch for the argument that Heston Blumenthal deserved his honorary degree in Chemistry. However, I recognised that we could discuss known facts such as boiling points, the basic taste elements, the types of food molecules and their use as energy.

I baulked immediately at Tracey's suggestion we could buy whole pigs and dissect them prior to cooking, as a biology lesson. She wasn't overly familiar with the traditions of some elements of the African community, many of whom might be Muslim.

'So why don't they eat pigs, then?' she asked when I explained. 'That means no bacon sandwiches. Ever. That's immoral.'

Her face took on a confused look as if she'd been asked to recite the first forty points of Pi, in Latin. After a moment it changed into one of recognition.

'Aha, but Baz eats bacon. So that can't be right.'

I explained that Baz and his mother Buke were Christians – as was Darius, although not practising in any particular manner.

'Around half the population in Nigeria is Muslim, and most of the rest will be Christian unless they practice some kind of local religion,' I explained. 'So, we need to be sensitive to the differences.'

I passed Tracey a pamphlet on the religion of Islam which she read with her jaw dropping lower with each word.

'There's a lot of bloody fasting with all of this. It's worse than the 5:2 diet,' she laughed as she continued to scan the paper. 'Praying five times a day? Good grief, no wonder they've no time to eat.'

She threw the pamphlet on the table in a gesture of dismissal. There was the sound of a car outside and I knew it would be Darius home, so I hoped Tracey would leave very soon. We might only have a few days to get everything ready for our 'first day at school' but I wanted him to myself. He'd been so busy recently we got little chance to catch up properly.

The latch went on the door, even though it was rarely closed, and I could hear the familiar sound of his size 12 feet on the hall floor. Pussy jumped up and down.

'Honey, I'm home,' screeched the parrot, a take on Darius when he used to use the expression in jest after I'd first moved in. It all seemed very surreal playing house and living together as a real couple, regardless of how naturally it came to both of us.

'Hi there Pussy,' I could hear Darius say in response. 'How's your day been?'

There was a purring kind of sound, then a scratch. 'Fine, thank you, very much indeed. Zirconium dioxide is relatively hard. Ding dong the dog's had its day. Not as hard as diamond. Eight point five, eight point five.'

Darius laughed as he walked into the dining room where I was pulling together all our papers and Tracey was stubbing out another of her 'fags'.

There was a sound of a burp, followed by 'sorry' from Pussy's cage. We all laughed. We'd employed the services of a bird trainer to help us re-educate her in the use of language. It was early days.

'The parrot is definitely getting better although I dread to think what the trainer is teaching her. At least she's not swearing quite so much'

'Bollocks,' said Pussy. She always liked to have the last laugh.

'Hello, Tracey,' Darius said as he leaned down to kiss the top of my head. 'How's things?'

'You know; same old, same old. Baz nowhere to be seen, Buke always busy.'

'You have your new career, though, Tracey,' he said as he nodded towards the school teaching paperwork. 'Rather exciting, don't you think?'

Tracey looked thoughtful and considered taking another cigarette out of her packet then looked at Darius and then me before thinking better of it.

'Yeah, I guess.'

Darius pulled up a seat, loosening his tie and the top button of his shirt. He sat with his large, powerful legs spread wide and I just wanted to take him upstairs there and then.

'You're worried. What about?' said Darius in his usual caring way. He'd an ability to drag people's thoughts from their head before they'd even processed them themselves. I know, he did it with me all the time.

'Well,' said Tracey before pausing. 'I never went to much lessons.'

'Many,' I corrected her.

'Wha?'

'Many. Never went to many lessons,' I repeated.

'Oh'. Tracey looked puzzled. Darius was smiling, as he often did with my concern for the correct use of English grammar – often arguing that as long as people communicated it didn't matter how they did it. It was something about which we agreed to differ.

'Anyway,' she carried on. 'My school was a bit crap. Lessons were boring, I didn't learn nothing.'

I restrained myself. I so wanted to tell her it was 'anything' and that she'd used a double negative, so implying she'd learned something. I didn't even look at Darius as I know he could read my mind and was teasing me telepathically for my pedantry.

'What if I'm no good and they all think I'm rubbish?'

Poor old Tracey, she gave out such an aura of complete confidence, yet underneath was a seething mass of insecurity. Ask her to face up to a kidnapper or steal a car to make a fast getaway and she'd be up for it as quick as you like. Give her something she thinks is in any way meant for a person with a different background to the one she's had, and she panics.

'I can't see any reason why they would think that,' I said, and Darius nodded.

'I agree,' he said. 'You've got lots of life experience that they can't ever possibly hope to achieve. They'll be fascinated by you.'

Darius winked in my direction as he spoke, knowing full well that Tracey would be something of a novelty to the group of African girls who had never so much as seen a white woman in the flesh before, let alone one with bleached hair, body piercings and shoes the size of small mountains.

She would be guaranteed to capture their attention from the very first minute.

CHAPTER THREE

It was opening day at the Outreach Centre and Buke was in her finest form, dressed as ever in the brightest colours and the most flowing fabrics. Her highly painted toenails were occasionally visible beneath her floor length gowns, as she walked along the corridors of what was our old prison. They peeked out daringly from the confines of her leather sandals, like the first purple crocuses of spring, giving a clue as to what might be hidden beneath.

It was peculiar walking around the centre, with our old prison completely renovated and refurbished with desks, chalkboard and motivational posters, ready to receive the first students rather than prisoners. Our old cell had been turned into a library which gave it an entirely different atmosphere to when we were locked up. Even 'The Art of Statistics' looked invitingly readable.

'And here we have the central classroom which can seat up to twenty of our students at one time,' Buke said to a group of delegates who were following her round with looks of strained interest. I couldn't help wondering if some of the older, male, contingent were as excited about the prospect of girl's education as Buke was. Political correctness was great PR but I wasn't convinced it was entirely engrained.

I knew that one of them, Toyin Remy, was a politician of some kind and also the major benefactor. He'd donated most of the funds to get the centre off the ground but Buke had said she thought it was a publicity stunt exercise, designed to make him look like the good guy. There'd been some rumours about shady smuggling deals he needed to clear up and the general consensus was that he was hoping the rumours would go away following the handing over of a hefty community donation. Mr Remy's face barely changed as Buke enthused about silver linings out of clouds, and turning around the camp that had been a site for kidnap and crime.

'From what was a place of terror for the women we see here, we now have a sanctuary for growth and positive development,' she said while Mr Remy checked his mobile phone. He didn't look like a man whose dream of liberating young African women had come true. From what I knew about African politics I thought it was highly likely it wasn't just the community that gained from his ill-gotten gains. There would be a few misdemeanours swept under the carpet once sufficient funds had been passed over to the relevant recipients.

Tracey and I cast a glance of comradeship at each other. The room that had been transformed into the main teaching area was where our captors had threatened our lives; held us up to ransom for whatever our families could sell to ensure our release. It was where we'd been forced to tape messages to send back as proof of our incarceration – a sombre moment, despite the positives that had come from our experience.

'So, what's it like being back in your prison?' asked one reporter, who decided to hold back from Buke's tour which was heading towards the kitchen and toilet block. 'Does it bring back bad memories?'

Tracey laughed sarcastically.

'No, of course not mate. We had a riot didn't we, Cynth... Cynthia? Like a bloody holiday it was.'

She pursed her lips, cocking her head to one side in a warning to the young man from the African department of CNN to watch his words. He took heed and scuttled off to follow Buke who was now heading towards the canal area, where a garden and allotment had been designed so students could learn to grow their own vegetables.

The old oil drums and shambolic shower facilities had been removed and replaced with timber fences, proper toilet blocks and a large kitchen area complete with fridges and cookers, all run by electricity provided by an industrial generator rather than the dodgy contraptions our kidnappers had put together. Apart from a general hum of the water moving along the canal and a smell that took me right back to that unfortunate time, it seemed like a different place to the one that saw us held hostage.

Darius came up from behind a group of people and gently patted my bum while he thought no-one was looking. I jumped, even though it was a regular occurrence.

'Oi, you two, get a room!' said Tracey, ever the eagle-eye who'd witnessed the not-so-subtle expression of affection. Darius laughed.

'You could have our old room, ' laughed Tracey, pointing over to where the shack that housed us for what seemed years while we read our way through old copies of *OK* and *Hello* magazines. We passed the time in any way we could in the constant hope we would hear of our imminent release. As the days dragged without good news, plotting our escape became something of a major occupation. Looking back, we were both rather resourceful all things considered.

The new library was small but had seating for up to six students at a time, access to computers and a fair number of books. Nothing like we'd have at home for anything that called itself a library but, by local standards, it was luxurious. Not only that, there was intermittent internet connection and so what was lacking in physical books could be complemented with knowledge from the World Wide Web. I only hoped the girls would take good care of their internet activities. I knew from personal experience that everything isn't always as reliable as you might think it would be when it comes to online research.

Fourteen girls had been chosen to take part in the first term of school. Some of them walked for over ten miles to get to the centre, equipped with little other than a bag to carry small items of clothing – in case they didn't get home again that night – and some bread or fruit expected to sustain them throughout the entire day. Others came from slightly better circumstances but had been accepted because of some kind of family trauma. We'd been told one girl had lost her brothers and father at war, and her education was the only hope for her mother and younger sisters to be able to survive.

I thought back to the days of my children going to school. I'd be up the night before until all hours making small cakes (without raisins because Bobbie told the others they were rabbit poo and they believed her until well into secondary school), creating interesting sandwich fillings and hoping that the flavours of crisps and drinks I'd chosen were acceptable. That was all before taking them to school myself, wishing them all a good day, prior to heading home to prepare their nutritiously sound, if somewhat predictable, supper — and possibly an evening of enhanced homework supervision followed by a perfectly calculated bedtime in clean sheets, complete with hospital corners.

I wonder how Bobbie would have reacted if told she'd have to walk for three hours to get to school with very little to eat and then walk the same distance back, probably in the dark and with little prospect of an evening meal, let alone a choice of TV channels to slob in front of beforehand?

I can imagine the response, and it involved an inventory of my faults, a catalogue of complaints and a number of words not encouraged for use in polite company.

The girls at the Outreach Centre were of various ages, sizes and levels of competence and were waiting cheerfully in a classroom with a teacher and a doctor, despite having very little idea of what they were to expect in their new surroundings. All were due to be enrolled but only after a doctor's report confirmed they were fit to be in a school environment.

'What do you mean? Some of them could have AIDS?' Tracey asked when we were advised about the levels of care we'd need to take in any kind of medical emergency.

She had displayed the anxiety I was doing my best to avert.

'Many children in Nigeria have been born with HIV,' explained the doctor, who added that in only a very few cases this may develop into AIDS.

'Treatment is so much better than it was, and diagnosis is no longer a death sentence,' he added, as he drew a needle back from beneath the skin of one of the student's slender arms. She was the last in the queue – the others all seated with large, proud, plasters where their blood had already been harvested. The last girl, small and frail looking, faced the procedure full on and showed no fear. Apart from HIV, the girls were being tested for a range of problems that would be associated with malnutrition – such as anaemia.

Tracey drew in a deep breath on the sight of blood filling up a test tube. 'Ooh, don't take any more, she might need it poor thing,' she said, turning away and covering her eyes with her hands.

The girl being tested looked directly at Tracey and as predicted by Darius, seemed to find her fascinating. She said nothing but watched all the time with a piercing glare from deep within the pearly whites of her dark eyes. Tracey looked back at her and was clearly unnerved, particularly when met with a beaming, broad smile.

'Wow. Look at your teeth. They're so white!' commented Tracey.

'Like your hair, Miss,' said the girl quietly, pulling down the sleeve on her shirt to cover up the evidence of her bloodletting.

Tracey pulled at a strand of her bleach-blonde hair and looked confused. She was protesting that her hair wasn't white, but golden oatmeal (as that's what it said on the packet) but her voice was drowned out when Buke made her grand entrance into the classroom, followed by the delegates. I noted Mr Remy wasn't with them so he'd either made his excuses and left – or managed to sneak off when she wasn't looking.

All the girls stood up and remained silent. I couldn't imagine that happening in any of the schools my lot went to and I was struck by the sense of respect. In Surrey schools there was a general sense of middle class entitlement, from the parents as much as anyone. I have to admit to a few occasions of being overly forceful with my questions as to the abilities of the teachers to recognise the varied talent of my offspring. It took me a while to recognise they were middling to average and not, therefore, likely to require any special treatment or attention.

It was no wonder there was a general disinterest in teaching where we lived in the UK. Most people would prefer to join the prison service on hard duties.

'Hello, girls,' said Buke and immediately they all stood to attention and responded with 'Hello, Lady Osolase' in perfect synchronicity. They stood bolt upright, their hands by their sides and anyone could be forgiven for thinking they'd completed a full round of military training.

Buke introduced everyone around her including the Head Teacher, a marvellous young South African man called Tony. Enthusiastic to the point of exhaustion, he was on a gap year from a Christian organisation called the 'Right Hand Brothers' which Tracey said sounded like a group of teenagers who couldn't get laid.

He'd brought his own books, footballs and a supply of pencils, pens and notebooks donated by the members of his local church – along with fifteen packets of Kendal Mint Cake which one parishioner had told him would keep him from starvation, should he find regular food supplies to be rare.

Rumour had it an older man from Tony's village stole some of the mint cake, only to result in terrible toothache of such voracity the new teacher was considered to be some kind of witch and immediately respected by all the villagers. His belongings were protected from that day by a ring of terror and full knowledge that 'Mr Tony' could impart punishment of the kind usually reserved for the most revered gods. By all accounts he found his new status rather refreshing, given the less than mediocre levels of popularity he'd experienced at school and university. For some reason, which may marginally have had something to do with his selection of Dr Who T-shirts and a life-long fascination with Play Doh, he was mainly considered something of a twerp. It was all rather refreshing and gave him a glow of extreme satisfaction which he tried very hard not to attribute to his own abilities.

My friends from the Bridge Club had offered to put together a parcel of 'goodies', as Mavis liked to call it, for my new position. I stalled them as I wasn't sure what we could end up with. We never found out what happened to the knitted Elvis dolls that had been sent to a Sri Lankan children's home after the Tsunami.

And unless you were a particular fan of the breed, a patchwork English Bull Terrier – made from recycled dusters — would have limited use at the best of destinations. I said I'd be in touch if there were any desperate requirements and suggested that maybe a fundraising event would be preferable. Mavis is always happy with a fundraiser – a great opportunity for her to organise a bit of a do in a church hall and make cupcakes in the shape of penguins.

Things moved on a little – some of the important delegates continued to listen to Buke as she described her vision for the Outreach Centre while the rest of us chatted in groups of two or three, in the hope that lunch would be served before the small talk ran out.

Tony organised a game with the girls, which I suspect came from a training manual about getting people to talk to each other. They all individually had to tell the others something about themselves they didn't think anyone would guess.

'I have six toes,' said one girl who told the group her name was Omolade, but was happy to be called Mo.

'I can sing the alphabet backwards,' said a larger girl called Esther who had to be stopped at 'W' on account of the fact her version of singing didn't quite match the universally accepted description of the activity.

Colin, may he rest in peace, once told me he'd played a similar game at a management teambuilding event. A very bossy woman had barked that he should have found something more interesting to tell the rest of the team other than he'd only ever worn white underpants.

Desperate to be more dynamic he then told his colleagues, falsely, that he'd run two marathons in bare feet. They were so impressed they cajoled him into running a third in aid of a favoured charity. He managed to find a way to wear training shoes for the event but unfortunately couldn't get out of actually taking part.

'I'm not cut out for this,' he'd tell me, having barely managed two laps around the village green. Being of the 'short and fat' variety of male he wasn't genetically suited for the long runs he was supposed to do and often took himself to the park where he'd sit and watch the other joggers rather than notch up some miles himself.

On the day the trainers, which he managed to convince everyone he needed on account of a badly placed corn, weren't any kind of comfort and nor did they protect his toenails, all of which fell out only seven miles in. He stopped at a St John Ambulance post for plasters but had to wait for over twenty minutes while paramedics dealt with a woman who was running with a cardboard cat on her head. It had cut through her ear and there was some debate about whether it would need to be stitched back on – the ear, not the cat.

Colin finally got the plasters he needed before limping the rest of the way, coming to the finish line very much crestfallen and well after it had been packed up and everyone, including his colleagues, had gone home. He never really recovered – physically or emotionally. What he found particularly damaging was that he was narrowly beaten by a 99-year-old man dressed as a Sherbet Dip.

Tony continued with the 'Getting to Know You' style games which worked well with the group, all of whom wanted to impart yet another glimpse of information about themselves. Friendships were made before our eyes and it was rather heart-warming to see camaraderie develop so quickly.

The positivity continued as within an hour the girls were given the all clear in terms of their health and formally admitted to the Outreach Centre as students.

I couldn't help but breathe a little easier. It was nerve-wracking enough to know I could so readily be in the firing line for their innocent criticism, without also being in the firing line for whatever transmittable diseases they might have.

CHAPTER FOUR

It came as a bit of a shock to hear that Gowon and Chiddy had been released. As guards they had been gentle with us and very easily influenced by our feminine charms. So much so they slipped up to the point they were blamed by their bosses for our escape which can't have been good for them. Their bosses were hardly working hard towards a life of integrity. On that basis I did think they might not have as fond memories of us as we'd like to believe – feminine charms or not.

'They gave us all a lot of information about the main perpetrators of your kidnap,' said Chinaza as she sat at our kitchen table. 'That secured them both very short prison sentences and the promise of support getting new work when released.'

I was glad Tracey wasn't around. She would be bound to say something about the guards who had watched over us during our captivity – and what we did in order to gain their trust. I'd sketched over the details with Darius, referring only to the fact we played games with them to get them on side. He didn't need to know the games were of an overtly sexual nature, and he never asked.

'There is some talk of getting them to help at the Outreach Centre,' she added, crossing her legs over in her tight dress and showing the shine of her smooth legs. She reminded me of a baby giraffe I once saw at Chessington Zoo. All limbs, lips and eyelashes. I looked at Darius to make sure she'd had no obvious effect on him. Thankfully he was opening some wine and not looking in her direction.

'How do you mean?' I asked, suddenly realising the implications of what Chinaza had just said.

'I'd heard that, too,' said Darius. 'Something about using their local knowledge and practical skills so they can give back to the community rather than spend more time in prison.'

I wanted to gulp but my throat was stuck. I took a swig of wine and could barely swallow it and started coughing like an old man with a 40-a-day roll-up habit.

'You OK, Cynthia?' asked Darius as he rubbed my back. 'You've gone a bit pale.'

'Yes, fine,' I squeaked. 'I'm still not used to this African wine.'

'It isn't African,' said Chinaza. 'My father brought it back from France.'

Darius was standing behind her when she made the statement, which had clearly defined her status as a rich girl among the poverty stricken. Not only did her family buy French wine instead of the local varieties but they sent her to the best English schools money could buy, so that she would know the difference. He made a face as if to say, 'you see what I mean?' because he was always trying to tell me there was nothing he found attractive about the woman who seemed to have everything. Coming from the background he did, which was hardworking and successful but not privileged, he preferred people who were a little more down to earth.

There was a sound of the telephone ringing.

'Is that real, or that bloody bird?' said Chinaza.

'That bloody bird,' Pussy shrieked from the hallway, at the same time as the ring continued.

'I think that answers our question,' said Darius as he went to answer the call.

I watched his back as he made his way out of the kitchen. His pale pink shirt was gently stuck to his sweat, from where he'd been leaning against a chair. I could see his broad shoulders, slim waist and pertly formed buttocks clothed in perfectly fitting suit trousers. If there was going to be a black James Bond, it should be him, I thought.

I imagined him finding out the truth about my little dalliance with Gowon. In hindsight the whole escapade was designed to win over the people who were holding us hostage. Gowon and Chiddy were our main guards and were easy to impress, thanks to their youth and lack of experience with the opposite sex. I told myself our actions, particularly mine, were a necessary part of the getaway plan. I imagined having to confess to Darius and had already put in place a victim mentality, one where I felt the only weapon I had was my femininity. The more I thought about the imaginary conversation, the more I was sure that he would understand. However, I'd really rather he didn't find out.

'I have a slight problem with the name of your programme,' said Chinaza when Darius was out of the room.

'Oh,' I said, thinking that if she hadn't been so helpful with all the school lesson planning and her colour coded systems for just about everything then I would just like to punch her in the face. She had a way of being overly assertive, while smiling in what she probably thought was a very charming manner. 'Why is that?'

'I might be being a bit paranoid, but think of the initials,' she said, gently sipping a small amount of her father's wine – brought as a gift to accompany the meal she shared with us. 'I.S.I.S' she spelled out. 'Isis. Did you realise it spells out Isis?'

I thought about it for a moment while she swilled her drink delicately around her mouth and I could only come up with Isis being the name of the Egyptian Goddess of Magic and Life. I knew it because Lord Crawley called his dog Isis in *Downton Abbey*. It was all very ironic when the poor mutt died and created a wave of British sorrow – which was neither magical nor lively.

'I think it's very appropriate,' I replied haughtily. 'What could be better than to offer life and magic to young women in an otherwise impoverished world?'

Chinaza looked at me with a sideways glance and remained silent for a moment. She suddenly laughed.

'You nearly had me there, Cynthia,' she said as she swilled some more wine around in her mouth while smiling in what I could almost think was a generally good-humoured manner.

'I'm not one to criticise anyone's ideals, I promise you,' she said with that 'I've done a management course, so I am trained to be patient' smile. 'But we live in an unstable environment and maybe advertising your allegiance to such a strong image might not be the best way of integrating into this society.'

Again, she'd made me feel small while coming across as a good mate who was passing me some very valuable information. Unfortunately, I didn't know what the woman had against *Downton Abbey*. The programmes I had chosen to watch in the past, when my life was very different, were entirely my business and were unlikely to have any impact on what Nigerian people would think of me. It was quite clear to me that she hadn't seen the series or the film, otherwise she would understand that Maggie Smith and the powerful women in her family would be a marvellously strong image to align with.

'That's hardly an issue for a small school in the middle of nowhere, for students who mostly won't have ever seen a television let alone watched it for any length of time, or even heard of a cinema, ' I said, rather annoyed that I had to justify myself to a woman at least thirty years my junior. She might be clever, but what did she know about children, teenagers and how to motivate them?

'OK,' said Chinaza after another pause. 'Maybe you have a point about the lack of exposure to the media. It does keep people away from much of what is going on. I just thought I would make an observation. But please be careful with everything you do. We might have caught most of the bad boys involved in your kidnap but there are still a lot of other nasty people about, many of them see women and westerners easy prey.'

There was a piercing scream from the hallway and a loud bang.

'Stop, thief. Stop, thief,' shouted Pussy.

'Oh, do be quiet,' said Darius as he walked back into the kitchen, holding a very crumpled envelope in his hand.

'That was Tracey,' he said, as he looked at the yellowing document. 'She wanted to know where she could buy hairdressing equipment.'

'Dear me,' I replied. 'What does she want that for?'

'I didn't ask,' said Darius. 'But she told me anyway. Apparently, she is going to set up some beauty classes for the girls at the centre.'

'Good luck with that,' laughed Chinaza, flicking her expertly straightened locks behind her bare shoulder. This time Darius *was* looking at her and my heart sank a little bit.

He leaned over and I could feel panic rising until he picked out a small feather that had attached itself to the top of Chinaza's head.

'One of Pussy's, I believe,' he said as he threw it into the sink behind him. 'I think she's moulting. Talking of which...'

He spread the envelope out on the table. It crumbled and left some dusty remnants on the table as he spread it out. On the front I could just make out my name, in very faint lettering.

'What on earth is that?' I asked him.

'It came out of Pussy's cage. She's been scratching underneath the floor for a couple of days. I thought she seemed aggravated so had a look to see what the problem was. She actually passed this to me with her beak. It was as if she was trying to tell me something'

'Clever bird isn't she?' I said, picking up the envelope and opening it.

'Thank you,' said Chinaza, pretending I was talking about her and laughing at her own joke. Darius was going to politely join in until I glared at him and they both stopped. I pulled out the piece of paper from the envelope, which had been folded many times and creased badly.

'It looks like some kind of official document,' said Darius peering at it first with squinted eyes and then through my reading glasses, which he borrowed automatically these days. His age was starting to catch up with mine, I was pleased to notice.

'I can barely read any of it,' he said.

I looked and even with my retrieved glasses couldn't make out much other than something about 'extraction' and 'agents'. It made no sense. Chinaza's more youthful eyes were no better.

'I'll take this into work and see if I can get one of the forensics team to sharpen the wording,' said Darius.

'I wonder what it is?' asked Chinaza. 'It could be something very exciting.'

'I doubt it. I was left Pussy by a man called Bill from Brighton.

He lent us a car when we escaped. He didn't seem very interesting,' I said. 'His wife left him for a younger man and he never really got over it,' I added, remembering the rotund stomach of a man who came to his premature death on a diet of saturated fat and a life time of unsatisfied dreams and ambitions. The most motivated I could imagine him getting was over the possibility of an All-Day Breakfast at a service café. He had been very nice to me, however, and for that I would always hold his memory dear.

'Worth having a look as you never know what secrets there are that can make one man more exciting than another,' added Darius while he licked his top lip with the tip of his tongue. I still don't think he realises what that does to me.

'Sorry we haven't any coffee,' I said, gulping what was left of my wine and picking up Chinaza's half full glass on the way to the sink.

'I haven't quite finished...'

'It's been so lovely seeing you and thanks so much for all your help, but I've a lot to do to get ready for Monday so I hope you don't mind if we call it an evening now,' I said.

Chinaza was from good stock and wouldn't dream of over-extending her welcome. Tracey, on the other hand, would have known exactly what was going on and made some lewd comment about what I wanted to get up to with my 'toy boy' as she liked to call Darius.

But then Tracey knew me far too well.

CHAPTER FIVE

Tracey and I both made our separate ways to our first day at the centre by local bus. Darius had suggested getting me a car, but I thought it might be better to live as the locals do. I already stuck out like a ham sandwich at a Jewish wedding and didn't want to alienate myself further by looking like I didn't want to join in with the local customs – and transport systems.

It was an interesting journey for both of us as we found out in our later discussion. I sat next to a woman carrying a boxful of chickens that repeatedly pecked into my arm which was nothing to Tracey's ordeal. She'd had a small child placed on her lap while its mother dealt with some goats' cheese that was leaking from a shopping bag. The child had been sick, and Tracey had managed to point it into the direction of a young man who got the full force of it in his lap.

'Kept moaning like it was my fault,' she said, adding that he'd followed her off the bus and she was worried he was going to insist she did his washing. 'Mind you, it stinks to high heaven that goats' stuff — like a cat has pissed in yer sandwich.'

That didn't seem as sinister as it might have been, as the man with sick in his lap had apparently tried to start up a civil conversation so I suspected Tracey had, yet again, just attracted some local attention.

I wasn't so sure my journey was quite as innocent, particularly as I was followed by a white man wearing sunglasses, a pinstripe suit and a very large hat. Every time I stopped to look at him, he'd turn to a window or pretend to be doing up his shoelaces so I never got a look at his face. I half wanted to laugh as it was like something out of those very old silent movies and I expected him to slam into a lamp post at any moment or slide along the road with a banana stuck to his undersole but, inside I was more than a little frightened.

I lost him as I turned into the centre's entrance and when I made a final check he was nowhere to be seen. There was something quite familiar about him but maybe I was being paranoid. We had just been kidnapped and kept hostage, after all.

Tracey had got to the classroom before me and was in discussion with the head teacher, who looked about as qualified for the job as a cat was qualified to nurse mice.

'It's about self-esteem, innit?' I heard Tracey explaining to Tony whose usual enthusiasm had diminished as he watched her set out various items for her 'Hair and Beauty' class.

'I'm not sure I recall this element of the curriculum,' he said, looking around at the boxes of hair grips, shampoos, bleach and perming lotion. 'I thought it was going to be a health lesson.'

'Healthy mind, healthy everything else,' said Tracey as she wrapped her own hair into a twist and pinned it up with two grips she'd had, until that point, in the corner of her mouth. 'I could give you a bit of a going over,' she added as she picked up Tony's fringe and dropped it back down into his eyes.

Tony looked suitably defeated and made a hasty exit from the classroom, calling the students who were lined up outside to come in. Mo's fascination with Tracey hadn't subsided and she made a beeline for the chair in front of her, keen to be in prime position to observe. It was like watching a child at a zoo.

I busied myself at the back of the classroom. As the designated Head of Subject, I was expected to supervise Tracey who was officially titled my Classroom Assistant, but this was her area of expertise. My only understanding of anything to do with hairdressing was the occasional trim or, if it was a very special occasion, a semi-permanent rinse. I once had a demi-wave, back in the sixties, but looked like I was wearing an old cauliflower on my head so never risked it again.

'Sit down where you like,' said Tracey, puffing with pride in her new role. She seemed surprisingly comfortable in the setting, considering her initial concerns about her lack of academic understanding. She caught me looking at her and blushed, so I knew to look away before her confidence started to ebb. It was a very fragile thing that could dissipate at the drop of a hat, or the slightest judgemental remark.

I turned away from Tracey's eye line to concentrate on looking through some planners for my own lesson, which would be next. It didn't matter how hard I tried, I just couldn't think of ways of integrating home-made pastry with the development of early civilisation. It wasn't as easy as anyone might think.

'So, who knows anything about hairdressing?' said Tracey. The girls were mostly staring back at her with their mouths open, star-struck by the woman with curly blonde hair with dark brown roots.

After a moment Mo put up her hand.

'My mum uses that stuff to straighten her hair. It stinks,' she said, nodding to the perming lotion.

I always thought perming solutions made curls, but apparently I was wrong. Tracey was full of information about what you could and couldn't do with the different products she'd purchased for the class. It did concern me about the interest they expressed in bleaching out their colour so they could dye their hair in a variety of different shades. I didn't see how we could justify that bit of education to the funders of the Outreach project. But there was no doubt it had caught the girls' imagination.

Soon they were a bubble of energy, telling stories of their own mothers' desires for straight, black hair – having mostly all been cursed with the thick curls often associated with the African race. I thought of our cleaner, Ada, and her quest for the same. I thought of the hours of work she would put in so she could afford her monthly hairdressing bill. I could see no other way she would be able to keep the sleek look she seemed to see as a badge of sophisticated beauty.

'It's worth every bit of the cost,' Ada would say. 'It's important to look your best,' she'd add, as she'd potter round the house looking as busy as possible. I often wondered if she feared losing any of her jobs in case it would mean cutting down on those hair appointments. I wondered how she would have coped with any kind of lockdown or solitary confinement. She'd literally be tearing her hair out.

'Well,' said Tracey, triumphantly. 'I'm going to teach you all how to do it yourselves so you can help your mothers, and yourselves, when you want to either straighten – or curl – anyone's hair.'

She undid her mop of curls and invited a volunteer to start the process. The response was overwhelmingly exciting for the students and although I doubted Tracey's understanding of the education system I could see she was a natural motivator. Everyone wanted to have a go at transforming their teacher's hair, much to her absolute delight.

I left her to it, surrounded by a babble of young Nigerian girls who'd most likely never even seen shampoo, let alone all the chemicals Tracey had managed to obtain through whatever methods — methods I didn't like to consider. They were pecking around her tresses, each owning a section for themselves, and willingly taking instruction on what to do next.

The day passed remarkably well. My Home Economics class was buoyed by the enthusiasm of the girls' previous lesson which seemed to have involved a variety of procedures, all demonstrated on Tracey – despite the fact she'd managed to purchase a practice head from a wholesaler. She packed up to go home with her hair wrapped in a towel immediately after she'd finished, while the model's was as untouched as the day it was made. She tucked it under her arm to take home and from a distance looked like she had a girl in a headlock.

'I've got to go and wash this bleedin' stuff off,' she said. 'Me head's been itching for the last twenty minutes. Anyone would think I've got fleas or summat,' she added as she gathered up her bag, adjusted the grip on her plastic model and dashed from the room. 'Seeya later.'

The pastry wasn't as edible as I might have liked. Despite reminders of thorough washing, the girls' hands smelled of bleach and perming solution which permeated through even when cooked. I also noticed a few stray hairs neatly embodied into the cases. I made a note not to eat any of the food the girls had made.

In terms of bringing in the concept of civilisation I informed the class that, of course, different elements must come together before a human community reaches a level of sophistication that is considered civilised.

'The first is the existence of settlements classifiable as towns or cities. This requires food production to be efficient enough for a large minority of the community to be engaged in more specialised activities — such as building or developing a government,' I told them, reading from an extract from Wikipedia.

'Everyone gotta eat,' said Esther who, of a size similar to that of my garden shed, probably knew a thing or two about that concept. I wasn't quite sure how she had managed to avoid the levels of under-feeding that everyone else in the room seemed afflicted by. Maybe there was something in the concept of being 'large boned' after all.

'Yeah but white people eat shite,' said another girl. 'They are all killing themselves with sugar and dat. We might not eat much, but we eat good.'

She had a point and I immediately felt very stupid, teaching them to mix up white processed flour with fat to make a food product. I was thinking of the cost but hadn't given much thought to using local supplies which were more likely to be unrefined and whole meal. That's what comes of a lifetime where all meals cooked from scratch start in a Waitrose.

'OK,' I said. 'I would like you all to think of what grows in Nigeria and what meals you can make. Perhaps we can share ideas so we can see the best way of providing for a family within a set budget.'

'We haf no budget,' said Mo. 'There's no money in our house, only what we might get selling my mother's paintings.'

I remembered what I'd been told about Mo's background and again felt pulled up by my own assumptions. Her family, what was left of it, would live hand to mouth and often on charity. No index-linked, government-guaranteed final salary pension for them.

'Your mother is an artist?' I asked Mo, suddenly aware of what she'd said. 'And she sells her paintings? That is marvellous.'

'She is very good. But not many people can afford the luxury of art, Miss,' said Mo.

'I would love very much to see one of her pictures, if you wouldn't mind bringing one in?'

Mo looked embarrassed and hung her head.

'I'll ask her. She doesn't do as many as she used to,' she said. I was intrigued to know why her mother had been stalled in her talent but felt the story behind any explanation might be a little difficult to handle. We went on with the lesson and the girls took part enthusiastically throughout, despite one making an effigy of her brother out of some of the pastry and sticking forks into its eyes. I couldn't help wonder what impact that might have, in a country full of wizardry and ancient rituals.

'Let's all clear up and get ready for the end of the class,' I said, feeling chastened by my first day with these remarkable young people. Whatever was going on in their homes they'd shown enthusiasm, interest and a passion for learning.

The door opened and Tony walked in carrying a tray loaded with plastic beakers and piles of biscuits.

'I thought we deserved a bit of a snack to finish off the day,' he said, almost dancing his way to the table at the front of the room that served as a desk. 'Oat Crunchies and chocolate milk – my favourite,' he added as he placed the tray down.

The girls clambered round him and helped themselves hungrily to what was on offer, stopping every now and then with their hands covering open mouths to say 'thank you' to the head teacher and ensure he understood their appreciation.

'I just wanted to quickly warn you,' he said. 'It might be something and nothing, but we've had a couple of unusual calls asking for details about you. Obviously, I didn't reveal anything but please keep an eye out for anything suspicious.'

Tony struck me as the kind of person who would think finding your teaspoons in the wrong drawer was suspicious, so I didn't take too much notice.

'There's bound to be interest in what we are doing. Probably someone hoping to sell something to the school and thinking I'll be a soft touch,' I said.

'Yes, you're right. Let's not worry about it and I'll make sure no-one comes here who shouldn't,' said Tony, looking around the room for Tracey. 'Where's your assistant?'

'She went after her lesson.' I said, shaking a hand at the offer of a biscuit. They looked like they might be something of a challenge to the bridge work on my teeth.

'So, how did that go?' he asked with a slightly worried look. 'Did the girls get anything out of it?'

'I think they got quite a few strands of Tracey's hair and some rather peculiar ideas of what they might be able to do to earn a living,' I said, trying not to sound too sarcastic.

Tony laughed and leaned against the table, only to quickly bounce back when Darius came unexpectedly through the door. I couldn't help feeling a rise of pride when the girls all turned to look – with many of them failing to hide a certain level of admiration.

'Don't mind me,' said Darius as he saw Tony's discomfort at his presence. 'I've just come to see Cynthia.'

'What is it?' I asked. 'Why aren't you at work?'

My heart rate started racing as it was unlike him to leave his office unless there was an emergency. I pictured each of my children, individually, in different accident scenarios before I could see there was no sense of concern on Darius' face.

'Don't panic. I've got some rather good news, I think.'

Tony picked up the empty beakers and plates and placed them on the tray before making his way to the door.

'Come on girls, I'm sure you've all got homes to go to,' he said, quickly realising that many of them probably didn't. Not ones they were keen to get back to, anyway. 'Um, school is finished anyway,' he added as he ushered them all out to their chants of disappointment. Their first day seemed to have been something of a success.

'I'll see you tomorrow, Mrs Hartworth,' he said and then nodded towards Darius. 'It's nice to see you again.'

'Don't rush on my behalf,' said Darius. 'This could affect you, too.'

Tony held back, balancing the tray with one hand and not

sure whether to close the door or keep it open. He looked like one of those mime acts you get on foreign beaches where they spray themselves gold and stay still for hours on end. If you stare at them long enough they start to wobble.

'Spill the beans, then. You're getting me worried now.' I told Darius. 'What's going on?'

Darius clicked on his mobile phone and held it to his ear.

'OK, you can come in now,' he said into it and within a few seconds my grandson, Tom, walked in through the door, knocking Tony off balance and bringing the contents of his tray crashing to the floor.

'Sorry, sorry, sorry,' said Tony, as he rushed around trying to tidy up without tripping over the beakers as they rolled about around his feet.

'My fault, mate,' said Tom. 'I didn't see you there.'

I could barely take Tom in and didn't recognise him as my grandson as he was totally out of context. I knew he was extremely familiar but for a moment I couldn't think where from.

That happened to me once with Lionel Blair. He was in a queue for coffee at Gatwick airport, just in front of me. He was so familiar I thought he was from the Bridge Club and had asked if he still preferred Rubber these days. He completely ignored me which, at the time, I thought was a bit rude.

When I got back to Colin, who'd witnessed but not heard the exchange, he just said *'Give Us A Clue'*. I said I didn't know what he was talking about and so the conversation went on with me getting increasingly irritated until I realised he was referring to Lionel's status as the host of the game show of that name.

I was mortified by my mistake and even more embarrassed by my comment when I realised how it might have sounded. I didn't tell Colin what I had said and have spent many a moment since telling myself that Mr Blair had been in my living room many times, albeit via a TV screen, so no wonder I thought he was a friend. It's not my fault he didn't know who the hell I was.

'Hiya, Cynth!' said Tom, lopping towards me like an over-watered Gladioli. He'd grown all stringy and gangly since I'd last seen him.

'What are you doing here?' was all I could think of saying. 'How did you get here?'

'I didn't walk, if that's what you mean. I've come to do some work.'

I looked at Darius and then at Tom. They were both grinning like Cheshire cats that had found the cream and decided to keep it for later.

'Stop teasing me,' I said. 'Tell me what is going on.'

'Give us a hug,' said Tom, which was unusual as only a few months ago he barely spoke unless he was offered cake and certainly didn't entertain any bodily associations. He walked over and enveloped me with his long, tentacle-like arms. It was only in such close proximity I realised he must now be at least a foot taller than me.

'Right, you two, let's get you back and settled,' said Darius. 'Tony, this is Tom – Cynthia's grandson.'

Tony was still on the floor picking up fragments of Oat Crunchies and trying to capture an out of control beaker that rolled away the minute he got anywhere near it. He nodded awkwardly at Tom while shuffling along on his knees in pursuit of the errant drinking vessel. He nodded back, exchanging the soundless communication only certain people seem to manage. Usually those who live in villages in Lincolnshire.

'Dude,' said Tom, after a suitably 'cool' pause. Tony wasn't really sure what to say back, so he just stuttered for a bit and tried to maintain equilibrium with his now reclaimed tray and beakers, without much success.

'Tom has turned out to be a bit of a whizz with some of the stuff we investigate at Forensix, so I finally got the all clear to invite him out on a gap year,' said Darius.

I must have looked aghast because all three of them looked at me and frowned.

'I thought you'd be pleased to see me,' said Tom with a mock-hurt tone. 'I've come all this way, too.'

'Of course I'm pleased to see you, silly. I'm just a bit surprised,' I said, wondering how this had been set up and what Bobby thought about it all.

'What does your mother think about you coming out here? I bet she wasn't too pleased?' I asked.

'A lot happier than she was when she found out you had a Nigerian toy boy.'

My breathing stopped for a moment and my vision went slightly hazy.

So much for me thinking it was a secret.

CHAPTER SIX

'Why on earth are you wearing that headscarf?' I asked Tracey who'd come into the classroom wearing what resembled a tablecloth. 'Have you got toothache?'

'Baz gave it to me.'

'Really?' I said, concerned that Tracey's husband was trying to turn her into a submissive wife. To my knowledge he wasn't a Muslim but I wouldn't put it past him to pretend he was, in a bid to exert some control - something he'd so far not managed in his short marriage.

'Don't look like that, Cynth,' she said as she pulled the material from around her neck and then de-mummified herself by unwinding it fully to reveal her head.

'Oh my goodness,' I said. I couldn't help but sound shocked. Apart from a few wiry sprouts of stray hairs, Tracey was bald.

'What on earth has happened?'

'That bloody perming solution,' she said. 'I forgot to tell the girls to neutralize it, so all me hair has broken off. Baz is furious. He said I looked like a boiled egg with a face on it and told me to cover myself up before I was shot by hunters.'

She was taking the loss of her crowning glory with incredible pragmatism, I thought. Tracey was the sort of woman who grieved over the loss of an eyelash, so to see her like this - and taking it all in her stride - didn't compute.

'I suppose you could wear the scarf until it grows back,' I said, probably unhelpfully.

'Nah, I'm gonna get a wig. Always fancied being a red head,' said Tracey as she wrapped her scarf back round her head. I had to admire her attitude - very much the stiff upper lip.

'I suppose you won't be doing any hairdressing classes today, then?' I asked.

'On account of the fact I don't have any hair, that is unlikely,' Tracey said as she laughed. 'So I think we'll move on to facials and make-up.'

A noisy clatter from outside suggested Tony was about. He couldn't move around the place quietly like you might expect a head teacher to do, because he would find something to bump into, or drop. He almost fell into our room.

'Morning ladies,' he said as he came in clutching a pile of notebooks and pencils. 'I've brought these to give out to the girls.'

He looked at Tracey and did a good impression of a goldfish as he moved his mouth up and down.

'Oh. Hello. Sorry, I didn't realise...'

'Didn't realise what?' said Tracey.

'Um, your position,' he said nodding to the headscarf.

'Oh, don't you worry about that,' she replied. 'No drama, it will all be forgotten in a few months.'

I could see the two of them were at cross purposes but didn't feel inclined to explain anything to anyone, not least the fact that if there was anyone least likely to adopt the Islamic faith then it would be Tracey. Tony was a very obvious Christian, complete with a fish badge and very white teeth. I suspected many of his trousers would be slightly worn at the knees from a lifetime of genuflecting in the hope of divine exemption from all things shitty.

Although he had said on a number of occasions that he was tolerant of all religions, he clearly felt uncomfortable with Tracey's attire, assuming it to represent far more than a cover-up for a hairdressing mistake.

'Well, let's hope so,' said Tony, sliding the books and pencils onto the desk at the front of the room. 'Be good if we could all live in peace.'

'Yeah,' said Tracey, frowning behind his back. 'Give peace a chance, eh?'

'Ah, that reminds me. We've got a musician coming in today, going to give some lessons on popular music and how it represents modern culture globally and in Africa. He should be here after lunch, so I'll make sure to come and find you, so you can be introduced.'

Tony left the room, stumbling over a desk on the way out and catching his jumper on the handle of the door, which pulled him back into the room and into Tracey's path.

'Watch yerself,' she said as he ricocheted off her and into a bookcase. 'My Baz won't like it if he thinks other men have been touching me.'

She let out a screechy laugh which terrified Tony even further as he raced his way out and down the corridor at full speed. I couldn't help but feel a bit sorry for him. What with all the need to be politically correct – and all the Jimmy Saville stuff at home – young men were terrified of any physical communication without prior consent. Shaking hands the wrong way could be highly complicated for some, in case their sweaty thumbs were seen as a sign of sexual aggression. I could see there was going to be some fun between the two of them.

I'd come to work a bit earlier than usual. Tom's presence in the house was wonderful in many ways, but did put a stop to the morning shower activity.

'He's a grown man,' Darius had said when I buttoned up my dressing gown rather than leaping under the water with him. 'I'm sure he knows all about the birds and the bees.'

'Not when it involves his grandmother,' I said, slipping into the cosy slippers that had been tucked under the bed since I'd moved in. They had a very definite 'Woman at Bon Marche' look about them, and not in tune with the seductive tone I'd been trying to maintain.

'A very sexy grandmother at that,' he said as he swung his hips around in a circular motion so his penis hit both of his thighs alternately. I didn't really understand why such an intelligent and worldly man would resort to such childish behaviour, although I couldn't help but find it strangely attractive.

'Look, a helicopter impression,' he said.

'Don't tell me,' I replied. 'A chopper.'

I left him to it as he wiggled his hips around while soaping his ample thighs. It took a fair amount of willpower not to give him a hand, but I knew I'd get carried away and Tom could be traumatised by the whole scenario.

I went downstairs into the kitchen and tried to concentrate on breakfast, hoping that Tom would be happy with the strange fare provided by the African markets. At least the eggs were good, although I wasn't always sure they always came from chickens.

He was going to work with Darius and Chinaza on some of the online fraud investigations, helping with the technology side of their remit. Since our rescue, which was initiated by his ability to go through my computer at home to find out where I was after I was reported as missing, he'd been fascinated by the work of agencies such as Forensix. He'd been keeping in close contact with Darius and his team in the constant bid for some work experience, which had eventually been approved.

The idea was that once he'd settled into the job he could find somewhere of his own to live. There was a small salary, certainly enough to find him a room in a shared house or maybe accommodation at the university, subject to Buke's approval.

'His first job,' said Darius, 'Is to decipher that paper we found in Pussy's cage. It looks like it might be instructions on how to get to a specific place, which suggests Bill has something hidden that he would like you to find.'

He added that Tom would use enhancing equipment and a variety of other means to get some more clarity and then use some detective work to find out what the document was meant to communicate.

'How cool is that?' said Tom, pushing around his goat's cheese omelette with his fork before asking if he could make himself a sandwich. I could see his disappointment at the contents of the fridge and could see it might take a while for him to adjust.

I told Tracey about the plans and she got rather more excited than I expected her to, given the state of her hair. There was a time a beauty disaster would have occupied all her thoughts. Maybe repeated kidnap, criminal activity and the possibility of an early death through murder had changed her priorities.

'It might be treasure! Bill might have left you information about how to get to his fortune, or the key to a gold mine,' said Tracey.

'More like an old leaflet on how to work his boiler, or an ancient letter from Readers' Digest telling him he's already won millions of pounds if he could just keep sending £25 cheques for a book on the historic railways of Nantwich,' I said.

'Are there any historic railways in Nantwich?' asked Tracey as she scratched underneath her headscarf with such energy I thought she'd wear a hole in her skull.

'Actually, there are,' I said, remembering a day out I'd had with Colin where he had taken me to Crewe for the weekend, just for the purpose of a day at a stream train rally. No-one could have accused him of being an incurable romantic.

'I just happen to know that the Nantwich and Market Drayton railway became part of the Great Western Railway's double track Wellington-Crewe line, ' I told her, surprising myself with sudden recall that regurgitated facts I had no idea I'd retained for such a length of time. It's a shame the same clarity didn't apply to where I'd left my glasses this morning.

'It carried through-freight and local passenger traffic until closure in the 1960s. Market Drayton was renowned for the manufacture of gingerbread, hence the line acquired the nickname "Gingerbread Line",' I said, with some sense of pride as I hadn't remembered so much information at once in a very long time. Why I could remember details of things I couldn't care less about but often struggled with my children's names was a complete mystery.

'Whatever,' said Tracey, pulling out a variety of creams and lotions from a large bag she'd brought in with her. 'I just think you should keep an open mind about these things. I once knew someone who found two hundred pounds hanging out of a cash machine — made her day.'

'Did she report it?' I asked, casting my mind back to a time when I'd gone to a hole in the wall and pressed all the buttons only to walk away with my card but without my cash. When I returned a few minutes later it was gone, although I did see a very sheepish postman looking around in all directions as he walked up the road with what could only be described as a skip and a jump.

'Like heck, she did. She went straight to the bookies and put it on a 'orse, because she knew her luck was in,' said Tracey as she arranged all her various lotions into rows.

'Did she win?' I asked.

'Nah. Lost the lot on some donkey called "Easy Come, Easy Go" – it fell at the second fence.'

'Ironic, really,' I said under my breath. At least it couldn't have been my cash as I never take more than twenty pounds at a time, mainly because I have a compulsion to withdraw money every time I see one of those machines and would soon run out. Colin used to tell me he thought that I thought it was a slot machine and I was winning the money, not taking it out of what he thought was his account.

'What are you up to today?' I asked her as I looked at my planner to check the curriculum. I noticed with some horror that Sex Education had to be addressed before the week was out. This had already been delegated to Tracey but I had been having some concerns about how she might plan the lesson. She'd asked for some condoms and bananas, which gave me a clue and an image I couldn't shake off.

'Facials,' said Tracey. 'It's important to look after your skin. Cleanse, tone and moisturise.' She looked at the packaging on the different products. 'I hope these are going to be good. I got them in the market. The stall holder told me they are all natural.'

I looked at the picture that was on most of the boxes.

'Aloe Vera,' I said.

'Hello Cynthia,' laughed Tracey and I knew I'd never been able to look at an aloe vera plant again without thinking of her.

CHAPTER SEVEN

Darius and Tom had gone off on the first morning of his employment in comfortable companionship.

Over breakfast, they'd discussed the first project and I was amazed at Tom's levels of intelligence, understanding and maturity. In just a few months he'd turned from a geeky boy into a useful human being, which is almost more than I could say for his father.

'I need to work out why anyone would leave any kind of information in the bottom of a parrot's cage,' he said to Darius, who'd invited Tom out to Nigeria after his investigation team had told him his levels of understanding of the technology behind the 'Dear Beneficiary' scam were extraordinary. I thought all young people knew how to break into their grandmother's bank accounts, but apparently that was quite a rare skill.

'It's secure, I suppose,' said Darius, casually eating his toast while looking into the middle distance. He always did that when he was concentrating. 'Not many people would want to go too near Pussy, particularly before her rehabilitation.'

'I also need to work out why he would give the parrot, and the cage, to my grandmother,' said Tom. 'It's not like she'd easily work out the codes to whatever it is he was hiding,' he added, clearly oblivious to my sensitivities about his comments.

'Excuse me, Thomas, but I am very good at both Suduko and *The Telegraph* Cryptic Crossword. Perhaps Bill recognised my deduction abilities before he decided I was exactly the right person to bequeath Pussy to,' I said.

'Pussy's in the well,' screeched Pussy from her cage. Any mention of her name set her off. 'Ding, dong, dell, Pussy's going to hell. Four molecules of carbon.'

'Doesn't that thing ever shut up?' said Darius as he and Tom picked up their phones and briefcases from the hallway.

'Why does she talk about carbon?' asked Tom, looking quizzically at the cage. 'She might know more than we realise. Maybe I should try and talk to her on a regular basis.'

'Fuck off,' said Pussy and tucked her head under her wing.

'Good luck with that,' Darius said and the two of them went off down the drive towards the car in a very manly fashion. I couldn't help but feel a burst of pride.

As I was getting myself ready to go to the centre, Ada turned up to do the cleaning, even though it wasn't really needed. Old habits die hard and I'd already made the beds, cleaned the shower (which made me feel somewhat nostalgic and strangely excited) and washed up the breakfast things.

'You really don't need to do dat,' she'd said, taking off her hat and gloves despite the weather being roasting hot and particularly humid. Her hair looked as sleek as ever, which gave me a thought.

'I hope you don't mind me asking,' I said to Ada. 'But would you happen to know where I might get a wig?'

'What are you sayin'?' said Ada. 'I wear no wig. Dis is ma real hair, worked to this beautiful sheen by da girls at da salon!'

'Oh, I know,' I said quickly, keen not to upset the cleaner who was busy stroking her head as you might stroke a child that had just cut its knee when falling over. I half expected her to say 'there, there' to herself. 'It's just that a friend of mine has a bit of a problem and her hair has fallen out. I thought I could help her by getting her a wig; just until it grows back.'

Ada looked a little ashamed.

'Oh, I'm sorry to hear dat. Is your friend very sick?'

I realised she thought that Tracey might be suffering from a medical problem so rather than explain I thought I would work on her sympathy.

'She can be, sometimes,' I said, thinking of Tracey's sense of humour rather than any physical ailments she might suffer from. 'It can affect her day to day life a bit.'

'Leave it wit me,' said Ada. 'I haf the perfect solution for your friend at my home; I will ask my sister to bring it over.'

'There's no hurry,' I told her, but Ada was a woman on a mission as she jabbed at her ancient mobile phone. It doesn't matter how limited anyone's budget is in Nigeria, everyone has at least a basic Nokia – of the sort my grandchildren would deem suitable for a local museum.

'We don't want yer friend to be waitin' now, do we? I'm onto it,' she said as she put the phone back in her pocket, whipped out the feather duster from under the stairs and started flicking it around the hall. The main house phone rang.

'You don't be getting me this time, parrot bird,' said Ada. 'I'm getting used to yer tricks now.'

The ringing continued and I picked up the phone. It was Darius, who would often call once he'd got to work. He wouldn't ring my mobile because I'd usually forgotten to charge it or couldn't work out how to answer the thing anyway. Even when he did show me, if I didn't have the right glasses I couldn't see which button to press.

Darius often complained there was no point me having it although I disagreed. It was quite reliable as an alarm clock when I did remember to plug it in and it also had a rather good torch, which came in handy with my night-time excursions to the toilet which never abated despite me being well past the menopause.

Darius wanted to report that Tom had already settled in and was being looked after by Chinaza. Once Ada realised the call was genuine, she sucked her teeth and flicked her duster rather more aggressively than was acceptable over Pussy's cage. I pretended not to notice.

'Do you know what line of business Bill was in?' Darius asked.

'I'm not sure. He mentioned oil I think but I didn't really spend any time with him to find out more. Plus we'd just been saved from a car chase and the possibility of impending rape, murder and pillage, so wasn't really concentrating,' I said, remembering meeting Bill as an occasion filled with mixed feelings.

'It's just that he was enrolled on a science degree course at Buke's university,' said Darius. 'He was majoring in alchemy, which seems a little odd for someone working in the oil industry at a high management level.'

'Maybe he just wanted something to concentrate on after his wife left him,' I said, thinking back to when I got involved in the Bridge Club to occupy the lonely afternoons and evenings after Colin had died. It didn't really help, in hindsight, but people do funny things when their life changes direction against any plans they might have made.

He added that Tom was going to see what sort of work Bill had done at the university and also find some geographical points that might match with co-ordinates they think were printed on a basic map of the area between Lagos and Abuja.

'We're not sure if it's a map or just a drawing of something, with instructions of some kind we can't decipher. But I'm sure Tom will work it out, he's a bright lad,' said Darius.

'Takes after his grandmother,' I said and was met with a short silence.

'Indeed. Anyway, I'll see you later, honey. Miss you.'

Darius hung up as I spotted a woman who looked just like Ada, but with the more traditional curly hair of the Nigerians, walking up the drive. I opened the door to her before she had a chance to ring the bell and saw a car driving past at some speed. I assumed it had dropped her off.

Ada came shuffling out of our front room, still with feather duster in hand, to meet her sister.

'Did you bring what I asked?' she said to the woman who was puffing from the heat and her general lack of fitness. She looked like she desperately needed to sit down.

'Would you like to come in?' I asked, and gestured her towards the kitchen. 'Maybe I can get you a glass of water?'

Ada pushed her way in front of me, grabbed the bag and shut the door in her sister's face, just as I thought she was going to bless me for providing basic hospitality.

'She don't need nuttin',' said Ada and thrust the bag at me. 'This is wat yer friend be needin' there's no doubt.'

I looked inside the bag and wasn't quite sure what to make of the contents but figured Tracey would be happy with anything that stopped her looking like a very good impression of a Wot cartoon.

'Thank you, Ada,' I said as I looked through the window by the front door and noticed her sister crouched over the wall, clearly trying to catch her breath. The car that had sped off was coming back the other way and as I had made the assumption it had delivered her, I also assumed it would be her lift back home. 'Are you sure we shouldn't offer at least a drink of something.'

'Nene is like a camel. She needs no water,' said Ada who went to the cupboard and collected a duster and some furniture polish.

'At least she's got a lift,' I said to Ada, who gave me a blank stare.

'She ain't got no lift. We don't know no-one with money for no vehicle.'

I looked out the window and Nene and the car had gone, so thought little more of it, mainly because I realised I hadn't said thank you to Ada's sister for going to so much trouble.

I hoped I wouldn't be cursed for my extreme lack of manners.

'Diamonds are forever,' Pussy started singing, but to the tune of Incy Wincy Spider. Goodness knows what the trainer was doing with her. I suspected that only those with some kind of mental deficiency would find a career in parrot training and forgot about it.

CHAPTER EIGHT

I walked into the centre with the various plans I had for financial management lessons, mixed with some business modules and possibly a bit of geography thrown in. It was getting good fun deciding what information to impart to the girls, who were sponge-like in their absorption of facts.

Tony was scuttling down the corridor, head down and displaying large beads of sweat on his forehead. For a young man he had already lost a lot of hair which made most of the area much higher than it might be. I couldn't help but think of Bamber Gascoigne and then, perhaps less kindly, the love child of Frankenstein's monster and that science correspondent on the BBC – the one who looks like his head was overly stretched during the birth process and, despite every assurance to his parents, it never went back to normal.

'Good morning, Tony,' I said, in my "we're professionals together" voice and he lifted his head to reveal eyes that reminded me of a rabbit Colin nearly ran over one dark night driving back from his mother's.

'I'm sure it isn't r-r-right,' he said to me, bringing a stutter to his voice that I hadn't detected before. 'Is this r-r-really what educating girls is all about?'

His eyes widened further and I wanted to ask him to explain but he dashed past me.

'I'll be in shortly. We've got a visiting teacher, I need to keep them away,' he said and raced into his office, banging the door closed behind him. I shrugged to myself and made my way to the room Tracey and I had now started to think of as ours. Not just because of the teaching but because it had been where our lives were intrinsically brought together, through a set of circumstances and hardship neither of us would have imagined in a million years.

When I walked in I found Mo plastering Tracey's face with a thick, yellow cream while the other girls were taking in turns to massage her hands and feet with another lotion that came from the various packages she'd obtained at the market. Tracey was laid out across two tables like a cadaver at a post-mortem. She still wore the cloth around her head (although it had been pushed back for the purposes of the beauty class), a pink polka-dot bikini top and torn denim shorts that had gathered around the crotch area into a lump of captured material.

'Watcha, Cynth,' she said with a mouth half-closed, to avoid Mo administering the face cream to her tonsils. Mo's enthusiasm was admirable, if a little dangerous from Tracey's point of view. I hoped suitable instruction had been given not to try and rub her teacher's skin off.

'Good morning, Tracey and good morning everyone,' I said to the room and, as ever, the girls replied in unison.

'Good morning, Mrs Hartworth,' they chanted, as ever all eager to be part of the activity of the day.

'We are learning about how our skin works today,' said Mo, as she continued to scrub around Tracey's face with lotion. 'How we need to get moisture in, to keep us young looking.'

I didn't think retaining youthful looks was an issue for these students. Early childbirth and numerous pregnancies would have them sapped of all their basic life if they weren't educated in birth control.

'Shouldn't we be doing our biology lessons today?' I asked Tracey, emphasising the word I'd used as euphemism for sex education.

Tracey had her mouth closed so muttered something back which I didn't understand. I was about to ask her to repeat herself when there was the sound of a car outside, booming out loud music at a volume sufficient to burst the batteries on a hearing aid.

The girls immediately stopped attending to Tracey's beauty requirements and rushed to the window, crowding round to see who was responsible for the racket.

'Who is it?' they asked each other as the occupant of the car made his way, complete with sunglasses and an enormously oversized cap that he wore the wrong way round, through the front entrance of the centre. I couldn't see all of him as they'd blocked my view but there was a sense of familiarity about his general gait and also the music he'd been playing.

'What's going on?' said Tracey as she sat up from her prone position and wiped off the facial cream with a towel. As she removed the majority of it, her skin was revealed to be as pink as a piglet's teat, with the threat of a rash around the sides of her ears. Coupled with the sprouts of hair that worked their way under her headscarf, she was looking like Catweazle's homeless aunty after a particularly bad night.

There was a loud knock on the door but unlike most days Tony didn't just barge in, he waited.

'Are you decent?' he asked through the keyhole.

'Well, there's a question, eh Cynth?' said Tracey, rubbing at her face with the edge of her headscarf. 'Decent as we'll ever be,' she shouted back.

Tony came in, bringing with him the person who'd just arrived in the car with the booming music.

'Chiddy!' shouted Tracey as soon as she recognised our former jailer, turned friend. She jumped off the table, her ample bosom wobbling impressively inside the slightly-too-small bikini top. 'What the heck are you doing here?'

I thought I'd recognised him and it was only when Tracey shouted out his name that I knew where from. There was a buzz as the girls' anticipation grew. It seemed that any friend of Tracey's was a friend of theirs.

'Yo, sister,' he said, taking in a good eyeful of Tracey's assets before giving her a hug. 'What you doing here? Good to see you.'

'I'm doing a bit of teaching assistance, helping out old Cynthia here.'

'Less of the old,' I said, feeling about as old as a hill in a retirement apartment complex.

'So, you all know each other then?' said Tony, clearly confused by the association and looking like he was hoping he might be able to extract more detail.

Chiddy had his eyes fixed on Tracey, mesmerised in her company.

'I'm here to teach as part of my ambition to put something into da community. Doing my bit to spread the Chiddy word and all things about the great Chiddy Bang,' he said.

Tony sucked in his lips and rubbed the palms of his hands on the side of his trousers. Not a good idea when your hands are grubby and your trousers are white. He looked down to see an unsightly stain and flushed red, particularly around his neck. I suspected he was one of those kids at school that might have wet themselves if shouted at.

I couldn't help but feel a little nervous at the arrival of this new 'teacher'. On the one hand he was partly responsible for our imprisonment but I also recognised his and Gowon's help and information which had brought about our eventual freedom. I wondered where Gowon was and what his role would be in terms of social justice.

'So how do you know each other?' said Tony, looking a bit perplexed. You'd think someone would have told him the connection.

'We're old friends,' said Tracey. 'Ain't that right?'

Chiddy grinned and looked around at me.

'That right, missy. We're all old friends.'

Tony frowned, clearly not understanding the camaraderie. I wasn't sure I did and couldn't help worrying about what else Chiddy knew – including what went on during our time in the camp. As if reading my thoughts, he immediately put me at ease.

'We go back a long time and have shared many things together, Mr Tony,' he said before turning round and winking at me. 'What goes on in Chiddyland, stays in Chiddyland.'

I wasn't sure I felt that comfortable with my 'secrets' being in the hands of a rapper with a criminal record but hoped there was some honour among thieves. Even if I wasn't a thief, well, apart from the car or two when required for escape purposes.

Tony stood still for a while, possibly hoping for more of an explanation as to how we all knew each other to the point of such familiarity, but it was clear he wasn't going to get one. He finally left us all to it, muttering something about needing to do a lesson plan for the next day.

The music lesson was unexpectedly brilliant. The girls danced and used whatever they could in the classroom as a drum, or just clapped in time while taking it in turns to write lyrics about their own life. It was illuminating and humbling. Esther talked about being hungry and sleeping on the floor, another girl called Amia wrote about her brothers going missing and no-one knowing where they were and Mo told of her home circumstances which were so bleak but bitter-sweet, they moved both myself and Tracey to tears – although I made impressive efforts to hide mine.

Chiddy encouraged them all to write down their words so they could build on them and gave some basic tips on how to rap effectively.

He told them some tongue twisters and told them to practise every day. He also grabbed Tony's pencils from the front of the class, told them to put them in their mouths horizontally and bite on them as hard as possible while talking.

'You'll sound silly, yes,' he said. 'But you will train your tongue just by doing this for five minutes a day.'

The pencils were in something of a state by the time they'd finished and I could only imagine Tony's face when he saw what 'education' had done to his church's donation to the school.

As he was packing up, Tracey helped and asked questions I was a little nervous of asking.

'What was it like in prison, then? Did you get beaten up for being a grass?'

Chiddy laughed. 'No, we was treated well, man. Gowon and I shared a cell – so not much different to being here, although da food was better!'

'So, where is Gowon, then?' Tracey added, and I held my breath as he thought about the answer.

'He's training – science teaching,' he said. 'He goes to school and then he'll be teaching, too. We must both do one hundred hours.'

'Do you think he'll come here?' my voice squeaked out,

wanting to confirm what I had been told a few days before.

'I think dat might be da plan but who knows?' said Chiddy. 'But don't you worry, missus. He's a gentleman.'

He winked at me before turning to look at Tracey with admiration, not seeming to notice the blotchy skin and unlikely headgear.

'You look very beautiful,' he said to her under his breath but loud enough for Esther and Mo to hear. They both put their fingers to their mouths as if to vomit.

'Thank you,' said Tracey, who might have been blushing, but it was difficult to tell given the colour of her skin, which was increasing in its depth of puce as time moved on. 'Not so bad yourself.'

'I hope to see you here next time, maybe?' he asked, cocking his head to one side expectantly.

'Sure,' said Tracey, regaining her composure. 'If you're teaching here when I am, there's no doubt about it.'

Chiddy made his way out, to the rapturous enthusiasm of the girls who were keen to see him again. They chatted excitedly about how they could write songs, become famous and never have to work. If only it was that easy.

'That reminds me,' I said to Tracey as the incongruity of her outfit became even more ludicrous the more I looked at it. 'I've got something for you.'

I passed over the bag containing the wig that Ada's sister had brought round. I'd not looked at it in any detail but I understood it to be something of a family heirloom.

Tracey stuck her hand in and pulled it straight out again.

'Oooh, it feels like a dead animal. What is it?'

She braved the contents again and the girls crowded round her as she pulled out the wig – as black and as shiny as could be.

'I thought you could wear it instead of the scarf,' I said. 'It doesn't really go with the outfit.'

Tracey took off her scarf and revealed to the girls her baldness. They questioned her about what had happened and, no doubt in the interests of sparing their feelings, she said she had an allergy.

The wig was certainly something to behold. Worked into a sixties style bouffant, it gave Tracey the look of Marge Simpson coupled with Whoopi Goldberg and a badly groomed poodle. She looked in the mirror reserved for her beauty classes and stared at her reflection while the girls started to giggle behind their hands.

'I'm not sure it's really me,' she said, still staring back at herself and looking a bit moist-eyed. I couldn't make out if she was upset or overcome with emotion that I'd put some thought into her predicament.

There was a time when Tracey would have said exactly what she thought but I suspected she was being unusually diplomatic when she said: 'That's really very kind. I look forward to wearing it.'

The wig slipped a little and dangled slightly to one side, so Tracey adjusted it but pushed it too far the other way. She left it as it was and packed up her bags ready to leave for the evening. She looked a little like my cat the time we dressed it for Christmas in a pair of reindeer horns and a rotating bow tie that played 'Silent Night' very loudly.

I felt sorry for her. In the time I'd got to know her she had shown a heart of gold underneath her brash exterior and, although she'd not much idea about formal education, was quite happy to give up her time to people she considered to be worse off than herself.

'Why not come over for dinner tonight?' I asked as she was about to leave. 'You can meet Tom and find out what he is doing to protect all the other silly women like us.'

She stopped and turned quickly, causing the wig to shift position yet again – much to the amusement of the girls.

'I'd love to,' she said. 'Can I bring Baz?'

'Yes, of course,' I replied, thinking there was really no-one I'd like to see less. Baz might be Tracey's husband, but he has the charm of an angry wasp and the intelligence of a dead one.

I made a note to tell Darius to bring home plenty of wine.

CHAPTER NINE

There was no point in pretending otherwise. Tracey looked ridiculous in the wig. I wasn't sure if it was too big, too shiny or she needed something to keep it in position but every time she moved, the hair moved in the opposite direction. It moved like a three-legged cat.

'Oh take it off,' I said. 'I'll get you one of my scarves.'

When she thought I was out of earshot, I heard her tell Darius she was only wearing it because I'd been kind enough to get it for her, but it made her itch even more than the perming accident. Not only that, the hair was rubbing against the rash that seemed to be spreading across her face.

'Just cover yourself up,' I heard Baz comment as I came back down the stairs with a pashmina Colin had bought me many years previously, while on a business trip. 'Save us all having to look at you.'

'Shut yer mouth,' Tracey had replied. 'At least I have a reason for looking like a pile of crap. What's yours?'

'I'll have a beer,' he grinned and Darius, ever the host, obliged. He got one for himself and Tom at the same time, pouring Tracey and me some local wine which wasn't too bad, whatever Chinaza's father's snobbery might suggest. It certainly got better after the first few glasses.

Tracey wrapped her head up like an unwanted parcel while Tom stared as each tuft of hair got covered up.

'So, what's it like being out here with your grandmother?' asked Tracey, looking Tom up and down like a dress she was thinking of buying. 'Bit different to leafy old Surrey, I expect?'

'You could say that,' said Tom. 'It's a bit different here, that's for sure – in a good way, of course. The work is very exciting at Forensix, nothing like I'd be able to do at home.'

'What you doing there?' asked Baz, as he leant back on one of our chairs and nearly fell off. 'They got jobs for anyone else?'

Darius, looking a little startled, explaining how Tom's knowledge of technology and the internet had helped catch our kidnappers. Baz didn't look particularly impressed.

'I'll remember to keep out of your way,' said Baz, swigging down the rest of his beer in a couple of gulps before holding out the empty bottle by way of a request for another. Darius obliged, although he did bang down the next beer quite heavily on the table in front of our guest.

'I'm working on the map that was in the bottom of the parrot's cage,' said Tom by way of explaining his current role. 'It isn't very legible and so we're trying to enhance the images to see if I can understand it. There's enough there to suggest it could lead to something interesting, though.'

Baz's face lit up and he leaned forward in his chair.

'What do you mean by interesting?' said Baz.

'I don't know yet, but it is odd that Pussy was left to my grandma without any explanation. Most people would just re-home the thing, not pass it on to someone specifically.'

'Pussy's gone to hell,' screeched the parrot from the cage and so Darius went to cover her up. She made loud kissing noises and a belch before going quiet.

I asked Tom how far he'd got with his investigations and it seemed they were having problems identifying some of the wording and the map itself was very unclear.

'It's just a few lines, really, and some co-ordinates I can't quite make out. Apart from a picture of a car and a fish, there's not much to go on.'

'I used to get jobs like that when I was on work experience,' said Tracey, dreamily. 'I worked at a DIY store once and they sent me out for some tartan paint and a glass hammer on my first day.'

'Did you get it?' asked Baz and I wasn't particularly surprised that he was being serious.

'Course not, stupid. I did get the K9P, though. They didn't catch me on that one!'

'What's K9P?' I asked. 'Is it one of those oily things like WD40?' I was pleased I could show knowledge of household maintenance, although my experience with the latter was only to release one of my high heeled shoes from our decking.

'Let's just say I got it from the local dog kennels,' said Tracey, and Darius and Tom laughed immediately. It took me a little longer to get the joke.

'I'm surprised your employers got away with that type of behaviour,' I said to Tracey who told us she thought it was all 'a laugh' and made her think on her feet.

'It wasn't as bad as the butchers who brought their racehorse into work and told me they were going to turn it into burgers. I got my own back and threw me fag ends in their sausage mix.'

'That sounds very unhygienic,' I said. 'I don't think I would have liked to have bought those sausages.'

'At least I didn't pee in the mixer, like the delivery boys. Funny thing is we had queues of old ladies for them bangers, all telling us they were the best in the town and had something extra about them.'

'Yeah, your fags and a load of piss,' said Tom, looking with a vague look of awe in Tracey's direction.

'Can I have a look at the map?' said Baz, thankfully changing the subject. Darius and Tom looked at each other as if asking the other for permission to speak.

'Do you have a copy here?' said Darius, raising his eyebrows and I could tell he was suggesting that Tom should respond in the negative.

Tom didn't read the signal and readily produced the paper from his briefcase – the one his mother had bought for him to send him on his journey to Nigeria. A journey she probably never dreamed he would ever make and will no doubt blame me for at a future point in time.

'Here,' said Tom. 'It shows what looks like some kind of outbuilding with a fair bit of land and what could be a small factory or workshop. There are a few scribbles on here with numbers and letters which we believe should identify the geographical position, but we're finding it difficult to match the co-ordinates.'

'What do you think you're going to find there?' said Baz with more enthusiasm than I'd seen him show for anything in weeks – other than beer, of course.

'Who knows?' said Darius. 'But hopefully Tom is going to find out why Bill took a shine to his lovely grandmother.'

Tom and I blushed in unison. I wasn't convinced my grandson was entirely 'cool' with the fact I was sharing my bed – and a fair few other things – with a Nigerian man over twenty years my junior. I wasn't entirely 'cool' with the idea that he knew about it.

Dinner was ready and so I asked for everything to be cleared away. When I served up – a risotto style dish with plenty of herbs to disguise the taste of the unrecognisable meat that went in it – the table was bare and everything out of sight including the map.

'So, Tracey,' said Darius. 'What's the story with the hair?'

She told him how it had broken off during the hairdressing lesson but she wasn't too worried as she quite liked wearing the headscarf.

'I can sort of see why women say they like it. Saves all that bother with the bloody hair dryer and products, and you can wear different colours of cloth for different outfits.'

'You're going to have to get a bigger one soon to cover up your face,' said Baz, this time helping himself to another beer from the fridge rather than waiting to be asked. I wasn't sure if I was happy for him to be so relaxed in my home, as he stood in a wide stance while he tipped the bottle to his mouth.

'That's not nice,' said Tom, not one for being rude to anyone, particularly women. He received a warm smile from Tracey in response.

'Don't worry about it, Tom. I'm used to the miserable git. Don't appreciate me assets at all – might as well cover meself up completely for all the appreciation I get.'

'You know what I mean,' said Baz, fiddling about with something behind him, pushing whatever it was deep into his back pocket before he sat down again. 'You're not looking your best, babe.'

'You look OK to me,' said Tom quietly, lowering his eyes only to find himself focusing on Tracey's bust, so he brought them straight back up again, and coughed.

Tracey jumped over from her seat and gave Tom a hug, enveloping his head with her arms. He came out a few seconds later, barely breathing.

'What a love you are, a credit to your grandmother. But it's true, I don't look great. I think I'll go and get some more material from the market tomorrow. Will you come with me, Cynth?'

I thought about Tracey, the market and me. Last time we went shopping we ended up having to find our way out of a small room we'd been locked in, because yet more con men had taken what they thought was Tracey's cash card. It was only luck and a bit of quick thinking that got us both out of that situation. I shuddered at the thought.

'Yes, OK,' I said. 'I need a few things myself,' I added, thinking that maybe a guarantee against lightning striking twice might be a good purchase, if it was available.

'I'll give you a ride if you like,' said Darius, not stopping himself in time. Always prompted by his use of Americanisms, Tracey snorted with laughter.

'We'd all like a ride, eh Cynth?' she said, and I tried not to react. It was even worse when he'd first called her bum bag a 'fanny pack'. I thought she was going to explode with the amusement of the expression.

'That would be lovely, we can make a nice early start,' I said.

'I was hoping for a lie-in to catch up on me beauty sleep,' said Tracey.

'You'd need a few days for that,' said Baz and was promptly kicked by his wife under the table.

'Anyway, I think we ought to be getting home,' he added as he stood up, checking his back pocket as he did so. 'I've got things to do and all that.'

'Like what?' said Tracey, swilling the remains of her wine and then burping, which prompted Pussy to start a barrage of noises – all of which resembled a different type of bodily function. The key to this activity was knowing not only which was which, but what came from whom.

'Business, Tracey, business.'

Tracey raised her eyes to the heavens and followed her husband, clipping along the wooden floors with another pair of her unsuitable shoes. These ones weren't as high as normal, so she repeatedly stepped on the inside of her floor-length skirt as it trailed on the floor, tripping over herself as she did so. How she made it outside without ending up arse over tit was a puzzle to all of us as we watched them walk up the drive, Tracey a few yards back trying to negotiate her steps while hooking up her skirt and simultaneously trying to rewind my scarf around her head.

'There's something not right about that man,' said Darius as we cleared up after they'd left. 'I get the impression he's always looking for a way of tricking people out of something.'

'Has anyone seen the map?' said Tom, lifting books and papers that had been moved from the table onto a side unit. 'I can't seem to find it.'

We had a look around but it couldn't be found.

'Baz was looking a bit shifty, perhaps he took it,' said Tom.

'Well, good luck to him if he has,' said Darius. 'If we can't work out what it means I'm as sure as anything he won't find it of any use whatsoever.'

'I've plenty of copies in the system anyway,' said Tom. 'If you don't mind, I'd like to go to bed now.'

Tom still felt uncomfortable when it was just the three of us, I could tell. I wasn't unhappy about him leaving Darius and I alone. I still looked at him and wanted him just like I did when we first met and would still reel in surprise that his affections seemed genuine.

'Not here,' I whispered as he lifted me up on to the kitchen table and ran his hands up my thighs. I slid back down to a standing position, although his hands didn't move.

'Spoil sport,' said Darius, kissing my neck and using his thumbs to press me in a particularly sensitive spot.

'Upstairs. Now,' I said, deciding on this occasion to leave the washing up until another time. That never would have worked with Colin. The dishes would need to be rinsed then put in the dishwasher on a specific programme as he waited until the first part of the cycle had finished before feeling comfortable enough to leave the kitchen. This was all because of a minor leak seven years previously that had caused some damage to the recently tiled floor. The fact the insurance company wouldn't pay out was probably the start of his heart problem.

'Yes, missy,' said Darius in his mock-servant voice. 'Your wish is my command.'

He scooped me up and took me to bed, where I had to bite my hand rather than risk Tom hearing my response to my lover's expertise.

I felt like a teenager and it was bloody marvellous.

CHAPTER TEN

When we got to Tracey and Baz's house the next morning, she was up and ready, complete with suitably arranged scarves – two this time, one around the top of her head and the other covering the lower part of her face.

'You going for the full look?' said Darius.

'Look at me face,' said Tracey as she pulled back the bottom cloth. 'Don't know what was in that cream but I've come up like a washer woman's knuckles. You'd think I was the victim of an acid attack or summat.'

She scratched furiously with her long fingernails, creating red welts across the bottom of her chin and up the side of her mouth. It looked like a person with no artistic ability at all had been drawing on her face.

'Just wait until I find the person who sold me that stuff. I'll give 'em 'natural! There'll be no way they'll be natural again, that's for sure.'

It was good to see Tracey getting her feisty side back again. I was a bit worried she was settling into responsible living, with a desire to be seen as 'normal'. It didn't suit her.

'So where's Baz?' asked Darius, no doubt hoping he was nowhere to be seen. He told me last night, once he'd got his breath back, that he found it difficult being polite to Tracey's husband. That was an unusual statement for a man who had the charm of a thousand princes.

'He's gone off somewhere. Said something about being onto something big and for once he wasn't talking about me,' she laughed. 'Perhaps this time whatever he's doing will earn him some money. I'm fed up living off Buke, however gracious she is about her support.'

Tracey and Baz still lived in the house within the university grounds where Buke worked. Tracey received a small 'salary' that Buke told her was a fee for looking after the place. She said the place would be vandalised without her presence, a story designed to remove any embarrassment Tracey might have had about being financially supported.

'Does he still have his business interests?' said Darius, knowing full well Baz was as interested in business, in the proper sense of the word, as I was in the inner workings of a combi-boiler.

'Monkey business more like,' said Tracey. 'Although he got up bloody early this morning so whatever it is has kicked his butt.'

'Come on, let's go,' I said as I could see Darius was itching to give us our lift then get off to work. He'd let Tom make his own way to the office and had already said he was concerned to make sure he'd survived the bus journey without any major incident. I could tell he was already starting to think of my grandson as family and a warm feeling swirled around my midriff, which could only partly be attributed to the humidity.

Darius dropped us in his air-conditioned company car just outside the market. It was as busy and as colourful as ever. Chickens and other types of foul were running about loose while various stall holders pulled us by the arms to try and sell us what they had on offer. Their stock ranged from fruit and vegetables to household goods, textiles and even the hind quarters of an unfortunate animal that had been removed to bring its bearer some cash.

'Very good meat,' said the toothless seller, brandishing the bloody back leg of what might have been a deer, poorly wrapped in old newspaper and covered in flies. I hoped the beast had been put out of its misery before the theft of its limb and wasn't hobbling around in a permanent state of imbalance.

'No wonder half the people here are vegetarian,' said Tracey and I had to agree. Our butchers were, on the face of it, more salubrious although I suspected that behind closed doors the attention to health and safety was just as remiss. I made a mental note to ask Darius where our meat came from, as he placed the monthly order with a long-standing supplier, then wondered if that was altogether wise. Perhaps it would be better not to know.

'Now look at this lot,' said Tracey picking up a selection of different coloured materials from the back of a van. 'I could make a whole wardrobe.'

A small child came from behind the truck and stood on a stool to help Tracey throw different swathes of cloth around her. Silently she showed her how to dress in true Muslim style, firstly just the head covering and then a method of covering the whole face apart from the eyes. The young girl held her tongue out, clamped between her teeth, as she concentrated on the task until it was finished.

'There, you can hardly see me,' laughed Tracey as she put her sunglasses on over the top of the last 'outfit' she'd tried on. 'I could get away with murder like this.'

She then waved her arms through some gaps in the body area.

'Look, ideal for nicking stuff. Whip it under the outfit and into a bum bag,' she said. 'Who's gunna know?'

I frowned at her, hoping that the Islam people around us wouldn't take offence at this white woman dressing in their style and then making disparaging remarks about their traditional dress. I looked around at the various women but they didn't seem to care. The child, probably the only one in hearing distance, was only about ten years old and just asked for money. She was so delighted when Tracey agreed to buy that she jumped off her stool, smiled and busily offered to wrap the purchase with the brightest of tissue paper.

'No, no, don't worry,' she said to the girl as she paid. 'I'll wear it now, I might as well, eh?'

The girl took further time to adjust the material until Tracey was covered correctly from head to toe. She then glided through the market like a true local. No-one would know who she was apart from the occasions when she'd pull her mask to one side to light a cigarette.

When we got to the stall that had sold her the lotions that had given her the rash, her outfit meant they didn't see her coming. If they had, they might have had the sense to run away.

'You!' she shouted at the person running the stall claiming to be selling the purest Aloe Vera available. The woman, dressed similarly to Tracey, looked for where the noise had come from and their eyes met. It was about all that could meet as everything else was covered up.

'Look what you've done to me,' shouted Tracey. 'I'm a mess.'

It was difficult to understand exactly what she was saying, under all that material.

The stall holder looked back at Tracey, through her own head scarf. It reminded me of our postman when we had the dog. He'd always have a quick look through the letterbox before putting anything in it, in case it'd eat our post or, more importantly, his hands.

'And why is your face my problem?' said the stall holder. 'This is God's gift and if you suffer then you must need to learn a lesson.'

'Cheeky, bloody cow,' said Tracey pulling her bag up over her shoulder and raising her fists. I put my hand on her arm.

'Now come on. Let's handle this nicely,' I said, concerned that a full-blown fight might break out between the two be-robed women. No-one would be able to tell the difference between them if they did. It would be like two cats in a scrap, just a blur of colour and lots of sharp bits.

'She's a con woman,' said Tracey. 'I want my money back.'

'Then give me my lotions back,' said the woman. 'How do I know they were your problem? You white women have very bad skin. It could be the sun, or your love of the alcohol.'

Tracey went into full boxing mode and it was all I could do to more forcibly hold her back.

'Let's go,' I said. 'I know somewhere we can get a great coffee and some cake. There's no point fighting.'

I could swear I heard the stall holder growl but decided to let it go. We weren't going to win the argument. Not only that, a crowd had started to form around us.

I dragged Tracey's arm and pulled her through the crowds, all the while talking about subjects I hoped would take her mind off fighting.

We had reached the small café, run by ex-nuns from Provence, when I felt a thud in my back and I was pushed to the ground. I was swiftly followed by Tracey who lost her balance and fell on top of me. A man wearing striped trousers and brogues – I could only see his bottom half from my position on the floor – gave me a kick and dropped a message on the floor.

'Read that and take notice. We are watching you,' he said, before walking anonymously off into a throng of people. As I looked up from the floor all I registered was a highly polished cane adorned at the top with what looked like an opal. It flashed against the sun and straight into my eyes.

A couple of the stallholders came over and helped pick us up, asking if we were alright. We said we were, although I wasn't sure.

'What the bejeesus was that all about?' said Tracey as she adjusted her scarf which, to the amusement of some locals, had come off to reveal her scalp.

'I haven't a clue,' I said, with a rising and strangely familiar feeling of panic reaching my throat. 'But I have a horrible feeling we're being watched.'

'Don't be silly,' said Tracey. 'Who'd want to watch us?'

I showed her the note and her eyes widened to fill the gap that exposed them. The note said 'Hand over the information. Or Else.'

'Bloody hell, Cynth, what do they want with us now?'

'What information, though?' I said. 'And who wants it? I know no-one in this country other than Fasina and Chike who are in prison - and we know Gowon and Chiddy wouldn't hurt us, they helped us.'

Tracey screwed up her eyes and from what I could make of the expression – limited in the absence of being able to see any other facial movement – she apparently was thinking.

'What about that English bloke. Did he ever get found?'

'John Baker. I'm not sure. What would he want with us now? Surely he will be in hiding making sure if he didn't get caught that he never would be,' I said.

There was a loud bang and Tracey and I jumped so violently

we leapt into the air and into each other's arms. It was easy to be nervous after the experiences we had had. Some might even call it Post Traumatic Stress Disorder, but neither of us had really heard of that before. We'd just mentioned we'd felt a bit edgy sometimes. It was often a good excuse for a gin and tonic.

'Sorry ladies,' said a man running out of a café behind us, chasing two large silver trays that were rolling ahead and towards the road. 'I am so clumsy.'

I pushed Tracey away gently and I brushed myself down. I'd fallen into some mango which had squashed itself into my white trousers, leaving a stain in the shape – ironically – of a mango.

'Please, come and have some coffee. On the house,' said the man.

'I could do with a brandy,' said Tracey, flipping the cloth away from her mouth so she could light up a cigarette.

I glared at her. Smoking was still something of an issue. I couldn't see why she needed to do it. She couldn't see why I needed to care about it.

'No good trying to give up in this place, is there?'

We sat down and were soon brought coffee and some liqueur that we both downed in one go, prompting the man – who we established was the owner and was called Banjo, a nickname given on account of his ability to play the instrument of the same name – to bring two more.

'I saw you have a bad experience,' he said in lower tones. 'I'm sorry for this. Not everyone in our country is bad.'

'Do you know who that man was?' I asked. 'You know, the one who just pushed us to the floor?'

Banjo looked from side to side and then up and towards the door. He lowered his voice. 'There are always people from different authorities, doing this and that.'

'What part of the government and why would he be looking for me?' I asked.

'I didn't say government,' Banjo said, looking around to check who was listening. 'Only you would know who might be looking for you, my dear. Last time I saw him he was paying some boys for information about some of the stall holders. They were found and never seen again. Let's just say I have learned to keep my mouth shut and my eyes open.'

'Maybe it's the people who sell that dodgy Aloe Vera?' said Tracey, never one to give up on the possibility of revenge. 'They don't deserve to be seen again.'

Banjo pulled Tracey's scarf to one side and made a clicking sound with his tongue.

'You've been to see Ally, haven't you?' he said. 'She keeps getting told not to make that stuff. No wonder your face looks like a bad bottom.'

I coughed into my coffee to disguise a laugh which was more because of the look on Tracey's face at the man's bluntness, rather than at the description of her complexion. I doubt it was a comment she'd had before, even in south London.

'Wait there,' he said as he scuttled off behind his counter, coming back with a pot of Sudocrem.

'Put this on twice a day, it will help you,' he said.

Tracey read the details on the pot.

'That just about takes the biscuit,' she said. 'This is for bloody nappy rash.'

I stopped myself from saying it was proof she had a face like a slapped arse, mainly because it sounded so common.

CHAPTER ELEVEN

Darius was very cross about the incident in the market and told me to never go there again without him.

'This is a difficult place for anyone, let alone a white woman,' he told me. 'Not only that, Tracey seems to attract trouble wherever she goes.'

I explained that it could hardly be her fault when the message was clearly meant for me – they hadn't taken any notice of Tracey.

'The thing is, with all that gear she's been wearing it would be easy to think, for those who don't know any better, that she's converted or something,' Darius said. 'I'm just saying that although she might not have been mentioned she is rather noticeable. You have to be very careful in this political climate. We don't know who our enemies are.'

'Do you think it is anything to do with the map?' asked Tom. He'd told me, while Darius was out of the room, that he was still struggling to find out what it meant but was sure there was something significant because there were so many equations, marks and map references. He said he'd checked out different geographical regions, according to the numbers and letters, but they still didn't make any sense.

'I don't want to let anyone down,' he said dispiritedly. 'But I just can't seem to get anywhere with it although I just have this feeling it might be very important.'

He vowed he would keep working at it until he had a solution but I could tell he was losing confidence and just wanting some kind of breakthrough to prove that he could do the job. I was heartened by his integrity and wondered where he might have got it from.

'Don't you worry about it now,' I said to him. 'I'm sure whatever it is can wait. You're a clever boy and if there's anything to find out, I'm sure you're the person to do it.'

I wasn't so sure it was really of any interest but was glad it was considered of sufficient enough importance to keep Tom occupied on his work experience. It was nice having a member of my family with me and I hoped Darius hadn't persuaded his employers to take him on just on my behalf. I shared Tom's concern about it being seen to be valuable.

The door knocker went and before I had a chance to open it, Tracey came flying through while wafting away the remains of a cigarette I could see was still burning out on the driveway. I suspected she had given it the slightest stamp before coming in.

'The bastard's gone missing!' she shouted to anyone who'd listen, which at this point seemed to be mainly Pussy.

'Bastard,' shrieked the parrot before she jumped up and down making spitting noises and then repeating our phone number. Having her cage in the hall meant she heard me say it on a regular basis as I still couldn't get out of the habit of reciting the four last digits to any caller by a means of a greeting. I've been told many times it makes me sound very old fashioned but I'm not very good at picking up the receiver and just saying 'hello'. It sounds so rude.

'Who's gone missing?' said Darius, running down the stairs in bare feet and trousers with his shirt flying behind him as he attempted to put it on while on the move. I could see Tracey take an appreciative look at his magnificent chest and wanted to drag him upstairs and lock him in a cupboard.

'Baz, of course,' she said, pausing to catch her breath.

Darius slowed down, suggesting there was no longer any urgency.

'He goes missing all the time doesn't he?' he said, stopping at the bottom of the stairs to button up his top, which pleased me. His nakedness was mine and mine alone.

Tracey tottered through into the kitchen and opened our fridge, pulling out a bottle of beer, taking the top off with an opener attached to the wall and swigging a good half of it. She slumped into a chair.

'It's different this time. I didn't want to tell you as I thought it was something and nothing. But he took that map thing you had when we were last here. I caught him a few times going over and over it and he got very shady about why he wanted it,' she said, finishing off the bottle and handing it over to Tom who was looking shell-shocked by the invasion of her personality.

'Did he say anything about it?' said Darius, taking the beer bottle from Tom before it slipped from his fingers. He seemed overwhelmed by the force of Tracey's presence.

'Nah, course he didn't, not to me, anyway, although there were plenty of secret phone calls.'

'Secret phone calls?' said Tom. 'Who would he be making secret phone calls to? Do you think they were about the map?

'If I knew that they wouldn't be secret, would they?' Tracey snapped, searching for her cigarettes, finding them and then putting them back in her bag. 'One of his so-called business partners I expect.'

Tracey told us Baz had returned home as soon as we'd gone to the market and she hadn't been able to track him down since.

'I usually know where he is, but this time he's gone off the radar,' she added.

'You can't possibly know where he is all the time,' I said, thinking how slippery Baz could be when he was on the trail of one of his deals. If he wanted to disappear then no doubt he would.

'Oh, I do,' she said. 'I put an app on his phone that shows me where he is. It's for kids, so it seemed very appropriate at the time.'

I could see Tom was getting agitated and clearly found what he was hearing of interest.

'Would you mind very much showing me the app?' he asked. 'I might be able to find him for you.'

Tracey passed over her phone, wiping greasy residue from her various face creams off the screen with her sleeve before she did so.

'Look, you can normally see where he is on this GPS system but he's not on it anymore. It all went blank about two hours ago and he's not picking up any calls.'

'I'm sure I can trace him. Can you give me about half an hour?' said Tom, removing the phone away from Tracey's outstretched hand.

'Yeah, sure, why not, 'she said. 'If you do find him it might be wise to keep it to yourself for a while in case I get the urge to go after him and commit a very nasty murder.'

Tom raced away into Darius's office with Tracey's phone, wiping it on the top of his trouser leg as he did so. When I checked on him a few minutes later, he was deep in concentration. I left him to it and hoped his investigations wouldn't bring Baz back too quickly.

'So, he didn't say anything at all about where he thought he was going, or why?' asked Darius.

'Nothing, apart from saying he was going to make it big one day and everyone who doubted him would be sorry,' Tracey said, pausing as she twirled her wedding ring round her finger. 'But then he's always saying things like that.'

Darius went to join Tom, leaving me the job of trying to console an obviously distressed Tracey.

'Maybe he just wants to surprise you,' I said in the hope it would help, but she looked at me as if I was telling her I'd found the secret of everlasting life in the bottom of my handbag.

'There's nothing he could do that would surprise me anymore,' she said wistfully. 'I'm surprised out with his schemes. Anyway, what does your man say about the incident at the market?'

I didn't tell her the bit about him thinking she attracts trouble and glossed over his warnings about being white women in an African country. It wouldn't make much difference to Tracey anyway, as she tends to do as she pleases regardless of the risks, but I wasn't that keen on having my life limited by the threats of others.

With everything that had been going on in the world it would be difficult to know how to fully protect yourself, regardless. The infiltration of a murderous and cruel mentality is no longer confined to war zones or front lines. We can all be at risk of something most of us don't understand, something that can manifest itself while we are at work or leisure, peacefully minding our own business.

'He says not to worry about it too much and weird things happen all the time,' I said, crossing my fingers behind my back. I don't like lying at the best of times but particularly so when it relates to Darius as he is honest to the point of the ridiculous. I know, because when I asked if his family would like me, he said that was a stupid question as of course they wouldn't like me, not as a partner for their boy.

'You're old enough to be my mother and can't breed. So they might like you, but not who you are to them.'

I was stunned as I rather hoped he would sing my virtues and claim they would be sufficient to win over any negative points about our relationship. He did console me with the fact that he doesn't care what anyone thinks about us as I'm all he wants, and it isn't anything to do with anyone else.

'Neither of us should need approval for finding happiness. I doubt very much your family would like me, either.'

I thought of my children and shuddered. They would no doubt be very vocal in their opinions which would range from downright outrage to disgust, disappointment and then a rising swell of indignant loyalty to their departed father.

'Tom likes you,' I said, knowing that to be true based on how the two of them got on and shared a similar sense of humour. I hadn't thought that much about our cultural differences as they generally enhanced our relationship when it was just the two of us. But it's rarely just two people that make a good relationship; there are always other influences - good and bad - that come into play at some point.

Tracey shuffled about in her chair, sitting on her hands. The absence of a cigarette left them bereft of activity.

'Do you think that man was related to the kidnappers?' she asked. 'I don't mean Fasina and Chike, but the big bosses above them. The people the police haven't caught yet.'

There was no doubt she had a point. John Baker's name regularly cropped up in my mind but nothing seemed to have been done about him as far as I knew. Darius probably didn't want to worry me by admitting he was the only member of the gang who got away. Being British, he may well be somewhere back home, intimidating the likes of Mavis with promises to secure their money in a highly profitable pension scheme. Men like him can adapt.

'No, of course not, that's all over and done with,' I said. 'It is all probably just random and because we were in the wrong place at the wrong time. They probably don't like white women.'

Tom came back into the kitchen with Darius, holding Tracey's phone.

'I've found him,' he said.

Tracey jumped up and grabbed her device, looking at the screen and then looking puzzled.

'I can't see him,' she said. 'Where is the shrivelled little turnip?'

Darius took the phone and turned it on its side so that Tracey could see a dot travelling along a line.

'Here he is, seventeen miles north of the eastern road to Lagos. He isn't actually that far from here but seems to have been travelling in circles,' he said.

'Will you be able to go and get him?' Tracey asked.

'There doesn't seem to be much need,' said Tom. 'He's driving along very long, empty roads. He's bound to come back when he realises he isn't going anywhere.'

'That figures,' said Tracey. 'Going nowhere pretty much sums him up.'

CHAPTER TWELVE

The car drove past the front door twice. It was the same one that came by the day Ada's sister had brought round the wig.

'Is that car anything to do with you?' I asked my hard-working cleaner. She looked out the window and it had gone.

'There,' I said as it swept past the second time but, again, she missed it. She gave me a look through narrow eyes and was clearly assessing me for signs of Alzheimer's. Or 'Old Timer's' disease as one of my younger grandchildren called it.

'I told you, we ain't got no money for no vehicle,' she said, breathing out very loudly while staring into the middle distance. It was my cue to go.

'Probably something and nothing,' I said as I left the house in the charge of Ada. It was oven cleaning and sheet changing day which usually involved a lot of huffing and puffing, more than usual, all mimicked repeatedly by Pussy to the point it got them both into a bad mood.

I reached for my keys in my bag and, remembering an old self-defence class Mavis had organised some years back, held them individually between my fingers, a bit like a knuckle-duster. It made me feel like one of the Kray twins and certainly slightly more secure in terms of how I might be able to defend myself should any trouble arise.

'What you do,' she'd told everyone,' is point the sharp ends of the keys outwards from your clenched fist, as a weapon. Punch your attacker in the eyes until they are blind and when they are reeling from the pain, kick them in the groin and run away.'

I often wondered about Mavis and whether she'd watched too many murder mysteries as a child. She had a very blood-thirsty streak.

There weren't bus stops as such here. You had to work on the basis that the driver would see you waiting and putting your hand out and would be good enough to let you clamber on the packed vehicle, filled with lots of sweaty people, their chattels and usually their animals and children – often interchangeable in terms of behaviour – for your journey to wherever he or she might take you. Sometimes they wouldn't stop the bus, probably for the reason Darius suggested – I'm a white woman in an African country – but mostly they did, screeching to a halt at the last minute as if they weren't expecting anyone to be there.

I could hear that my transport was on its way. The women would often sing on their journeys, or chatter so loudly together they were like a vast group of migrating birds. Not only that the driver would be playing music through a radio that dangled from his rear-view mirror and there would also be copious amounts of back-firing, revving and general clattering.

I looked at my watch and it was going to arrive at yet a different time to every other morning. There was no timetable, probably because there was only one bus. When it got to its destination it went back to where it started and repeated the process until everyone had got to where they wanted to be, or the driver decided to take a break – which could last an hour, a day or even a week.

'Good mornin' missy,' said the driver, ever cheerful and oblivious to the cacophony of the occupants of his bus. 'Yous be going to your work today?'

I said I was and looked around for somewhere to sit. I don't know why I kept up that expectation as to that point there'd never been a seat readily available. Sometimes a younger woman would rise to let me sit, but mostly people were too busy hanging on to whatever space they could find to worry about anyone else. I found a frayed strap to hang on to and settled in for the forty minute ride to the Outreach Centre, as the bus lurched forward and then stopped abruptly enough to cause a sheep to come tumbling down the centre aisle followed by three large women, a basket full of geese and a bicycle wheel.

'You bloody idiot,' the driver was shouting out of his nonexistent window. 'Watch where yous going!'

We all looked out to see a car, the one that had been driving past our house, racing into the distance. I couldn't help but feel a little relief that the timing of my bus trip today was a few minutes earlier than normal. I held the keys in my hand a little tighter and said a little internal prayer of gratitude while telling myself at the same time, in the schizophrenic way that I can, 'There's nothing to worry about.'

Tracey was already at the Outreach Centre when I arrived. She'd taken to getting there early to help Tony, even though he clearly wasn't as appreciative as she might have thought.

'Bless his little socks, he's here all by himself and only a boy really. He always seems so nervous.'

Nervous of you, I thought. He'd probably never come across anyone like Tracey in his entire life, coming from a middle class suburb of Berkshire where the greatest scandal of a Sunday morning was the newsagents staying open beyond midday.

Tony was responsible for all the academic teaching, with a view to the girls being able to sit exams and get proper qualifications, whereas our remit was the pastoral and social development side.

'Sex education today,' said Tracey. 'I asked Tony if he'd come in and talk about it from the man's point of view, but I can't find where he's gone.'

I suspected he'd be hiding in the area reserved for his toilet facilities; the only place where the students, and us, couldn't get to him. The poor man looked haunted after any prolonged dialogue with Tracey.

'Is there any more news of Baz?' I asked, hoping she wasn't going to refer to her marital relations in the class.

'Nah, he still seems to be driving around in circles according to the app. I'm assuming he's on one of his missions,' said Tracey. 'Let him get on with it. He'll either make some money or get bored and come home with his tail between his legs.'

She laughed loudly and caught her breath, coughing at the same time.

'Or get eaten by wild beasts!'

I could tell the marriage was starting to show signs of complacency.

'Shall we get on with the lesson, then?' I said, nervously hoping Tracey had forgotten about it. I could soon see she hadn't as she produced the banana and a selection of various condoms, the provenance of which I suspected weren't entirely African. A number of them were stamped with the names of pop bands, with one specifically aimed at the gay community and another proclaiming the addition of a 'tickler tip'– whatever that was.

The girls had started to gather around enthusiastically. They knew what was on the agenda and the giggling had started before they came into the classroom. It's no wonder Tony, as the only male on the premises that day, had disappeared once Tracey got out the 'Pin the Tail on the Donkey' game. No-one would put it beyond her to ask him to join in.

After a number of discussions about what constituted a 'tail', Tracey's euphemism for a penis, and what to expect from it, the girls warmed to their teacher and wanted to know more. The next part of the lesson was on contraception.

'You got a boyfriend?' said Esther to Tracey, eyeing up the banana with an interest I suspected was more for its calorific value than its sexual connotation.

'I have a husband,' said Tracey, tugging at the ends of her headscarf and throwing them behind her neck.

'Did you have sex with him before you were married?' said Mo.

'Course I did. Got to try the goods before ya lumbered with 'em, ain't ya?'

I glared at her with wide eyes. I didn't think pre-marital sex was a good recommendation although I wasn't really sure of the protocol in Nigeria. If young girls were having babies at thirteen because they were married, it made a farce of the marital process. Legitimising paedophilia in my view but of course I was blessed with education, contraception and a vast support system. Not only that, my father would have killed anyone who'd come anywhere near my virginity before at least promising to take me away from home and become their responsibility rather than his.

As ever with Nigeria I found I was again in awe of how people lived. In this case, young girls oblivious to the fact some women could take control, even at their age. Unaware they could, with the wind in the right direction and with the right kind of help, make choices that would entirely change the expected outcome of their lives.

'The thing is,' I said, my heart pounding with the need to make my latest thoughts heard. 'Sex is a wonderful thing between two loving people. But it does have consequences.'

'Yeah, like having to make them breakfast in the morning,' said Tracey, winking at the girls who weren't sure who to look at. 'Or sleeping in the wet patch.'

I glared again but Tracey was re-wrapping her head with just a scarf rather than the full burqa. She decided 'less is more' after she was sat upon while on her way to work. Wearing all black and sitting in black surroundings, an old woman on the bus had failing sight and thought Tracey was, literally, part of the furniture. I'd have loved to have seen her face when what she thought was an overly-plump bus seat turned out to be an enraged white woman, hidden beneath a swathe of cloth.

'Who knows what those consequences are?' I asked the class as they shuffled forward, clearly captivated by the subject matter.

'My mum getting cross,' said one of the smaller girls, as she bit her bottom lip with her top teeth. 'And telling me I'm stupid.'

'Hey, it ain't stupid to have sex,' said Tracey, holding the banana in an upright position with both hands. Rather too tightly in my opinion.

'It is if you get pregnant,' said Esther. 'My sister is stupid. She's done it twice.'

'She got two babies then?' asked Mo, turning to look at her classmate.

'Three,' said Esther.

'That's three times, then,' said Mo.

'Triplets – she did it once without getting caught so did it again and had three babies all at once. She nearly died.'

'Bleedin' hell no wonder, poor thing — that must have been painful,' said Tracey. 'Having one is like pushing a cannon ball out. Three must be like the Battle of Trafalgar.'

She shook her head which had the effect of loosening her scarf. It was good to see her hair was growing back and the rash was going down.

'God bless her front bottom, it must have stretched itself to the size of a carrier bag. Any future rumpy pumpy will be like throwing a chipolata down the M1.'

The girls looked puzzled and I didn't try to explain. I wasn't a hundred per cent sure I knew exactly what she was talking about anyway.

'So,' I said. 'What are the other consequences?'

The girls looked around and shrugged their shoulders, as did Tracey. I'd forgotten her catalogue of dubious 'girl's problems' – the euphemism for a variety of sexually transmitted diseases — which all started as a result of the freedom women achieved in the swinging sixties and the 'birth' of the contraceptive pill.

Negating the risk of pregnancy turned women into sexual equals in the mating game, hunted by randy men only too keen to support the concept of free love, probably on the basis they were getting their end away with considerable regularity. This led on, in the case of Tracey's generation, to the scratchy seventies, itchy eighties and the nasty-rash nineties – and that was if you were lucky.

HIV and AIDS had a big impact on the generation below Tracey's. Too frightened of sexually transmitted diseases the condom became the 'norm' for new couples from the eighties onwards – until they both felt comfortable enough to go to the STI clinic together for a mutually acceptable 'all clear'. The clinic visit overtook farting in bed as the sign you were in a long-term relationship.

'Does it stop the devil getting inside you?' said Esther, and judging by the look on her face she meant it seriously.

'I don't think the devil exists,' I said, hoping to quell her fear.

'Oh, he bloody does,' piped up Tracey as she swung her legs back and forth on the desk, still holding the banana only this time between her legs. 'He's called Posh Git and he's married to my daughter.'

'My mother says that my father was the devil's spawn,' said Esther, waiting for an answer.

'Condoms stop spawn going anywhere,' said Tracey as she ripped the cover off a red 'Smiley Face' pack with her teeth (not the best start to the lesson) and proceeded to take out the contents with her lips – much to the enthrallment of her audience. Within seconds she'd manipulated the prophylactic onto the banana with her mouth, proclaiming 'Ta Dah!' once she'd secured it into position. She sounded like an advert for Boots make-up.

The girls were open mouthed, as was Tony who was looking through the window having come out from wherever he was hiding. I waved for him to come in, but he looked away rapidly, pretending he hadn't seen, and ran off in a direction nowhere near his office. I hoped he wasn't going to report Tracey for indecent behaviour.

'Forget about putting a ring on it,' said Tracey. 'Put a thing on it. Don't let him put his giblets anywhere near you without a coat on.'

'Giblets?' I couldn't help but say out loud.

'Yeah, that's what they look like, men's bits – chicken necks, or, if you're lucky, turkey necks,' said Tracey, laughing her raucous laugh.

I thought of Darius and his rather proud collection of genitalia and couldn't think of the resemblance, although it had been a long time since the butcher had given me any giblets, so to speak.

'Does it stop the devil, though?' asked Esther with increasing impatience.

'It stops a range of things,' I tried to explain. 'Pregnancy being one of them and then all the diseases you can catch from having sexual relationships.'

'Like AIDS,' said Mo, looking glum.

'There's AIDS but there are also a few more such as syphilis,' I said.

'Then there's gonorrhoea, chlamydia, smelly vag syndrome – or BV or something, don't know what it stands for,' Tracey added with enthusiasm. 'Herpes – that's a nasty one, scabies, crabs, trick, don't know how to pronounce the full word and, of course, thrush. Not that I've had them all, you understand. Never got scabies or herpes although one of me mates did and is now the leading expert on it.'

'Fascinating,' I said as the girls looked shell shocked at the sheer potential of infection.

'I don't think I'm ever going to have sex,' said Mo. 'It's very dangerous.'

'You might change your mind when you meet the right man,' I said, trying to instil a sense of the concept of making love rather than the current trend for sleeping with anything for the instant gratification it might offer.

'You might change it back again if you meet the wrong one,' said Tracey, unwrapping another selection of condoms ranging from fruit flavoured and fun, to large, sensitive and ribbed. She even had one with a battery attached which I asked her to hide not so much because it was inappropriate but because batteries are so expensive in Africa.

'One of these could stop a whole catalogue of disasters,' said Tracey as she blew up a blue condom before placing it over her head. 'Don't ever let any bloke say they're too big to wear 'em,' she added as she snapped the rubber back into position. 'If he is, you don't want to go anywhere near him.'

I saw Tony scurry past the window in the opposite direction to previously but he didn't look through the glass, no doubt fearing what he might encounter.

One of the smaller girls pushed herself to the front of the class. Wide-eyed but nervous she had her hand up but didn't say anything.

'What is it, Izzie?' I asked, remembering her name and how it reminded me of one of the TV programmes my kids use to watch.

'But what if you don't want to do it at all?' she said.

'Just say no!' said Tracey. 'You don't need to do nuffin' you don't want to.'

'Sometimes they don't take no for an answer,' said the girl.

I looked over at Tracey who looked back at me, then we both looked at Izzie.

'Who doesn't take no for an answer, Izzie?' I asked, hoping I sounded sensitive and the type of adult she could talk to.

'Those men who come into our village and do whatever they like to the women. My sister said we must pray it doesn't happen.'

I wasn't sure at first what Izzie meant but after some gentle coaxing it transpired that she lived in a rural area that had been affected by Boko Haram. Hundreds of women and girls had been raped having been locked in houses and at the beck and call of fighters who forced them to have sex, sometimes with the goal of getting them pregnant.

'One of them married my cousin and then she had a baby. She didn't want it but she was forced. They choose the ones they wanted to marry. My cousin shouted but they said they would shoot her.'

She went on to explain that the radical Islamist sect had taken over large stretches of territory in the country's northeast where she originally came from and targeted women, using 'marriage' as a way of justifying sexual violence.

'The men do what they want with their... giblets. They put them where they want, when they want. All in the name of their religion,' said Izzie, her voice rising with indignation at a regime that ruled through fear.

No condom could protect them from that.

CHAPTER THIRTEEN

'We've found Baz's exact location now,' said Tom as he came through the door, his shirt soaked with sweat. He still hadn't got used to the searing humidity of the country he'd come to for his gap year.

'So where is he?' I asked, not sure if I really cared whether he was found or not. There was something about him that always had an air of the miscreant and vaguely criminal, although to date I'd no evidence to support that. Tracey would often tell us he'd gone here, or there, with various excuses for his long disappearances. She believed his stories about his 'business' which was probably a blessing, in my view.

'He's been following your map,' said Darius.

'How do you know that?' I asked, curious that Baz would be the slightest bit interested in anything to do with me. I had the feeling he viewed my entire persona as irrelevant to him and his life.

'I was trying to find him at the same time as looking up some geographical details for some of the markings on the map. When I checked one after the other I realised there were some similarities. Baz has been heading for a building off the beaten track somewhere between here and the Outreach Centre.'

I wondered what he meant by 'off the beaten track'. It brought back some memories of when Tracey and I were escaping from our hostages. We certainly hadn't been on the main road when driven to the university by Luter, the one-armed taxi driver. It was very rocky terrain that took us to the seclusion of Bill's office and certainly could be described as 'off the beaten track.'

'Do you think it could be Bill's office?' I suggested. 'It's where I met him and Pussy, where he helped us – giving us another car to take us to the university as we thought Luter's was being followed.'

I thought a bit harder, trying to recall the exact location although it was almost impossible. Every bit of road looked the same – dusty, dry and relatively uninhabited.

'The building was like a small cricket pavilion with a couple of rooms – he worked from there I believe, because he liked being miles from anywhere. He might even have lived there. He didn't look like a man who wanted much to keep him comfortable.'

I remembered my first sight of the rickety, makeshift building. It had initially brought terror but was actually the key to our final getaway – and also the only sign of habitation for miles.

'High five, Grandma!' said Tom, raising his hand at me in a manner I wasn't overly familiar with. I realised I needed to smack it, but being shorter than him by a good foot, I missed and ended up smacking his chest instead. He shook his head in mild amusement.

'I think you might have got it,' said Darius picking up a copy of the map and studying it. 'You're right, if it is where you think it is, then the shed is the only building around there for miles. The terrain is pretty barren other than the road above, that just runs for miles with no real life to break it up. You clever old thing you,' he added, giving me a hug.

'Less of the old,' I said, although I did feel that my maturity had offered a sensible and experienced approach to the conundrum. 'It makes sense that he would keep anything of any value in his office. There was no one else there and I doubt many people knew about it,' I added, wondering if I might have made it as a detective had I ever given any thought to a career.

'I think we will need to deploy some of our resources tomorrow,' said Darius, which I'd learnt to understand meant him and Tom would be off on a mission the next day, one they would treat as if it were top secret and confined to the capabilities of the men of the household. It was similar to the issue of putting the bins out or tuning in the television. But probably more exciting from their point of view.

'What will you do about Baz?' I asked, vaguely hoping there might be proceedings for stealing my map and therefore conclusive evidence about his untrustworthy character; hopefully followed by a long prison sentence.

'I don't think we need to do anything other than follow him,' said Tom. 'If you're right, Grandma, then he'll be at the hut and we can deal with him then.'

'He might even have led us to an important clue about the map,' said Darius. 'So maybe we can let the matter of how he got hold of it drop, for everyone's sake.' Darius had read my mind.

Darius was no more of a supporter of Baz than I was, but we had both agreed a while ago we would tolerate him for Tracey's sake. It wouldn't do to get him into any trouble, not least because his mother would be on at him like a tonne of bricks. She still hadn't got over having to pay back Tracey the five thousand pounds he'd 'borrowed' off her before they got (forcibly) married.

We'd been invited to Buke's later in the evening for a meal. She was keen to catch up on the progress of our schoolwork, Darius's activity and Tom's involvement. We weren't sure how much to tell her about what had been going on with the map and Baz. We thought it best we kept him out of any conversations for the time being, so we agreed that any references to what was going on outside of the Outreach Centre would be kept as vague as possible.

'I'm so happy you've settled into the centre so quickly,' said Buke as she welcomed us into her vast, colourful home. 'I knew it was a good choice to take you on.'

'Thank you,' I said, feeling a little bit of a fraud when it came to our classroom activities. With regard to the education programme, it was clear that some elements had been more popular than others. Integrating geography with domestic science and home management was a success, but the matters of hairdressing and sex education hadn't quite gone as expected. Most of Tracey's condoms had made their way home with a couple of the girls and were used to make flour bombs by their brothers. I'd hoped that that news had been kept from her.

As it was, there was nothing she seemed to have missed and soon after arriving at her house I realised that Tony, for all his fumbling, was the eyes and ears of our host. He'd reported back everything other than minor details, the ones only missed because of him hiding in the toilets. I felt a little ashamed, although Buke seemed to be happy to gloss over the incidents I was feeling concerned about. Perhaps she expected nothing less from anything that involved input from Tracey.

When Buke pulled me over for a 'quiet word' I thought I was going to get a telling off. She was the sort of woman who could put you in your place, but so nicely you'd hardly notice. Thankfully I was wrong.

'I need to let you know we have a problem with one of the sponsors of the centre. I think you met him, Mr Toyin Remy, the politician.'

I only remembered him for his apparent disinterest in his investment so wasn't surprised when Buke told me she thought he might be reneging on some of his promises of further finance.

'It may be that we won't want to be associated with his funds, anyway,' she added, telling me that rumours were rife of corruption and fraud on a global scale.

'He has always been suspiciously wealthy, even for a politician in an African country,' Buke said. 'I was always concerned about his involvement but I've learned to never look a gift horse in the mouth.'

At that moment Tracey came through the door and towards us. She was warmly welcomed by her mother-in-law, who changed the subject of our conversation. I suspected she didn't want Mr Remy's possible exposure to blemish the reputation of the centre just yet and wasn't entirely sure Tracey's tongue could be trusted to stay still.

'I hear Izzie has been telling you of her cousin's life in one of the villages,' Buke said as one of her staff passed round a tray with drinks of an indescribable colour. I took one and sipped carefully – it tasted of aniseed. Tracey took one and swigged it in one go, following the tray to help herself to another.

'Bloody lovely,' she said, smacking her lips. Buke raised her eyebrows at me in a 'nothing surprises me about that woman' manner.

As I admired Tracey's constitution, I hoped the drink wouldn't have the same affect Buke's last cocktails had on my digestive system. I couldn't move more than one hundred yards from a toilet for two and a half days, and after that I built up particularly strong muscles trying to retain wind. I might be living with Darius but I didn't want to introduce permanent flatulence into our relationship just yet.

We both told Buke that we had found the conversation with Izzie distressing. Although we'd heard of these things happening, they came so much closer when told by a child who was directly involved.

"She will tell you it is her cousin, but it was her own family,' said Buke. 'Dat is why she is one of the girls chosen for our education. We wanted to get her out of da environment, one where the weight of guilt is heavy on those who escaped.'

'That is bloody awful,' said Tracey. 'These men need their knackers cut off. What's the matter with them, destroying these young people without a sodding thought for what they are doing to people?'

Buke explained that often the girls who escaped the worst of the treatment suffered from a kind of survivor syndrome. They worried about their families and couldn't always understand why they'd been spared by their god.

'It is almost as bad for those who witness the atrocities as for those who suffer them. All the girls get caught up in this shameful treatment and attitude to them.'

It was a sombre moment broken quickly by the arrival of Chinaza, dressed in a beautiful skin-tight dress made of a petrol blue material so sheer it might as well have been painted on. I cast a sideways glance at Darius and was again pleased to note her appearance still seemed to have little effect on him other than the usual warm affection for a colleague.

'Jesus wept, she's like a filleted anchovy,' muttered Tracey, looking her up and down with such vigour she resembled one of those nodding dogs people used to have in the back of their cars.

Well, I say people, but Mavis is the only person I know to have had one after winning it from her insurance company for completing a survey. 'I've seen more meat under a butcher's fingernails,' added Tracey.

Tom, unlike Darius, seemed incapable of maintaining his own equilibrium. Had his eyes grown any bigger they'd have flopped out on his cheeks and I suspected his 'giblets' were going through turmoil, judging by the way he was moving from side to side uncomfortably before he asked to be excused. Returning a few minutes later with evidence of a 'cold water splash' still trickling down the side of his face, he clumsily went forward to kiss Chinaza on either cheek, at the same time as spilling some of his drink onto his shoes.

'That's one way of cleaning them,' she said, joking with him to ease his tension. It didn't help, he immediately looked down and bumped his head against her glass, knocking the contents over the front of her dress.

Buke handed her a cloth which she used to delicately mop up the spillage, while Tom looked on with his cheeks burning to such a colour they'd be considered dangerous on a baby.

'You ain't going to offer to help out?' said Tracey, laughing loudly at her suggestion. She stopped quickly when Chinaza threw her a glare sufficient to freeze the gates of hell.

'Have you converted?' Chinaza asked, coldly.

'Whaddya mean?' said Tracey, looking uncomfortable. She was rarely thrown by sarcasm but seemed overwhelmed by the presence of this very beautiful woman.

'The hijab,' she said, pointing to Tracey's scarf.

'The what?' said Tracey. 'I ain't converted to nuffin.' She pulled the scarf over to one side to reveal her head, now growing tufts of wiry hair, mostly brown but spattered with grey at the temples.

Chinaza could barely contain her smiles, ignoring Tracey and turning to Tom.

'I hear you have broken through the code,' she said to him, while handing the cloth back to the waiter who was still occupied with delivering drinks. He wasn't sure what to do with it, so stuffed it in his pocket and then gave a look suggesting he wasn't impressed with the situation at all.

'Um, not really,' said Tom, barely able to lift his head and so looking at her from deep beneath his eyebrows.

Darius had told me he thought Tom had formed a bit of a crush on his work mate. Chinaza had been mentoring him since his arrival and had been very kind, showing him all the resources at Forensix and introducing him to staff who could offer their knowledge and support. Tom had fallen for her, drawn by her welcome, and by all accounts she thought he was very interesting. Chinaza was only five years older than my grandson. But at 23 seemed to much more sophisticated and worldly, certainly compared to him.

'The older woman, you see,' said Darius one night as he peeled off my linen dress and kissed my neck, tracing the shape of a heart with his lips over my chest. 'Totally and utterly mesmerising.'

I can't remember anything he said after that but lost myself in his caresses. After a number of months together he'd been like a student of my every need, learning exactly what would collapse any resistance I might have to his advances. Not that I could see any point in resistance. Had I known what I was missing when I'd been married so conscientiously to Colin, I might have had a very unhappy marriage.

'Oh, he's done brilliantly,' Darius said to Chinaza, always keen to support my grandson's work but in this case clearly boosting him up in front of Tom's crush. 'We're sure we know where we are going tomorrow and there's little doubt we will bring back the intelligence we're after.'

'Do you know what it is we might find?' she asked Tom who was so busy staring he didn't hear the question.

'Information, treasure, dead bodies, Lord Lucan, the secret recipe for Kentucky Fried Chicken?' she asked again, teasingly. Tom was jolted into the moment and stuttered that he wasn't really sure.

'There are some numbers, pictures and letters written in some kind of pattern, although I don't recognise it as code,' Tom explained. 'I'm hoping they will make more sense when we get there. Maybe they'll link up with something we find. It's a bit of a mystery really.'

Chinaza smiled warmly at Tom who asked to be excused again and disappeared out into the garden, where I could see him take a cigarette out of a packet and light it.

I could kill Tracey for offering him one of her 'fags' when he first came over. He'd got himself hooked and when he gets home his mother will surely blame me.

CHAPTER FOURTEEN

Darius decided it would be best for me to accompany him and Tom on their quest to find the building located on the map.

'If it's where you think it is, you'll recognise it,' he said. 'Anyway, I like it when you're with me.'

I like being with Darius even when he's working. Just having him near makes me feel safe, particularly after the incident in the market – and my concerns about the car I keep seeing around our house and by the centre. He said it wouldn't be anything to worry about and lots of people do weird things in Nigeria but I sensed he didn't really mean it. He wouldn't let me go anywhere on my own and had even said he would be driving me to work rather than let me get the bus.

It didn't take much persuasion for me to agree to go with them, despite my having concerns about whether my memory would be of any use. I often found I had blocked out a lot of detail surrounding the kidnap and how we escaped and wondered if I would remember the whereabouts of a shed I'd only been in briefly and had not seen for some months. Maybe being in the area again would act as a prompt, and I wanted to be helpful although my map reading and sense of direction has never been that great. When I started driving more after Colin died, I'd often find myself driving fifteen times round a roundabout trying to choose the right turn off to get home. That was after living where I did for over forty years.

I asked Tracey to look after the girls during my lesson, which was scheduled to be about nutrition but I suspected would end up being something else – like how to walk in stilettos in the snow (very practical advice here), or use nylon tights as a weapon. The class would often delight in her stories and talks although I wondered how much use they could ever make of

Tracey's gems. Still, I learned about algebra and have yet to work out the point of it or, indeed, the purpose of knowing that Lulworth Cove has a variety of rock types that provide a continuous sequence covering 80 million years of Earth history from the Jurassic to the Cretaceous Periods. I know the world has been here a long time but can't see what use it was inspecting the caves and arches for a week's geography field trip c. 1971. I hadn't been there before or since and it was this pointless piece of education that had me questioning school altogether.

The journey to the area of Bill's shed took longer than expected, not least because Darius allowed Tom to drive. I sat in the back of the car, slamming my right foot to the floor on a regular basis in the hope it might slow him down.

'Please, Tom,' I said. 'You'll have my nerves shot to pieces roaring round these bends.'

'You'll be fine, Nan,' he said. 'There's nothing to hit out here.'

Darius was monitoring where we were heading and gave us a regular report of how far we had to go. I think it was mainly for my benefit as we were never more than twenty miles away, even when Tom took the wrong turning and ended up in a turkey farm. Looking at the straggly beasts, I couldn't understand why they ever became our nation's favourite Christmas meal. I was minded of Tracey's reference to 'giblets' and for a moment considered becoming a vegetarian.

It took us all by surprise when we came across the shed and I immediately recognised it – not least because Luter's car was still parked outside. We had left it there and transferred over to the one given to us by Bill after we had explained to him that we thought we were being followed. Looking back, it was very helpful of him.

'There it is, there it is,' I pointed out excitedly although they both already knew.

We parked up and Darius checked the map again after opening his door to let some air into the cabin.

'These numbers don't make any sense,' he said. 'I don't think they are co-ordinates. They must mean something else.'

Tom stretched and leaned over Darius to take a look.

'I did wonder if they might be some kind of formula,' he said. 'They remind me of the things our science teachers would put on the blackboards.'

'Wasn't Bill studying science at the university?' said Darius, his voice drifting as he looked over to the shed and saw something moving inside. 'What's that?' he said, as he quickly left the passenger seat and crept, head out of sight of the shed's windows, towards the door.

Tom and I got out of the car to hear the sound of a series of squeals, none of which I thought could ever come from Darius's deep and mellow voice box. A few moments later, Baz emerged sheepishly through the door of the shed, looking like a teenager that had been caught looking at his father's collection of adult magazines. (I won't tell you how I know that face, but my son and I found out quite a bit about Reader's Wives on a fateful evening of 1975.)

'I wasn't doing anything, honest,' Baz was telling Darius who nudged him forward every time he tried to turn back. 'I just wanted to get away for a few days.'

'Funny you wanted to get away to here, isn't it?' said Darius, showing a rare sign of irritation. 'It would be nothing to do with stealing Cynthia's map, would it?'

Baz didn't say anything. He kicked random stones as he walked towards the car, where Darius forcibly placed him in the back before locking it, securing the child locks with the remote-control key. I hoped that I wouldn't have to sit next to him on the way home.

The inside of the shed was just the same, with the office to the right where Tracey and I had first hidden with Luter when we thought Pussy was a potential attacker. It was virtually as we last saw it – with Pussy's perch in the corner and the phone still on the desk.

'I really don't know what to make of it all,' said Darius, as he walked around opening drawers and cupboards that all seemed to be empty. 'What do you think, Tom?'

Tom was pouring over a piece of paper he'd picked up from Bill's desk. It was covered in similar notes to the map.

'I think these are chemical equations,' he said after a while. 'They're so like what I could never understand at school.'

'What is this, then?' asked Darius, pointing to one of the signs on the map that looked like a fish although it was very specific. 'Do you think he was some kind of Christian?'

'He didn't say so, if he was,' I said. 'He didn't strike me as the type.'

'Is there a type?' said Darius, smiling. He was teasing me again for my British stereotyping.

'Of course there is. They drink moderately and we know that Bill loved drinking to excess,' I said, teasing my lover by reverting back to the worst aspects of my middle class upbringing and ability to put everyone into a social box.

Tom and Darius smiled at each other and went back to looking around Bill's office which revealed his liking for Jaffa Cakes – three empty boxes were in the bin – and a disliking for his wife, as his divorce papers were framed and hanging proudly beneath a sign proclaiming 'Freedom is never given, it is won.'

'He likes his fish, they're drawn everywhere,' said Darius, looking at a notepad with a doodle of a fish exactly like the one on the map.

'It must mean something,' said Tom. 'What kind of fish is it?'

We listed as many as we could; seabream, trout, carp, goldfish.

'Haddock, cod,' said Darius.

It was when he added 'Perch' that Tom came alive.

'Brill,' he said.

'Is Brill a fish?' Darius asked.

'No, I mean brilliant. Look – a perch. Pussy's perch, perhaps it is a cryptic clue?'

They pulled at the bird stand and tried removing various bits from it. As they did so, Tom came across something that caught his hand.

'Ouch, that was scratchy,' he said, inspecting the end of the long metal tube that held the entire thing upright. He ran his hands over the top and then down to where to tubes met in the middle.

'Bloody hell,' he added, tugging at a small metal item with a prong at the end of it.

'It's a USB memory stick, stuck inside,' said Tom. 'What would that be doing here?'

Darius was busy shaking the perch, making it rattle.

'I think there's something else inside,' he said, turning it upside down. The sound of items moving was clear to us all, so he jabbed at the end, revealing a rubber stopper which was easily removed. As Darius tipped out the contents, it became clear that Bill had something to hide.

'Good grief,' I said, not able to contain my excitement at the fact a multitude of precious stones fell from where Pussy once held court. I bent down to look through them and there was no doubt the diamonds, amethysts, opals and other jewels were a minor treasure trove.

'No wonder Baz was here sniffing around. He must have guessed there was a chance of finding something of interest,' I added as the sound of the car's horn started blaring outside. It would do that if you moved enough while shut inside when it was locked.

'You think he's that bright?' said Darius.

I had no time to answer before there was a loud bang behind us. Baz was brandishing a large metal bar and waving it in our direction as he ran towards me, pulling my arm hard to bring me in close.

'I'll kill her if you move as much as one muscle,' he shouted while I wondered what had got into him. I'd never been frightened of him before and just considered him with contempt, but he was scaring me now. Baz certainly seemed very agitated and my concern for my welfare increased the more he shouted.

'This is my treasure,' Baz said as he pointed to the stones on the floor. 'It is my lucky break, time to make something of myself. I was here first, so give them to me.'

Darius was reluctant but as Baz strengthened the grip on my arm and I winced, he scooped them up and put them back into the perch before handing them over.

'You stay here. Don't move,' Baz added, picking up a key from the desk. He pitched me forward so I lost my balance and hit my head against a shelf. I thought I saw him look worried, particularly when he saw the blood that was running over my eye and blurring my vision, but he shook his worry away, turned and let me go.

Tom moved forward as if to hit him but Darius pulled him back, shaking his head. Baz picked up the few stones which had not been put back in their hiding place before turning away and locking us in the building. Seconds later we heard the car start and the sound of tyres screeching along the gravel track.

'Are you OK Cynthia?' asked Darius. 'I'm so sorry I let that happen to you.'

'And me,' said Tom, joining Darius to inspect the bruise that was starting to throb around my left eye. 'What a pig!'

'I'm fine. It wasn't your fault, either of you. I wonder where he'll go now,' I said, thinking it could be the last we might see of Baz and, although Tracey might be upset for a bit it would only be from a sense of rejection, not from any feelings of genuine loss.

'As far away as possible, I hope,' said Darius as he got on to his mobile phone and called the Forensix head office, while at the same time dabbing my cut with a clean hanky from his pocket. Colin always had to have a neatly pressed handkerchief rather than ever use a tissue and it seemed it was the one very small thing I could find he had in common with my lover.

'He didn't get this, anyway,' said Tom, holding out the USB stick in his hand. 'I can't wait to see what's on it.'

Darius told us that help would be on its way very soon and, sure enough, we were released quickly – having had only enough time to sweep the entire premises and find nothing else at all that would give any clue to Bill's intentions regarding the map and my involvement in his scheme.

CHAPTER FIFTEEN

We got the call that Tracey and the girls at the centre were being held by a masked man moments after we got back home. They told us there had been an ambush but no reports of any injuries. The authorities were dealing with it and would keep us up to date...

I wanted to immediately go and find out what was going on but we were warned not to get involved and told that the situation was under control and unlikely to escalate. It didn't stop me worrying though, as I thought back to Tracey and my kidnap. We probably weren't in any real danger, but it certainly didn't feel like it.

I wondered if anyone had been able to contact Baz, although I wasn't sure how much he'd care about his wife being kept hostage yet again.

The team from Forensix had released us from the shed, a process they found easy enough as we'd only been locked in with a single Yale lock and Baz had left the key in place. Had it been necessary we could have got out by ramming the door or smashing a window.

The two men who came to get us were from the company's security team and asked a few questions about what we were doing, but Darius and Tom didn't want to explain what we'd found. They wanted more time to investigate the situation themselves, so Darius handed over some cash 'for a drink for all their help' and asked for the incident to remain unreported. I suspected Darius wanted to deal with him in his own way, possibly humiliating him in front of his mother, something he would find thoroughly embarrassing and far more of a punishment than anything the local authorities could administer.

Pussy had been dancing up and down making phone noises

and so we nearly didn't answer when it rang for real. I think she was miffed we'd been away for so long and left her on her own with no-one to talk to. Ada had been in, but I suspected she covered her cage the minute she arrived.

The police told us there'd been an official report of someone going into the centre just a few minutes before our return. The person was refusing to let the girls in the class go home and had been shouting demands at Tracey, but no-one seemed sure what those demands were.

Tony had managed to escape because he'd not been seen by the intruder – no surprise there – so the captor wasn't aware he was in the school. The police officer told Darius that when Tony heard the screams of the girls, and the man's shouts, he'd made a dash for it and called the police. They went straight to the building to surround it and then tried to make contact with those inside.

'Why didn't do something?' asked Tom, bewildered that a young man would leave a group of fourteen girls and a woman on their own. 'What sort of a bloke is he?'

'Probably a very sensible one,' said Darius. 'We don't know what we're dealing with. There have been many cases of people being taken by radical groups. They can be dangerous. We can only hope this isn't what we have here.'

We'd been home for over an hour and still no news had come through from the centre to suggest what was going on. The information we had was that negotiators had tried, and failed, to get some communication going. They could hear a man telling everyone to keep quiet and that they wouldn't get hurt. Other than that, there were no particular conditions being made known. The good news was there was still no suggestion anyone had been hurt.

We were asked to meet at Buke's house as it was thought that any demands could be directed to the centre's management. Lady O was a well-known figure and could easily be a target in her own right. Just before we left our house, we had another call from the police but it wasn't offering any update, it was to let Darius know that his car had been found in a café a few miles away from Bill's shed.

'I suspect he's managed to find cover somewhere and he's hiding low,' said Darius. 'No-one has seen or heard of him.'

He organised for Forensix to send a driver to collect the car with a spare key and to investigate further, although no-one was particularly concerned about Baz at this point. The main issue was Tracey and the girls, and what was happening at the centre.

When we got to Buke's house I was asked to describe the nature of the girls' temperaments, and Tracey's likely stability, to the police. They needed to know if there were going to be any specific problems they would need to deal with. I just hoped my friend didn't run out of cigarettes or she might get very tetchy indeed.

'Let's pray Tracey keeps her cool,' said Buke. 'She can be a bit of a hot head sometimes.'

I thought back to when we were kidnapped and through all the days we were kept hostage. She had a tendency to get emotional, particularly in the light of nicotine withdrawal or getting to the end of a second bottle of wine, but there was nothing to suggest she wouldn't do all she could to protect the students. I had seen her grow fond of them and, knowing her as I did, suspected she would do something to surprise their captor.

I thought about Baz and whether or not anyone should at least try and leave a message for him about Tracey's predicament. Then I thought again. He had shown no signs of caring very much about anyone, least of all his wife.

Buke wasn't yet aware that her son had tried his own bit of hostage taking at Bill's office, proving with his treatment of me that he hadn't learned any lessons about being a decent human being. Darius, Tom and I had agreed to keep what he'd done under wraps until we knew what was going on. There'd been no harm done, other than a slight black eye and a small cut which I'd managed to hastily cover with some make-up. He'd made off with some jewels but there was little he could do without trying to sell them. When he did, we were sure we'd trace him as he was too stupid to be cautious. I felt sorry for Buke knowing how disappointed she would be in her one and only son when the truth came out.

Tom was itching to look at the memory stick he'd found but

had been asked to stay with us while the situation at the centre was looking serious.

'Whatever is on the stick will still be there tomorrow,' said Darius. 'It might be nothing, anyway. Let's just make sure we stay safe and that we can help secure the release of Tracey and the girls.'

'Has anything suspicious happened to you recently?' asked a police offer, sent in to gather information about all we'd done at the centre. He wanted to know pretty much everything Tracey and I had seen and done since we'd started work. I decided to keep the sex education classes to myself. I didn't think the ability to blow up a condom like a balloon, to the point it would fit over your head, would have any bearing on the matter in hand.

I told him about our desire to teach the young girls about being independent and making choices but he didn't seem interested, so I told him about the market, when Tracey and I were pushed to the ground and I was given the note saying I was being watched. The officer asked why I hadn't reported it and I stopped myself from suggesting that they probably wouldn't have been very interested anyway.

'What did this person look like?' asked the officer, as he took notes. 'Can you describe him or her?'

'He had very nice shoes,' I replied. 'And suit trousers with a stripe in them. I couldn't see much else from the floor, other than his walking cane which was quite fancy. It looked like it had a green stone in it although it could have been the light reflecting back.'

'What about the car you thought might be following you? Can you remember what that looked like?'

I'm not very good with cars. I had a Toyota all through the school-run days, but I thought it was a Honda. I also knew it was blue and that it had a fifth gear which I didn't know about for three years.

'It was a sort of green-silver colour and quite big, like a Jaguar or Volvo,' I said, realising I was probably making up what it might be, as I didn't have a clue. 'It went past very quickly and disappeared every time I saw it.'

The officer seemed frustrated with my lack of information

and snapped his notebook closed. He went to answer a knock on the door, being on guard duty, and Chinaza made her way through to where we were all sitting.

'I'm so glad you're all OK,' she said, giving us all a hug which I found strangely peculiar but welcome. She wasn't a hugging sort of person, being very angular, but her soft perfume and affectionate embrace lent a warmness I hadn't expected. I was pleased she didn't linger over Darius. I didn't want her smell on him next time we got close.

Buke brought in some tea and had just set it down when the officer's phone rang. He went off into another room to answer it.

'Does anyone have any idea what is going on?' said Chinaza, looking genuinely concerned. 'Do we know if Tracey and the girls are OK or what is wanted of them?'

The officer came back in the room and asked everyone for quiet.

'It seems there is some new information which suggests there might be a terrorist organisation behind this incident. Paperwork has been found relating to ISIS and we understand that one of the people involved is a recently converted member of the organisation.'

There was an audible gasp as everyone expressed their concern. We had been talking only recently about Boko Haram and the threat to world peace. I couldn't cope with the irony of escaping from scammers, only for Tracey and the girls to fall into the hands of these people.

'We have everyone working on this and I can assure you we will do our best to resolve the situation as quickly and calmly as possible,' added the officer who was visibly shaking.

'Where was the paperwork found?' said Chinaza. 'How does anyone know it relates to ISIS?'

The officer explained that a car, believed to have been used by the captor, contained a package of paperwork about some kind of system designed to bring down the community – it had been isolated by a bomb squad but had clear markings on the top.

'There was also a lot of explosive type of liquid and a range of different hijabs and burqas of the kind the terrorist groups insist their women wear. This would strongly suggest an extremist cell of the type we've seen develop in recent years. We believe the clothing is for the girls and that the captor will make the students wear it.'

My chest tightened and my palms started to sweat. Tracey and the girls had become a surprisingly dear part of my new life and to think of them in any danger was like hearing my flesh and blood family was under threat.

'What can we do to help?' said Buke, looking as uncomfortable as I'd ever seen her. I suspected she was fonder of Tracey than she'd want to let on, plus she had a vested interest in the girls who she wanted to educate not subject to even more terror in their young lives.

'There's something more,' added the officer, helping himself to some tea and settling down in Buke's best armchair without asking. 'And it is rather puzzling.'

'What's that?' said Buke, overly sharply. I got the impression she was fed up with the languid style of the policeman and his disregard for her upholstery.

'Another man went into the centre, separately from the original intruder, and he took your friend. He left the original attacker and the girls behind. We can't work out if he is working with the first person or if this is totally separate from him.'

Darius sighed and Buke frowned.

I knew it was now time to be worried.

CHAPTER SIXTEEN

It was all over the news. An English woman had been snatched in a surprise attack, while fourteen Nigerian students of the Outreach Centre remained in captivity, held by a man believed to be closely linked to a terrorist organisation.

The television reporters seemed to be enjoying the fact there was a possible terrorist link to the situation and the police relished the puzzle of two men being involved, not knowing whether they were working as a team or separately.

'The hostages were overwhelmed by the swiftness of the ambush,' said the man on the news. 'A man then somehow got through the barricades at the back of the centre and took a white woman hostage, leaving behind all the others including the original attacker and a number of female students,' he continued in the dispassionate way newsreaders do. Doesn't he know that 'a white woman' is called Tracey, and that she's my friend?

'How did a guy manage to get through the back of the centre while it was under police surveillance?' said Darius, almost angry. It was rare to see him agitated but he'd been told Forensix couldn't get involved in the situation and he was frustrated. I know he would have had a team on it far quicker and better than the Nigerian authorities could provide.

'What on earth is going on here, and why would anyone want to kidnap Tracey?' he said as we continued watching the broadcast on the kitchen TV. The story had gone international and created a wave of concern across the world.

It was a good question. What would anyone want Tracey for? She had no money and certainly no knowledge about anything that could be useful to terrorists. Not even hairdressing, as we'd come to find out. It was even stranger, but perhaps coincidence, that two people seemed to want her but no-one knew if they were working together or apart.

'Perhaps they've mistaken her for someone else,' said Tom, still in his pyjamas despite it being eleven in the morning. I call them pyjamas but he was wearing some lengthy underpants with buttons at the front and a faded T-shirt bearing the slogan 'Keep the Dream Alive – Go Back to Sleep.'

I couldn't think who they would mistake her for, unless they were looking for someone with an alopecia problem and a nasty skin rash.

The phone went and Pussy remained quiet. She hadn't mimicked it for some time and in fact had been generally subdued. Darius thought it was because we'd finally trained her, although my suspicions were that Ada had covered her over so many times, she'd lost the will to live.

'She doesn't like that bird,' I told him, and he raised his eyebrows at me.

'Who does?' he said, and he had a point; her use of a particularly offensive swear word, when the local priest had been here seeking donations for his church roof, had been very much to the point. We tried to explain it was the parrot but the Rev Michael, as he liked to call himself, sucked his teeth at Tom and told us he wouldn't be bothering us again. I, for one, was quite relieved and Pussy grew further in my affections.

'Yes, that's right,' I heard Darius say to the person who had called. 'Of course, that's no problem at all.'

He came back to the kitchen and flicked on the kettle. It didn't have any water in it so it made a banging noise and flashed. I got up to take over and was glad of my abilities on a domestic level. With all this stuff going on I was beginning to feel a bit useless.

'That was someone claiming to be Tracey's son-in-law. He's seen the news and realised that either you or Tracey were in trouble. He's coming over with Tracey's daughter. They're on their way to 'sort out all this mess' as he put it,' he said. 'Seems they think it's just a matter of coming over and telling the nasty kidnappers to give her back.'

Oh God, I thought in an uncharacteristic reference to a deity

I wasn't sure I believed in. That will be Posh Git. I realised I didn't know Tracey's daughter's name.

'I've heard about him,' I said. 'By all accounts he's a bit of an issue in the family. Tracey calls him Posh Git and he won't allow her into his house.'

'Bit like Dad, then,' said Tom, without appearing to think about what he'd said.

'What do you mean?' I asked, wondering why he thought my son-in-law was anything like Posh Git. I hardly saw him, anyway.

'He always goes out when you come round,' he added. 'Mum's always shouting at him about it.'

I was taken aback and felt wounded. I'd always been polite about his interest in his cycling and only once said that people on bikes were a nuisance and should pay the same road tax as car drivers. I even bought him a bicycle helmet once. It was from the charity shop but didn't look very used, apart from the slight crack at the top.

'I don't think it's that bad,' I said, looking across at Darius who, thankfully, was deep in thought. I'd always told him we had a close family and everyone adored everyone else. That's not altogether true but it is the kind of impression everyone wants to give about their blood relatives. I might not like some of them, but nobody else is allowed the same opinion.

'Dad's a bit weird anyway,' added Tom, reading through a local newspaper while I wondered about the times I'd been to Bobbie's house and her husband hadn't been there. That's the last time I buy him a fifty pound Halfords voucher for Christmas, I thought.

'There's something in here about the school, look,' said Tom.

He was pointing to a picture of Buke with Toyin Remy. Even there, posing for publicity purposes, he looked disengaged.

'He doesn't look very interested, does he?' said Tom, continuing to read.

'That was at the opening. I don't think he stayed very long, just enough time to get his photo taken,' I said remembering that Buke said she wasn't all that keen on him but was happy enough to take his money.

'There are few people with that kind of cash to give away to something that supports young girls. They aren't the priority of many of our politicians,' she said, and I realised how pragmatic even those with the most integrity have to be when it comes to money.

'Well, well, well,' said Tom, scratching at his chest while rubbing his spare hand through his hair. It reminded me of a day trip to Whipsnade Zoo when I thought it would be fun to go to the chimpanzee's tea party with my grandchildren. It wasn't.

'What?' I asked him, while thinking how that day at the zoo only seemed like a few months ago when in fact it was probably fifteen years in the past. Time is so deceptive. You hardly notice it going by until you look back and take notes. I should take more notes along the way..

'It seems Mr Remy has been arrested for getting up to no good,' said Tom, continuing to read with great interest.

'He's a politician, what do you expect?' said Darius, who'd had his eyes glued to the television in the hope of more news about Tracey. Maybe he cared about her more than he wanted to let on, like Buke. I knew the feeling, as she's a bit of an embarrassment as a friend. At the same time you wouldn't want anything to happen to her. She sort of grows on you. Her name should be Rose or Ivy.

'Let me have a look,' I said, and Tom passed the paper over as he shuffled out of his seat. I read the article which talked about fraudulent activity, investigations and possible seizure of all Mr Remy's funds. It was an unusual attack, as many African politicians widely used corruption and any other unsavoury means to get what they wanted. To make it into the news he must have done something pretty big.

'I'm going to get dressed if we've got visitors coming. I was hoping to start work on the memory stick today, to see what I can find,' said Tom.

'Haven't you done that yet?' I asked. I'd forgotten about it what with everything that had been going on. I wasn't really that interested. Baz had taken Bill's treasure so there wasn't likely to be much else to discover.'

'I managed to have a quick look. It's in an old format so I've just got to download a programme to open it up and read it. Shouldn't take long,' said Tom. 'I best go and get sorted before Tracey's family turn up. When are they due?'

'They're on their way,' said Darius.

'What?' I said, more loudly than I meant to, as Tom made his way up to the bathroom. 'Do you mean they're on their way from England? How long before they are here?'

I was thinking about the housework. I didn't want Ada around while all this was unfurling. She had wanted to be, to get the gossip, but Darius had paid her wages for the week and told her to take a holiday. Poor old Ada almost looked disappointed, although Pussy seemed much brighter, if less vocal. Whatever everyone thought, it meant the business of getting the house suitable for guests would be down to me.

'They called from the airport.'

'Which airport? Gatwick? Heathrow?'

'Lagos,' said Darius, still not realising the enormity of what he was saying. We had visitors about to arrive and I hadn't changed the beds, polished the mirrors, checked the bathrooms for stray hairs, bought flowers for the guest rooms, and so on. Had the man no idea about entertaining?

Then I felt a panic set in. Tracey called him Posh Git so would he expect a certain standard of hospitality.

'Have we any French wine in?' I asked Darius who looked at me as if he was about to laugh. He put on an African voice which he often does when he's teasing me, or we're playing the butler game where he has to do everything I ask. I had a sense of rising nausea associated with needing to give a good impression, regardless of who to.

'We will haf da African wine,' he said. 'Den we will feed dem our own goats wit a stew of der own blood,' he added, laughing so hard I couldn't help but feel left out. I just couldn't be that relaxed about unexpected visitors and hankered after the delicatessen's delivery service at the end of my road in Surrey.

'You just don't understand,' I said, hoping we at least had some cold beers in the fridge. I could feel the wrath of the Posh Git already.

Darius cocked his head to one side as he came over and picked me up, carrying me upstairs and telling me I needed to relax.

'I know just the thing,' he said as he put me back on my feet when we got to the landing.. I could hear Tom in the shower, something that would take him at least fifteen minutes for some reason I didn't want to consider.

'We haven't got time for all that,' I said as he pushed my blouse apart and stroked my nipples very gently with the insides of his thumbs before kissing my neck. I could feel his interest growing from beneath his loose, linen trousers and decided housework could take a running jump.

I didn't like the sound of Posh Git anyway.

CHAPTER SEVENTEEN

'What sort of a hell hole is this?' said Posh Git as he dropped down two real leather (and obviously very expensive) holdall cases in our hallway.

'Paul, by the way,' he added, holding out a hand for some time before Darius took hold of it.

'It's my hell hole,' said Darius, smiling. 'Nice to meet you, Mr By-The-Way,' he added, looking over at me and winking. Posh Git didn't notice the sarcasm as he was too busy looking over the top of pursed lips at our home. He clearly wanted to make sure we knew he wasn't impressed.

I could tell we might have fun with this silly man, although it was a shame we had to meet under such strained circumstances. He was as Tracey described him, irritatingly unpleasant and smug, with the sort of face you want to slap. Hard.

Darius had a way of coming across as very charming even when he'd probably have no concern about committing murder if it was necessary. I could see him looking at our visitor with a contempt that was disguised so well that even I found it hard to detect.

This part of my lover was very attractive to me as it made him very masculine; protective and endearing. His manliness drew me to him yet again, particularly in the cosy afterglow of our morning session which concluded around the same time Tom shouted for a clean towel. Darius shouted 'airing cupboard' at a critical moment and it sounded like he'd found the key to the meaning of life.

Tracey's daughter was a surprise. Donna, as she called herself – being short for Madonna – was quiet, flat-chested and mousy-haired. She barely spoke as Posh Git told us of their horrific journey via Nigerian Airlines, how the plane smelled of burning chicken and the toilets were flooded. I asked if they'd had turbulence and Donna said she'd taken some tablets for it before they left.

'I can be prone, particularly when I'm nervous,' she said in a clipped voice that suggested cheap and ineffective elocution lessons.

'So what the bloody hell is going on, then?' said Posh Git, throwing himself down into a chair in our living room, before being invited to do so. Darius made a big show of bringing up a foot stool for him, which he immediately used to put his feet on – without taking off his shoes.

The man clearly has no breeding, I thought. Tracey might easily be influenced by his booming Home Counties accent which can easily be developed by watching the right television as a child, but I could only think of him as Pompous Twerp rather than Posh Git. I suspected he earned a lot less than he let on, too.

'So, what do you do?' I asked him, delaying any offers of refreshments because I didn't feel inclined to be hospitable.

'Banking,' he said.

'Figures,' said Darius, this time not smiling but keeping an entirely unreadable look on his face.

'Pardon?' said Posh Git, looking affronted.

'Lots of figures, numbers and things,' Darius added, looking pleased at the effectiveness of his trap. 'Not much good at maths myself.'

'Oh, yes, I see,' Posh Git said. 'Do you have a job?'

'I am a servant,' said Darius, watching as our guest wasn't sure how to respond, although his demeanour would suggest he wasn't surprised at the answer.

'Of the Nigerian government, working on fraud investigation, scams and international corruption.'

Posh Git did an exceptionally good impression of a surprised carp, rounding his mouth and then closing it again. Words had failed him and there was little at that point that could have made me feel better.

'We're very worried about your mother,' I said to Donna, who was still standing at the door of our lounge, looking like a rabbit in the headlights.

'What's the silly moo been up to, now?' said Posh Git, swinging his feet down onto the floor from the foot stool and leaning his head on his hands. 'Never ceases to amaze me how bloody stupid she can be.'

'She isn't stupid,' I said to him. 'This is a very volatile country, anything can happen.'

He looked at me as if I'd crawled out from a drain. I wanted more than anything to punch him on the nose. No wonder Tracey had given up on him and harboured secret desires to turn him into kebab meat.

'I recognise you from when the two of you got caught up in all that kidnapping? I was surprised to find that you're still here.'

'Why wouldn't she be?' said Darius. 'Not everything in Africa is unappealing,' he said as he gave me a sideways glance and a secret wink.

Posh Git snorted loudly and Donna looked ashamed.

'Don't be rude, darling, please?' she said quietly, hanging her head. I suspected it might have taken a bit of courage to stand up to the man she called her husband. If he were anything to do with me, I'd be calling him my mistake.

'I'm just stating the facts, and that's all; you women will do the stupidest things without any thought. It's a good job you've got us to look after you, isn't that right Denzil?'

'It's Darius.'

Tom walked in from the office, having heard the noise of the guests arriving and introduced himself. Posh Git nodded, Donna looked like she was going to faint from the pressure of meeting yet another person and so Tom left us to it.

'How's it going with the memory stick?' Darius called after him and got a mumble that included the word 'nightmare' so his response didn't sound overly positive.

'What are the police doing about this situation, then?' asked Posh Git. 'Do they know what's happened, have they got people trying to find my stupid mother-in-law?'

It was strange to think of Tracey as a mother-in-law. She

didn't look the type, if there was a type. My mother-in-law, by comparison, was a woman who knew what day it was by what she was cooking for dinner. Stew on Saturday, a roast on Sunday and sausages on Monday. She wore support stockings from the age of forty-seven because she thought they helped to hold her up in the queue at the butchers. She had the same lipstick for nine years, wearing it only to weddings, funerals and once when she went to the theatre. She didn't like that particular outing because she said she knew the actors were all 'making up' what they said, and she never went again.

'We haven't had any significant news yet but I understand an officer will be on their way very soon to give us an update,' I said, wanting to usher these people out of my house and back to where they came from.

'We need to find her!' said Posh Git, so vehemently I thought maybe he was a better person than he came across, the he had real concern for Tracey and just needed to get to know people before turning into a human being. I swiftly dismissed my first impressions, giving him the benefit of the doubt. He perhaps thought more of my friend than had first appeared.

'Yes, we want that to happen very soon,' I said, looking over to Donna and indicating, for the third time, that she should sit down. She slowly and seemingly reluctantly moved towards one of the vacant chairs by the window and hovered, looking over at her husband nervously before finally taking a seat. There must have been a mix-up at birth, because Tracey would never be cowed in such a manner. Either that or the poor girl's father was a mouse.

'She has some papers that we needed her to sign. We sent them over but had nothing back, so I've brought new copies over with me. She's probably lost them knowing her,' said Posh Git.

'Papers?' I asked thinking it strange that Tracey would be required for any kind of official purpose.

'Yes, we are...' started Donna.

'Don't tell people our business, Don. It's nothing to do with them.'

I pressed my lips together between my teeth and Darius

moved out of the room saying he wanted to make a call. He might normally have used his mobile, but I suspected he needed to be away from this odious man. I thought I was going to make myself bleed with the pressure of restraining myself from coming out with an expletive that I usually reserved for news reels involving Donald Trump.

'Tosser!' came the voice from the hallway, unfortunately sounding uncannily like Darius. 'Bollock-brained arse wipe.'

I couldn't have said it better myself.

Darius came back into the lounge as Posh Git was standing up, puffing his chest and preparing to be annoyed; very annoyed indeed.

'So sorry,' he said. 'Just sorting out a few domestic matters.'

'What did you just say to me?' said Posh Git, facing up to Darius and then realising he'd more than met his match, being around a foot shorter and far more flimsy in terms of girth and projected strength.

'Tosser!' came the voice, this time clearly not from Darius.

'Pussy,' said Darius, which made Donna snort back a giggle. Her husband glared at her and looked around the room by which time Darius had brought the offending parrot into full view of our guests.

'Hick, hick, hooray,' she said and jumped up and down on her perch. 'Three blind mice fell up the hill.'

The nursery rhyme exercises, which according to the bird trainer would teach Pussy better language than she was used to, were still in a state of confusion. I did wonder if the trainer even knew the rhymes herself.

Darius took Pussy back into the hallway while Posh Git stood smoothing his shirt down with his hands and looking completely discombobulated. I could see Donna smile very slightly and hoped that underneath her aura of obedience she was planning revenge and retribution on the man I could now only refer to as Pompous Twerp. He might be a git, but definitely not a posh one.

I could hear Darius dialling out on our phone, no doubt to get in touch with the relevant authorities. We'd been assigned a liaison officer who was supposed to keep us updated on any progress but so far the level of information he had was akin to what a flea knows about landscape gardening.

'There have been some developments,' he said, as he came back having finished the call, interrupted throughout by Pussy's rendition of 'Happy Birthday Humpty Dumpty' at the top of her voice. Nobody could accuse the bird of lack of enthusiasm.

'And?' barked Pompous Twerp. 'What are they?'

'We need to go to a meeting with those involved. By all accounts the top security teams have been enlisted which suggests they're taking this matter extremely seriously.'

'So they bloody should. We need this mess sorted so we can get what we need and get home.'

I wondered how a so-called man like this could go about his day-to-day life without having his lights punched out. I noticed a small scar on the top of his right cheek and hoped it was where someone had taken a sharp knife and deliberately made him bleed.

'Tracey will be so pleased to know of your concern,' I said and noticed Donna drop her head so directed my comments to her. 'I'm sure she'll be fine, you know.'

But I wasn't at all sure. It was all sounding very ominous.

CHAPTER EIGHTEEN

'The biggest concern is the terrorist threat,' said the officer leading the investigation. 'The items found in the unknown vehicle, which we believe was used by the hostage-taker to drive into the centre, suggest he has connections to a known radical group.'

He explained again that the Muslim dresses, alongside a variety of items that might be seen as gifts and therefore offered to lure the girls to their fate, were worrying signs of potential future radicalisation.

'They use these items among other things to gain trust and flatter the girls. Once this has been achieved, they will marry them to other members and then they will consider them to be their property. That's when the problems begin.'

I couldn't see Tracey agreeing to any such plan. Even she was ever hopeful that the institution of wedlock was based on romance. Not only that, she was married to Baz, for better or worse — mainly for worse in her case.

Some of the girls' mothers had turned up to find out what was happening to their daughters although I was surprised at how few were there. Darius said it could have been lack of funds or other commitments that would have stopped more coming along, a fact that wasn't as surprising for him as it was for me.

'They probably have many other children to consider and no money for transport. They will pray and hope for their daughters' safety and put their trust in God and whatever they think is meant for them.'

I couldn't imagine that happening in Surrey. Parents protected their children with the biggest four wheeled cars, designed – they thought – to ride rough-shod over pavements, obstacles and anyone else's child should it be in the way. They'd pay for ballet lessons, make-overs, private dentistry and modelling contracts, all in a bid to protect them from any kind of unpleasantness such as disappointment, failure, or a lack of suitable friends to invite to a sleep over.

In Africa, mothers accepted that one or more of their children may perish before adulthood. They'd give them their last bowl of rice and the shirt off their back, but so many times giving everything they had just wasn't enough. It made Jemma Troy-Rowland's objection to the 'unflattering colour of the school gym kit for girls with auburn hair' pale into insignificance.

'Do we know who the man is, or do you have any clue to his identity or motivation?' asked Darius. He was wearing the trousers I really like because they stretch tightly across his thighs, barely able to contain themselves against his power. I knew the feeling.

'All we know is that he is on his own and we don't believe he intends any harm. There have been no suggestions of him having any firearms or other weapons, for which we are grateful.'

There was a commotion at the back of the room and Chinaza walked into the meeting, waving to the man in charge to come over to her, and he immediately did as he was told. I'd noticed that many men were only too keen to obey whatever instructions she gave and could see why her career had been so successful. There was a power in sex that so many women couldn't or didn't utilise. When in the right hands – or the best brains – it turns men into puppies.

'Oh, I think I've found Tom somewhere to stay,' said Darius, moving round to face me. He was so close I could smell the sweetness of his breath and his after shave. It would be good to have the house almost to ourselves again.

'Really?' I said, trying not to sound too enthusiastic. Tom was my grandson, after all.

'Chinaza said she has a spare room and would be happy to put him up for a while. She won't want much rent, just something to cover the bills. She's taken quite a liking to him, so I think she'll look after him.'

I thought of Tom sharing the same space as the woman he no

doubt had a huge crush on. I imagined him never being able to speak in her company, not even to ask how to use the washing machine or which cupboard to put his beans in.

'Is that a good idea? You do know he's got a huge thing for her.'

'Lucky boy,' said Darius, winking at me. I thought how he was getting a little more relaxed with me these days, with his sexual references and playful approach to my middle class demeanour. That's what comes when you share a bathroom with a man. He's seen what I do with cotton buds and baby oil, so the barriers come down. I like it. Colin would never acknowledge anything to do with private parts. If I didn't know better, I might have thought he didn't have any.

'Have you told him?' I asked.

'No, not yet, I thought I might let her ask him herself. That way he won't feel like I've set it all up. '

I just hoped he'd be able to answer her if she posed the question.

'I don't suppose he'll want to take those pyjamas with him,' I said. Even Tom couldn't believe they would be acceptable to any woman other than his grandmother.

The man leading the investigation made his way back to the front of the room. The mothers of the girls had started talking among themselves with concerned but not overly excitable voices. Despite regular reports of kidnaps, this didn't feel the same and they said so. Their optimism was palpable and I wondered if they were like this about every trial or tribulation they faced in life.

If so, it was a lesson to us all, particularly the members of the Bowls Club at the end of my road, four of whom had anxiety attacks so severe they required medical intervention – just because a family of moles unearthed most of their competition green the night after the Summer Fair. The committee claimed it was sabotage – and that the moles had been specially brought in, like some kind of 'attack mammals' – because the West Sumpting team didn't agree with a decision made by what they considered to be a 'biased' umpire from the Hastings region. The matter even made the local newspaper, it caused such serious uproar, although the committee wasn't happy with that either because they spelled the chairman's name wrong and he's been called Mr Crap ever since, instead of the correct, Mr Crop.

'I would like to update you on the information,' the policeman said, as he took his seat and the mothers of the girls turned their attention to the front of the room, bustling in their clothing and shifting bags around to gain the optimum view.

'We already know that the Outreach Centre has been entered by another male and we can confirm that he has taken the teacher, Ms Tracey Osolase, and left behind the first, masked, intruder with the girls. He has been followed but escaped and, so far, has not been found. We are obviously very concerned about the safety of his hostage and whether she will be used as a bargaining tool for the girls' release.'

There was a murmuring among the mothers, one of whom – dressed in colourful robes and with a tired look that permeated across her face – put her hand up to speak.

'Do you know if our children are safe? Have they been hurt or asked to do anything they don't want to do?'

My heart went out to the calm and quiet woman whose concern for her child seemed to have taken every ounce of energy from her otherwise depleted body.

'Our men on the ground have not reported any matters of concern,' he said. 'There is only the noise of quiet talking and, at one point, loud music. This would suggest there's no need for immediate worry and that we will be able to resolve the issue,' he said.

Darius asked why no-one had gone into the centre and how did another man get in when authorities were surrounding the buildings.

'The second man, we believe, had knowledge of the area and the centre. He gained access via the waterway and a boat which hadn't been cordoned off and then slipped in through an entry point at the back of the buildings,' he said, before explaining that plans were in place to storm the centre very soon.

'We just need to know we are not putting anyone in danger.'

He shuffled up his papers and went to leave the room, on his way being grabbed by two of the mothers, asking him to get their daughters back safely. He nodded but without confidence and the room fell into a silence which was broken a few minutes later by a trolley bringing in tea, sandwiches and cakes. The women swept towards the refreshment which occupied their interest, each of them inspecting the fillings and sniffing the bread, choosing carefully which one to take as their own.

Chinaza walked up and asked to speak to us out of the earshot of everyone else.

'This might sound like a strange question, but have you had anything to do with Baz recently?' she said.

Darius went to speak and then looked at me. I wasn't sure what to say, either.

'Why do you ask?' he said.

'Well,' said Chinaza, pulling us both closer to her. 'We have found his passport and a number of items that suggest he's been up to no good.'

'So?' said Darius. 'That's about normal for him.'

'There's something else, so it would really help if you could tell me anything you know.'

Darius took in a deep breath and told her about us following Baz to Bill's office and how he locked us in and made a getaway in the company car, which had been discretely recovered.

'That makes sense,' she said. 'The items were discovered in a stolen car – probably one he swapped for yours knowing it might be tracked – and we also found a selection of precious and semi-precious stones, often used as gifts to young girls when being encouraged to join some of the radical religious groups. There were also a wide selection of hijabs and burqas, around fifteen, all of different colours, and so enough for all the girls being held in the centre. These form the uniform of the women of these organisations. Plus there was a selection of liquids originally believed to be of an explosive nature, although on inspection were just bleach and other commercial liquids so whoever thought they would be dangerous doesn't understand science. Is Baz a sympathiser?'

I laughed out loud and Chinaza looked at me with the tip of her tongue under her top lip. She wasn't impressed. Although I knew I shouldn't, I felt a strange glow of superiority

'I'm sorry, but I think I know what has happened here,' I said. 'Those are Tracey's clothes. We went to the market recently because she wanted to buy different colours of cloth to wear after her hairdressing and facial incident. She must have bought around enough to make fifteen outfits, at least. As for the liquids, they would be peroxide and hair perming solutions.'

'That doesn't explain the precious stones,' said Chinaza, still retaining an air of disdain at my outburst.

'I can explain that,' said Darius and went on to tell her about the jewels taken from us in Bill's office.

'It might have been good if you'd bothered to tell me this before,' Chinaza said. 'You should not be keeping such information to yourself.'

He apologised and said we considered the matter of the map to be private business as it related to a bequest from Bill to me and had no relevance to anyone else.

'Oh but it does, Darius,' she said in a haughty tone.

'Because we found the stolen car just outside the centre and we believe it is Baz who is holding the girls hostage.'

CHAPTER NINETEEN

It was difficult to believe that Baz would want to hold his own wife hostage and I couldn't think of a reason. She would pretty much do anything he wanted if he asked, even though she didn't much like it that much recently.

As it was, he hadn't managed to execute his plan very successfully. He'd only been in the centre for a few hours before another man entered the building, seemingly over-powered Baz and escaped with Tracey, leaving Baz and the girls behind.

The officers who were supposed to be watching what was going on missed everything and were only alerted when a fast car raced past them with Tracey in the passenger seat. They tried to get into the centre to release the girls but found them to be still kept hostage by a man who was crying and shouting that someone had stolen his wife.

'I don't know how they didn't work it out,' said Darius. 'They had police surrounding every corner of the place and yet this other man gained entry via the canal, took Tracey, and then made a clean getaway – again without being seen.'

Chinaza, now less prickly about not being told about Bill's legacy – and my deduction that Baz was the 'terrorist', said it was if the second intruder knew the place in great detail.

'If he came through the back then, as the police have said, he would have had to have come to the rear entrance on water and know exactly where to get into the centre. It's not an easy route or obvious to anyone unless they have intimate knowledge of the area,' she said.

It was a mystery. To get held hostage was bad enough, but then to get kidnapped on the same day might be considered careless even by Tracey's standards.

'Do you think it has anything to do with that man at the

market?' I asked Darius, as I searched for any reason why Tracey would become a target. 'He said he was watching me.'

'That was you, though,' he said. 'If they wanted Tracey then I'd have thought they'd direct their message at her.'

'What man at the market?' said Chinaza, and I could feel the prickliness rising again. She clearly didn't like being left out of the loop when it came to information.

'Oh, it was nothing really,' I said, thinking that it was now feeling very definitely like something, although goodness knows what. 'I haven't seen him since.'

She asked if there had been any other strange activity and I said no, although I felt a little guilty about not telling her about the car that seemed to be following me. I didn't want to say anything in front of Darius as I knew he would be worried and get cross that I hadn't mentioned the last time I thought I'd seen it.

A couple of times, I'd seen the man drive past the house. He never stopped but always slowed down and looked into the window. I'd caught his eye a few times, at which point he hit the accelerator and disappeared. It occurred to me that maybe he was just curious about the older white woman living with a younger black man. It wasn't exactly the norm where we were living.

Ada had also seen the car, saying it gave her the creeps and she felt it was following her, so it could just be a man who likes to drive around a lot. Had something more specific happened I might have felt obliged to report it earlier rather than waiting until being asked by the police but being weird isn't a reason to get someone arrested. If it was, we'd all be in jail.

Ada also said he had 'a look about him' which reminded her of a dog she once had.

'It would look like dat and then have a fit,' she said. 'Poor thing was mad as a hatter.'

That didn't make me feel much better but at the time I still thought it was nothing to really worry about. If he was going to do something awful, he'd have made a move then surely? Anyway, I had more immediate things to worry about.

Another team of police had been despatched to try and find Tracey but with no information to go on, it was going to be tricky. I'd tried calling her phone but it just went to voicemail so either she didn't have it, couldn't get to it, or it had run out of battery. House to house inquiries led to nothing and so the only hope would be for the authorities to get access to the centre and talk to the girls. They must have seen everything.

Posh Git was getting apoplectic with frustration that his mother-in-law had gone missing, not out of any concern for her welfare but because he was obviously very keen to get her signature on whatever paperwork it was he needed to get signed. I couldn't imagine what she had over him that he needed her so badly, but it pleased me she had a bit of power over the obnoxious little toad.

I saw the way he treated Donna and often tried to talk to her when he was out of hearing, but she remained fiercely loyal – refusing to suggest he was anything but the perfect husband. Her manner would change every time he came within range and she would go rigid though; she'd fidget and not be able to make eye contact with him. On one occasion I thought I saw her flinch, not from any threat of physical violence but from a potential barrage of verbal abuse.

He was the sort of man who kept his woman 'in her place' by making sure she felt as low as she could. I overheard him saying her 'arse looked like a couple of puppies in a blanket' which was totally unreasonable. She hardly had an arse and what little she did have was very firm. I quite envied it. I thought it was a poor insult considering his backside resembled a balloon full of blancmange and he had legs like chicken drumsticks.

Thankfully Buke had managed to find the two of them some accommodation near the university which would keep them out of our way, although despite ungraciously accepting the nicer house for as long as he might need it, he would spend his time leaving numerous voicemail messages on our phones, all of which we ignored.

'So what's happening now?' said Darius to Chinaza, who seemed to be on the pulse of the rescue operation, despite there being little official input from Forensix. This wasn't seen, after all, as a fraudulent action or one involving any technical scam. If it was anything to do with Baz it would just be a totally random act of an idiot with limited reasoning abilities, so expert advice and investigation wasn't a requirement. But Chinaza knew everyone and was keen to take an active interest and so had been granted special permission to offer support and any help that could be professionally provided by the government agency.

'They're going to storm the centre very soon, I think,' she said. 'The aim is first to ensure that Baz, if it is him holding the girls, does not have any access to any kind of weapon.'

She added there had been concern about the apparent explosive materials in the car which had so far been holding them back.

'I've informed them this is likely to be related to hairdressing, so maybe the threat will be downgraded and they'll take the calculated risk of going in. If they take him by surprise and he's on his own, they should be able to get the girls out safely.'

Her phone rang and within minutes we were aware that the girls had been rescued and Baz (for it was indeed him) had been arrested.

Chinaza clicked her phone shut and told us he'd virtually given himself up and was crying like a baby. He denied any links to terrorist organisations and said he just wanted to take his wife away, but she wouldn't go with him, so he had got 'a bit angry'.

'By all accounts he was unarmed and wasn't at all threatening to any of the girls, but he was cross with Tracey. Something about helping with his business, but she kept telling him she was happy where she was.'

Baz was about to leave when the other man stormed in through the back door, pushed Baz aside then grabbed Tracey and took her out of the building.

'The girls claim she might have known who it was as she was entirely unflustered and went calmly, if not happily. They couldn't see exactly who it was as he was wearing a scarf and hat to cover his face. This would fit in with the belief that we think the person concerned has been to the school before,' said Chinaza.

'The girls are being interviewed now by a special team, so hopefully we will know more soon. The good news is that it didn't sound like they were frightened at any time or that Tracey felt herself to be in any danger.'

I couldn't think of any man who might have been to the centre before, other than those who went to the opening. Perhaps it was Toyin Remy or one of his political cronies wanting to capture Tracey in the hope of getting off the fraud charges? But she didn't seem high enough collateral for that option, so I mostly dismissed the idea from my mind. If it was Toyin, she could deal with him easily. I was suddenly overwhelmed with relief knowing Tracey was likely to be OK.

'Maybe one of Tony's friends went in and got her?' Darius said. 'You know, the head teacher who called the police,' he added after noticing that Chinaza looked puzzled.

She laughed.

'I doubt it. Apparently, he's been in quite a state since running from the building and asked for an immediate transfer to a school in Lagos. Something about not being suited for the job.'

I couldn't disagree with the sentiment. Tony was a bit of a wimp.

CHAPTER TWENTY

The girls' mothers were in high spirits, chatting among themselves and waiting to be reunited with their daughters. Plenty of tea was being provided and I was surprised to see Ada among the group.

'What are you doing here?' I asked, having made my way over to the women.

'You remember my sister?' she said, pointing out the woman who I now recognised as the one who brought round the wig for Tracey. 'One of her daughters, my niece, goes to the school.'

'Why didn't you tell me?' I said, surprised it wasn't ever mentioned. She knew I worked there and my relationship with Buke, who had recommended her to us when we were looking for a cleaner.

'We don't want no special favours,' she said, raising her head in the air and standing straight. 'We're good, hard working people.'

It took some interrogation for me to work out who Ada was related to and I soon realised it was Esther. Ada had once mentioned in the past there'd been triplets in the family, but I hadn't made the connection.

What did take me by surprise though, was the realisation that Ada wasn't working to just pay for her hair – by all accounts, hairdressing was a family trade. She was, in fact, working to keep her family in food, clothes and education – where possible – but she was too proud to admit it.

Esther's mother spoke quietly but with a steely determination. Her marriage hadn't worked out, she explained, and she was left with the children and grandchildren. She'd taken up hairdressing and wig making to make ends meet but with so many hungry mouths – including the particularly hungry mouth of Esther — to feed, she had to rely on Ada's contribution.

It's funny how you can have a view of someone and it completely changes with one fact. The woman who I thought was vain and irritable was giving up her time to earn a living for others. She used her hair as a cover for her real motivation and I felt humbled.

'Esther is a fabulous student,' I told the two women and they visibly beamed with pride, swaying their heads very slightly as if I was only telling them something they already knew.

At that point the girls came running in to the room, having been brought by the police in a mini-bus after their interviews.

'Mother,' shouted Esther across to Nene who ran towards her daughter with her arms open wide.

'I'm so happy to see you, my child,' she said, and a tear trickled down her face. 'You're safe, you're safe.'

'Of course she is safe,' said Ada. 'Look at her! Nuttin' to worry about at all!'

A lonely figure stood away from the crowd of people who were gleefully re-uniting. Not sad but definitely alone. It was Mo, so I went across to her.

'Hello, Mo. Is your mother going to be coming along?'

Mo smiled broadly showing a row of wonderfully white teeth and I wondered how, in such poverty, they didn't have the rotten gums you might expect.

'She will be here. I know it.'

'How are you?' I asked. 'Did you get hurt, or were you frightened?'

She smiled again.

'Oh no, not at all. The police don't believe us but really everything was fine. It was quite good fun in some ways although I'm glad it's over and I was worried for my mother's concern.'

We were both drawn to someone trying to push open the heavy door into the room. A frail figure carrying a large, flat package was pushing it, using their behind and walking in backwards.

'There she is,' she said. 'I must go and help her.'

Mo ran to her mother and immediately took the package from her, grabbed her hand and pulled her over to talk to me.

'This is the teacher I was telling you about,' said Mo, and a watery eyed woman looked back at me with a rheumy glance. I could only hope it was from gratitude rather than a chronic infection.

'I can't tell you how important I think education is,' she said, catching her breath and holding her chest as if in pain.

'Let me get you a drink,' said Mo, and went off in search of some tea, leaving me alone with this woman who looked as if she could pass out at any moment.

'I'm sorry, it has taken me a long time to get here and all the time I was worried,' said Mo's mother as she regained her composure.

'Cynthia,' I said, holding out my hand. It was eventually met, shyly, by the damp and bird like fingers of the woman who told me her name was Alala.

'It means a loud cry in Greek,' she said. 'Ironic, don't you think?'

'What's in the package?' I asked, looking at the parcel, wrapped in brown paper and tied with string. I was captivated by this African who was coming across as educated but exhausted. The regime she lived in stripped so many women of their dreams, even those lucky enough to start with good opportunities, and left them with all the responsibilities but none of the freedoms of life.

'It's some of my artwork,' she said. 'I have a buyer nearby who said he would take it from me but wanted it delivered.'

'Could I have a look?' I said. 'I love African art.'

'Why do you think it is African?' said Alala, then smiled knowing she had unnerved me by pointing out my assumption. 'You are right, of course.'

She laid the package on the floor and gently undid the wrapping as if taking the clothing off a newborn baby. She was deferential and methodical, as if about to reveal the secret to eternal life.

As the covers came off it was clear this woman was talented. Her work was vibrant, real and strangely emotive.

The picture was of a black couple, embracing erotically while wrapped in sheets of multi-coloured hues, lying on a bed made of gold and red cushions. It was sensitive and evocative and reminded me of the first time I slept with Darius, the beauty of touch and connection.

'I would really like to buy this,' I said, surprising myself at the reaction I had to the painting. I'd never been one for pictures in the house other than a few Constable prints in suitably gilded frames that matched the shape and tone of the light fittings, or the colour of the wallpaper.

'It is already sold,' said Alala. 'But I could paint you another one.'

I had an idea and wondered if it would be offensive. As I considered how I might phrase a specific request, she helped me out.

'You can tell me anything you want,' she said, her eyes glistening with mischief and a deep understanding of the human psyche. 'You wouldn't really want a black woman in your picture, now, would you?'

My heart leapt with anticipation of being able to commission my own artwork, creating a permanent vision of how I saw myself and Darius. A memory of that electric, physicality of our love, likely to remain long after my old bones had lost interest in dancing around for the benefit of sexual completion.

'Not necessarily, I suppose,' I said. 'Nor one that young, either.'

I looked her straight in the eye and she almost winked, as if by being in my proximity she read right into my soul.

I remembered what Mo had said about her family and something about her mother's strength failing. I wanted to ask what was wrong but didn't think it appropriate.

'I would like to pay you in advance for your work,' I said. I had to be careful not to patronise or belittle Alala although she was probably a good negotiator.

'Fifty per cent up front,' she said, forthright and direct.

'That's absolutely no problem,' I said, trying to remember how much cash I had in my purse; probably not enough but maybe a gesture so she could start on some ideas.

'That will be five thousand naira,' she said and held out her hand. I recognised the need, which fell just short of desperation. It didn't pay to miss chances in this country.

I did a bit of working out in my head as I still couldn't figure the value of the Nigerian currency. When I did my sums, twice because I was so unsure of my accuracy, I wanted to cry.

Alala wanted just sixteen pounds as a deposit, so little more than thirty pounds for a picture that would be sold even in African galleries for at least ten times that amount.

'I would like to pay you more,' I said, pulling ten thousand naira from my purse as discreetly as I could.

'You must only pay what I am worth. That is five thousand now and five thousand when I've finished the work,' said Alala.

I wanted to argue but knew pride would come into it and that was more valuable than the cash to this world-weary woman.

'It's a deal,' I said and started to anticipate giving Darius his anniversary present.

We have been together a year in just nine weeks' time.

CHAPTER TWENTY-ONE

'Why on earth would Chiddy want to kidnap Tracey?' I said, completely shocked at the news Chinaza had just given us.

Darius had made me breakfast and we were going to have some 'alone' time as soon as Tom had gone to work, before she had rudely dropped by with the latest information.

'I don't think it was a case of kidnap,' she said. 'According to the girls she had a massive row with Baz and then willingly went with him. That is why Baz got so angry. He was calling her all sorts of names and not all of them very friendly.'

I could just imagine him jumping up and down if Tracey didn't do as she was told. He still thought she was someone to be pushed and pulled around at will. Considering his mother and all her achievements and strength you'd think he might have more respect for the fairer sex.

Buke often mentioned it and blamed his father.

'No-good waste of skin,' she said about him once. 'Better use of breath in a floppy balloon.'

I guessed he hadn't been around that much, although Buke said that on the times he did visit, he would bring toy guns, war games and books on mortal combat.

'Not that he'd know what to do wit any of it. He frightened of his shadow, as well as spiders, thunder and green vegetables.'

The girls had been interviewed as a group but it wasn't until individual sessions later into the night and the morning that they gave more detail. The authorities didn't want to pressurise them as soon as they'd been released. They decided they'd probably been through enough, although from the sound of it most of the girls thought the whole episode to be something of an adventure.

'Baz came in with a large metal stick which is why at first everyone thought he was being aggressive. But it turned out to be some kind of holder for a load more jewellery, would you believe? Looked like part of a broom.' We hadn't told the full story, so this was only news to her.

Chinaza added he'd demanded Tracey came with him right at that moment and leave the country as he was going to make his fortune selling diamonds in Europe.

'She told him not to be so stupid and carried on teaching, which made him get even more cross. Tony left at that point without Baz knowing he was even there and alerted the authorities, which is how they got involved.'

I remembered it was Tuesday and the day we'd agreed Chiddy would come to give some more music lessons. That would be why he was at the school. Not only that, he'd know the way in through the back entrance, having lived there for so many months.

'Where did Chiddy take her then?' I asked, remembering how easily Tracey had formed a relationship with our rap-obsessed guard.

'No-one knows at the moment,' said Chinaza. 'It would seem that he worked out something wasn't right, so disguised himself as an intruder to throw Baz off the scent. This was enough to take control of Tracey although once she knew who it was, she was apparently more than happy to go.

She went on to add that they still didn't know their whereabouts however, and there was concern that another scam had been set up by Chiddy's previous bosses.

'It is particularly worrying as he has only recently been released from prison so might be looking for money and being involved in a kidnap could be a way of earning some. So, I thought this might be something we could put Tom onto, as the police don't seem to have a clue.'

Tom looked surprised by the suggestion. He'd been struck dumb by her presence and had sat staring at her, possibly imagining the things that teenage boys do when looking at a beautiful young woman.

'Er, yeah,' was all he could muster. 'I can give it a go.'

'Excellent, then you'd better come with me,' she said, holding out her hand as a mother might to a child. He ignored the gesture and muttered something about getting his bag.

'You may as well pack a few things, then you can come to mine and we can work on a few ideas tonight. In fact you might as well get as much as you need so that you can move into my spare room,' said Chinaza, shouting up the stairs after Tom.

He came clattering back down with his eyes wide open and I thought I'd seen deer in headlights that looked calmer.

'Sorry, what was that you said?'

She repeated the suggestion and I wondered if Tom had heard properly as he didn't move for what seemed like minutes before turning on his heel, rushing up the stairs and making a strange guttural noise which could have been one of pleasure, excitement or terror. It was difficult to know the difference.

'I hadn't told him of your offer yet,' said Darius. 'I thought it best coming from you.'

Her smile weakened when she saw Tom had packed a suitcase which he'd dragged into the hall along with a selection of different pieces of technology, varying in size and possible noise levels.

'It's OK, I've got headphones,' he said when she was giving it all a good look over. Judging by the amount of stuff he'd gathered I guessed he wanted his stay to be a long one.

'Has anyone told Donna and her husband what has happened yet?' I asked, trying to alleviate the rising sense of anticipation that was filling the room, mainly from Tom who could barely keep still.

'I believe someone has been in touch and told them what is going on but they just received a barrage of abuse. As soon as there is something more positive to report, they'll be on to it, I'm sure.'

Chinaza looked round at Tom who seemed very ready to leave our company. She took the hint.

'Come on, let's get you settled then maybe we can start getting some results on those projects of ours,' she said, kindly.

'What has happened about the memory stick?' asked Darius. 'Did you sort the format out OK?'

'Nothing on that yet,' Tom said. 'But I did get a weird response from the university about the lettering and numbers on the map. They're some kind of recipe for making different types of material. They're going to get back to me.'

'Are you going to share this information?' said Chinaza, raising her eyebrows and reminding us that she didn't like to be kept in the dark.

'If it is relevant, but for the moment it just relates to the items that Bill seemed to have wanted Cynthia to have – nothing sinister just yet!' said Darius.

For the first time in some while the house was now empty. Tom had left, willingly, and although I thought I might miss him, I was pleased to be able to do those things you do when on your own or in a couple.

'This is nice,' I said, as Darius started to place the breakfast items on a tray. I frowned, pretending that I didn't know what he was planning.

'You thinking what I'm thinking?' said Darius as he nodded down towards his waist.

I could see that he was very pleased to see me.

CHAPTER TWENTY-TWO

'I don't know where she's gone,' said Baz while being questioned not only by the police but by Tracey's daughter and the lame excuse for a husband.

Darius and I had gone along to the station to help deal with Donna and Posh Git, who by all accounts was causing trouble.

'He must know where she is,' said Posh Git, banging his fist down on to the table in front of him while Donna jumped. 'He's her bloody husband for goodness sake!'

'She went with that man. She ignored everything I said, telling me she didn't want to come to Europe and help my business,' said Baz. 'She chose a kidnapper over me.'

Darius raised his eyebrows to the officer to see if he had approval to continue the questioning. He seemed happy enough as his own questioning was getting nowhere.

'What business would that be?' asked Darius, picking up some of the jewellery that had been laid out in front of Baz as evidence. 'Anything to do with items you might have taken that weren't yours?'

We hadn't officially reported the matter of him taking my map and going to Bill's office. I still considered it a private matter and until we got to the bottom of the mystery felt there was no need to involve the law enforcement agencies. That didn't mean Baz wasn't concerned we could drop him in it and add further fuel to the police fire.

'I've taken nothing,' he said, folding his arms and pouting. He raised his head defiantly towards Darius who smiled.

'That's not entirely true, is it?'

The police officer didn't react and didn't appear to be in the slightest bit interested in Baz, Tracey or anything else that was happening. One of his colleagues had brought some lunch and he kept looking at it with more interest than he was showing anything else in the room.

'What's he taken?' said Posh Git. 'Is this man a thief?'

'This man,' said Darius, 'is your step father-in-law and has a name.'

Posh Git flinched and Donna tried to stifle a giggle. It was the most relaxed I'd seen her since she'd arrived, which I put down to the knowledge her mother was likely to be safe.

I'd explained to her how Tracey had engaged with Chiddy on the matter of rap music and because of their friendship we'd been able to work together to ensure our escape when we were kidnapped. I left out the bit about drugging them and Tracey tying them up as I thought it best to see her as the clever negotiator rather than a dominatrix manipulator – even though that could be the bit Chiddy liked best.

'Let's call it a day,' said the police officer, picking up his food parcel from the desk and ushering the rest of us out of the room. Baz got up to leave and was pushed back.

'You're staying here until I know what has happened to your wife,' said the officer. 'You're not in the clear yet.'

As the door closed behind him, Baz was making a number of different sounds ranging from shouts to sobs with a number of expletives between, some of a very personal nature towards the police.

'Think I might just mislay the keys to that room,' said the officer. 'I'll see you later.'

Posh Git was still ranting on about needing to find Tracey so she could sign his paperwork while Donna seemed less concerned about the issue. She still wouldn't tell me what it was all about, on the grounds that her husband 'wouldn't be happy'. Posh Git not being happy clearly had implications.

Darius and I made our excuses about needing to get home and dropped them off back at their university rooms which, despite their international five-star status was still a 'hell hole' according to Tracey's son-in-law.

'Someone's going to pay for this,' he shouted back through the window as we drove off and I suspected it might be Donna, although she was showing a bit more mettle as the days went on. Only that morning I'd heard her tell him to 'pipe down' and he did, rather quickly as well.

'Thank goodness we've got rid of them,' said Darius. 'Although I'm not sure where this saga is going to end.'

Baz hadn't actually done anything the police could charge him with. We'd not reported his theft, or his locking us in Bill's office, and Tracey had apparently gone off on her own accord with Chiddy. There was the matter of keeping the girls hostage in the centre but none of them claimed they couldn't have left had they wanted to. If anything, they seemed to enjoy the whole episode as something of an adventure. It was obvious to everyone involved that Baz was only interested in taking his wife and no-one else.

When we got home there was a smell of cigarette smoke and a noise coming from the kitchen.

'Is Ada here today?' asked Darius, and I told him she wouldn't be as she'd gone with her sister to be with the family after the ordeal of the supposed hostage situation. Besides, Ada didn't smoke.

'Only me!' came the familiar voice of Tracey, clutching hold of the cafetiere which appeared to have some tea bags in the bottom. 'I wish you'd get a bloody teapot.'

She had a cigarette in her hand which I looked at, then so did she.

'Sorry, Cynthia but I just had to have one. I'll put it out,' Tracey said as she trotted off back into the garden. She was still wearing a headscarf only this time slightly down from the top of her head so I could see her hair was growing back in grey and brown wiry clumps. It looked a bit like the back end of a guinea pig.

Darius looked at me as if to say, 'What on earth?' and I looked back with a similar expression as we watched her come back into the kitchen.

'How did you get in?' I asked, as I'd been careful to keep the house locked since the various incidents with the strange man following me, the blue car following me and then the forced tumble in the market.

'You never lock your back door properly,' said Tracey. 'Look,' she added, as she showed how a double push upwards, coupled with hefty shove with a shoulder, would force the lock. She leaned against the open door, blowing the smoke from a fresh cigarette into the garden.

'What are you doing here, anyway?' said Darius. 'There are police and lots of other people looking for you all over the place.'

'Really?' she said. 'Why's that then?'

'Why is that?' said Darius, raising his voice. 'Because everyone thought you'd been held hostage, first by some random man and then kidnapped by another one who broke into the centre.'

'Baz is certainly very random but he didn't hold me no hostage,' said Tracey, who displayed a look of understanding slowly spreading across her face. 'O.M.G. No-one realised it was him?'

She started to laugh and coughed at the same time, the actions of which caused her scarf to fall off completely. She had a sort of Judi Dench look about her with such short hair but without the air of success and adulation.

'We know it was Chiddy who took you,' I said.

'Took me?' said Tracey, perplexed. 'He didn't take me anywhere. I asked him to get me away from Baz, cos he was getting on me tits, and I needed some fags. He'd come in to teach but then saw that Baz was being a dick and completely understood my situation, that's all.'

'So why were you gone so long?' I asked. 'Everyone's been really worried about you. And you left the girls there on their own with that madman!'

'It was only a couple of nights. Chiddy's car broke down then a mate of his came by and gave us a lift to his. It all ended up as a bit of a party. And the girls were fine. They were making dough balls like you showed them last week. They weren't taking any notice of Baz. Think they thought he was a bit of a dick but that's all.'

'A bit of a party, and you didn't bother to tell us where you were?'

'Me battery was flat,' said Tracey, pouting. She didn't like being told off and was about to sulk, then her face changed into a broad grin.

'I met up with one of your old friends,' she said, looking directly at me.

'Gowon sends his love,' she said, mischievously, and I knew she was warning me not to give her any trouble.

I panicked a bit, thinking I wouldn't put it past her to provide some graphic reminders of how I enticed one of our kidnappers. I didn't want Darius thinking I was a complete trollop for anyone but him. Not to be outdone I thought I'd shake Tracey's world up a little with my own piece of news.

'Your daughter is here with her husband. He says he's got something he wants you to sign.'

The effect was immediate and Tracey's guard dropped. She walked out into the garden, pacing up and down.

'Did he say what it was he wanted signing?' she asked. 'How's Madonna? Is she OK?'

I told her what had happened and about them contacting us because they thought she was missing and them then coming over.

'It wouldn't be out of any concern for me,' said Tracey, pausing for thought while half closing her eyes in a look of total contempt.

'Don't you think I should tell them you're OK?' I said, and Darius nodded.

'Nah. Let 'em sweat. Might do 'em a bit of good,' she said. 'Right, let's make some more tea!'

Darius boiled the kettle and made tea the 'Tracey way' for us all, while she told us of her trip out with Chiddy and what fun he was. She was careful not to mention Gowon again although I was still nervous she might. I believed that what happened in camp should stay in camp.

'Baz is up to no good again.' Tracey said as we sipped our drinks and nibbled at some shortbread biscuits Darius had been given by a visiting diplomat from Sweden. I'd never thought the Nordic countries as being into biscuits but guessed they were something the visitor had picked up at the airport – and definitely not in Lagos nor a rejected prize from a Bridge Club. They were delicious.

'We know,' said Darius who proceeded to tell her about him taking the precious stones that were hidden in the parrot perch in Bill's office.

'Shit for diamonds,' said Pussy when she heard her name and the mention of stones then went into a screeching fit which involved more expletives and a lot of wing flapping.

'So that's where he got them, the little turnip head,' said Tracey. 'He was banging on about some business deal and ow we was going to make our millions. He's so full of crap I guessed whatever he was doing would be bent or useless.'

It hadn't taken long for the shine to diminish on Tracey's relationship with her husband. We always knew he'd not married out of love, but as a punishment inflicted by his mother for cheating a white girl out of money. It seemed the tables had turned, and Tracey was no longer interested in him at all.

'He wanted me to take him back to England and start again,' she said. 'But I can't be bothered. Marriage isn't all it's cracked up to be. Best you don't bother, you two,' she added, nodding towards us.

I blushed as I hadn't ever thought of Darius and me married. That would certainly shock the Bridge Club, let alone my family, who'd probably be more worried about their inheritance than anything.

I could imagine Mavis and the rest of them deciding what to wear and what present to buy. They'd be concerned that the buffet would contain the meat of unknown animals and they'd have to shout at Darius because he's 'foreign' so might not understand them otherwise. My children would stand on the side lines and eventually designate one of them to discuss the 'family assets' and all of them would wonder what he sees in me and possibly vice versa, although they'd raise their eyebrows at the girth of his thighs and his marvellous chest. Tracey was right, marriage would be a bad idea.

'What do you want to do then, Tracey?' asked Darius. 'We

should at least tell the authorities that you are back and safe, so they don't waste any more resources looking for you.'

Tracey laughed.

'They found me twice. We were stopped when the car broke down because it was blocking the road. The police asked for ID and we both gave it. Then I got into trouble over the singing.'

'What singing?' I said, wondering at which point it had become a criminal offence.

'Karaoke in Chiddy's bar. I got some of the words wrong and they sounded like something else,' she said. 'I hadn't meant to be offensive, but the police were called. I got a caution for obscene language and imitating a terrorist.'

'Imitating a terrorist?' Darius said, hardly able to keep a straight face. 'Because of the scarf?'

'No. Well, possibly. It was because of what I was singing and possibly the way I was dressed. But that hardly matters now,' she added, obviously trying to change the subject. 'The thing is they weren't looking for me as they'd found me. They knew who I was. If you must know I gave them money to keep quiet because I was having such a good time.'

I sighed and asked Darius to just let Chinaza know what was going on and ask her to tell the relevant authorities that the matter had been resolved.

'Just don't tell Baz where I am. I need to think about what I want to do,' Tracey said.

'Don't worry, he's still under arrest,' said Darius. 'And the way the police feel about him I think he might be there for a while.'

'Suits me,' said Tracey. 'I'm hoping it's OK to stay for a bit?' she added.

I nodded, telling her I would change the sheets in Tom's room.

'Where's he gone, then?' she asked.

I told her he'd gone to stay at Chinaza's while they worked on a few projects together. Tracey expressed her surprise saying she didn't think that Darius's colleague would like company, but then conceded that maybe even Tom's was better than none.

'Great! Room for a little one, then,' she said gleefully, as she kicked off her excessively high shoes and settled down to making herself at home.

I wondered if Darius and I were ever going to get any alone time.

CHAPTER TWENTY-THREE

'Just sign it, will you?' said Posh Git to Tracey who was sitting in her dressing gown taking up two chairs in the kitchen, sitting on one and balancing her feet on the other while painting her toenails. She had to force herself forward in small bursts while holding her breath to do each toe.

'Sign what?' said Darius, walking in wearing just his pyjama bottoms and looking like a chocolate Adonis. He made Posh Git look like something that had been made out of a wimp's leftovers.

'Never you mind,' he said, getting closer to Tracey and leaning over her waving some papers. 'Why won't you just bloody sign them?'

Darius casually walked over to Tracey and looked over at her toes.

'Very nice,' he said before turning to Tracey's son-in-law and whipping the documents from his grasp. 'As Tracey's legal advisor, I think I should have a look. Is that OK, Tracey?'

He looked at her with wide eyes as if to suggest that looking at the papers might be a very good idea. She nodded, flinching away from Posh Git, whose agitation levels were getting to the point anyone watching might think his head could explode. I personally wished it would.

'Yeah, if you don't mind, Darius,' said Tracey. 'I've never been much good with papers and that.'

'Just hurry up then,' said Posh Git. 'I haven't got all day. We want to get back home and sort some things out.'

Darius patted the papers on his hand without looking at them.

'Actually, I'm a bit busy at the moment,' he said pouring some tea from the cafetiere and sitting down on the chair opposite

Tracey. 'Perhaps you could come back later when I've had time to fully digest the implications of any signatures.'

Tracey looked up from under her scarf and smiled appreciatively. I'd never seen her look as intimidated by anyone as she had by this ineffectual bully of a man and wondered what made him different from genuinely scary people like our kidnappers.

'He's married to my daughter,' she explained when he'd gone. 'If I upset him, he might take it out on her and while she's been a mare, ignoring me and that, she's still my girl. Donna was never like this before she met him.'

Darius was reading the papers that had been left behind before Posh Git had stormed out in a fury. He told us he'd left Donna in the rooms packing their bags and getting ready to go. 'She'll be furious,' he barked at Tracey, but she didn't respond, although I suspect she might have given in to his demands had we not been there.

'How long has she been with him?' I asked, thinking it seemed strange a girl bred from Tracey's loins would put up with such treatment.

'Too long,' said Tracey, leaning back and admiring her paint job. I suspected her eyesight might be failing, as it does with middle age, as she couldn't see that half the paint was on her skin.

'Do you know what these papers mean?' asked Darius, looking concerned.

'Nah, haven't a clue,' said Tracey. 'He's been mithering on for ages about getting stuff sorted but I don't know what the bloody hell the stupid brainless fat arse is going on about.'

'So, you don't like him then?' I laughed. Tracey was nothing if not straight to the point if she took against someone.

'He's a tosser. Always after summat for nothing. I don't listen to him, to be honest.'

'Mmmn,'' said Darius, still reading the papers. 'Would you mind very much if I dealt with this for you? I would just like the chance to put the man in his place.'

'Be my guest. As long as it don't cost me nowt!'

'Oh, it won't cost you anything. I will make sure of that.'

Tracey's phone rang.

'Ooh, it's Chiddy,' she said and ran out into the garden, then ran back again realising she had no shoes on and the pathway was gravel. 'Ouch, ouch,' she said, picking her feet up quickly after each other before seeing a pair of Darius's shoes by the back door and putting them on. With her scarf, wiry hair and flowy dressing gown, and now oversized man's shoes, she looked like she might be thinking of auditioning for a circus.

'Hi babe,' we could hear her say. 'How are you?'

Her voice was soft. She walked away from the house so that we couldn't hear what was being said.

'Isn't she supposed to be going to the station to sort out Baz?' said Darius.

In timely fashion, the doorbell rang. It was Buke.

'Is Tracey here?' she asked, floating in with a rainbow of colours surrounding her. She had the ability to wear what looked like tablecloths and turn them into a fashion statement no-one else could mimic.

Tracey was still on the phone in the garden when she turned round and saw her mother-in-law. She snapped her phone shut and shuffled back in, unable to keep Darius's size thirteen shoes on her feet so they flapped noisily as she made her entrance.

'Goodness me,' said Buke. 'What have they done to you?'

It was clear she didn't realise Tracey hadn't actually been kidnapped but for the sake of appearances we all kept quiet.

'Are you alright, my girl?' Buke asked tenderly. 'You have been through the wars.'

She looked down at Tracey's bare feet and took in a sharp intake of breath at the red splashes over her toes.

'Good, aren't they?' said Tracey, tightening up her dressing gown. 'The colour would go with your dress,' she added, nodding towards the scarlet swathe wrapped around Buke's expansive waist.

Buke looked shocked and shook her head very slightly, frowning and taking a second look at Tracey's feet. A wave of realisation washed over her face and she started to laugh.

'I thought the kidnappers had cut off your toes?' she said and it occurred to me that maybe Buke needed to go to Specsavers, she could go with Tracey.

'Kidnappers?' said Tracey, and Darius and I stared at her. It didn't seem appropriate at this time for anyone to know that her absence was entirely voluntary. 'Oh, them,' said Tracey. 'Nothing I couldn't handle.'

'I'm sure,' said Buke. 'We need to go to the police station and find out what they are going to do with Baz.'

She went quiet and looked to the floor for a moment.

'Of course, it's entirely up to you whether you want to press charges. I know he's not treated you well and wat he did was inexcusable. If da is any way I can persuade you to let him go without any further slur to his name, dat would be just wonderful.'

Tracey sniffed in an expression of defiance.

'Yes, he's done a lot of things that ain't right,' said Tracey. 'But I don' want to press charges.'

Buke's chest filled with air as if she'd been waiting to hear that news. She might not like her son very much, or what he got up to, but he was the only family that we knew about.

'You are a very good girl, Tracey. You will git your rewards in heaven.'

'Whatever,' said Tracey, who was more of a fan of instant gratification than of jam tomorrow. I also knew her views on heaven.

'There'd be nobody there I'd wanna be with,' she said during one of our conversations when shut up in the camp. 'Boring bunch of do-gooders; send me down where the fun is.'

'I need to get dressed if I'm going down the station,' Tracey said, and made her way to the hall, kicking Darius's footwear in the process, having tripped up twice in the rush to get in from the garden. Darius went after his shoes and hid them under the stairs, picking off a bit of red nail polish from the edge of one of them as he pushed them way out of anyone's sight. He was quite protective of his shoes – something to do with not having any when he was growing up.

'What do you think they might do to him?' I asked Buke, who'd taken Tracey's seat. For the first time I'd ever seen, she looked exhausted. The indefatigable force had been spent.

'Oh, I don't care about him,' she said. 'He'll git what he deserves.'

She took a deep breath.

'We haf much bigger problems, Cynthia – the money promised for the centre has been stopped. I haf no idea why but a letter has come to say our sponsors cannot honour da next payment.'

It took me a while to understand what she meant. I thought money had come through to ensure the future of the school and to pay for the students' education until they had enough qualifications to secure a career or at least some better opportunities.

'I thought you had government backing,' I said, and could hear Darius grunt in the background.

'That doesn't mean what it does in the UK,' he said. 'There are no such things as promises with our authorities.'

Buke's mouth drooped and her eyes were watery. Everything she'd worked for, and been so pleased to achieve, appeared to be disintegrating.

'I haf no details but it is unfortunately a fact of life dat we can't rely on our government or people in power. Corruption, deceit, manipulation are da watch words for dem.'

Tracey came clattering down the stairs in some wedge-shaped sandals that meant she couldn't quite bend her knees properly as she walked. I suspected she was wearing them because they showed off her varnish work. She'd coupled the look with a red headscarf and matching lipstick.

Pussy started singing 'We Wish You A Merry Christmas' at the top of her voice which was quite a surprise as we'd never heard that from her before.

'Shut up poxy bird,' said Tracey. 'We ain't nowhere near Christmas.'

'Ding dong, humpty dumpty, happy birthday to Pussy,' she screeched back in response before getting hiccups and racing up and down her cage in an apparent attempt to get away from them.

The two women left, and Darius and I were just about to embark on our game of 'What Else Can We Use The Kitchen Table For,' when Ada came tripping through the front door.

'You got a bad back?' she said as she saw me clambering off the table into an upright position. She'd missed Darius pulling back on his trousers, thankfully because he was doing so behind the door.

'Something like that,' I said and was just thinking of sending her away when I realised why I hadn't seen her for a while.

'How is your family?' I asked, hoping to keep her attention while Darius sneaked his way past her without being noticed.

'They is good,' said Ada. 'They's just getting over the shock but all fine.'

'Think I'll just go for a shower,' I said as I saw Darius waving at me from the stairs.

'I'll do down here then. There'll be plenty to keep me going for a while,' she said as she looked around at the array of cups and paraphernalia. I'll be coming upstairs later,' Ada added.

Me too, I thought and made a mental note to lock the bathroom door.

CHAPTER TWENTY-FOUR

Tracey told me they'd let Baz out with no charges although they threatened they would be watching his every move.

'He's not very happy with me,' she said, scratching the skin around the top of her ears where long, wispy hairs were creating patterns of their own making.

We'd gone back to the café in the market as I was hoping to see Banjo and find out more about the man who'd pushed me over and given me the note. I'd seen the car again, but it had kept its distance, it might not even have been the same car.

'Maybe it was because you went off with another man while he was declaring his undying love,' I said, looking through the menu which implied the only hot food or drinks you could get would have been provided by a goat. I decided to have a local beer, it was safer.

'He wasn't declaring any such thing,' said Tracey. 'He wanted me to go to London with him so he could sell those jewels to me mates. He was talking about me shoving some of them where only a few people have been.'

More than a few, I thought but let the idea go as quickly as it came.

'Why would you have to do that? No-one would know where he got them from,' I said.

'It's known, isn't it? Jewellery smuggling, there's lots of it goes on around here,' Tracey said, as she looked through the menu and threw it down in disgust. 'Chiddy told me.'

A bored looking waiter came and took our order for two beers. I asked where Banjo was, and he just shrugged although a couple of older men at a table in the corner of the café looked round when I mentioned his name.

'He's gone,' said one of them as he chewed something around

in his mouth. I hoped it wasn't that nasty stuff that people liked to spit on the road when they'd finished. I thought chewing gum was bad enough until I found out about beetle juice or whatever they called it. It was everywhere on the pavements and looked like very small animals or even beetles had come to a very sticky end – frightened the life of me when I first saw it.

I wanted to ask where he'd gone but they both turned away and carried on with their game of Scrabble which was very popular in Africa as a way of improving English. However, as is common with so much of the country, they were cheating and making up any words that suited their selection of letters. Either that, or 'plyagz' had entered the Oxford English Dictionary without me noticing.

Tracey surprised me with the knowledge she'd picked up and the detail she'd understood about the gemstone business in Nigeria.

'There's a whole thing going on with illegal mining,' she said. 'The Nigerians are desperate to earn a wedge from abroad, cos they can't make it here.'

It seemed that Baz had been very motivated to get involved and even clever enough to get in touch with some people in the Jos area, once he knew what he had, in terms of his haul of my gemstones from Bill's office.

'Jos is where it all happens, the mining and cutting and that, and there is some legal, some not,' Tracey said very animatedly. She seemed to have taken a lot in.

She went on to explain that there are many real gemstones and also lots of fakes. Sometimes it doesn't seem to matter as it is very difficult to tell the difference. Chiddy had told her the whole business had got very professional, very dangerous, but also very lucrative.

'The main thing is the big boys need overseas contacts to build up their business,' added Tracey. 'Baz had known all about this for years but didn't know where to get the jewels, otherwise he would have been on it like a shot — anything for an easy buck.'

She went on to explain that illegal miners will get gemstones from wherever they can – real or fake – and sell them on to a whole range of people only too keen to buy. Few fakes are realised to be a con before the originators have made their money and run away.

'Although there is an official market, all above board and proper, the people Baz was talking to, use runners like him to smuggle out stones and cut out the red tape. There's big money to be made and he really thought this was going to be his road to riches, stupid man.'

If Chiddy was right then the lure of the gemstone market was huge and created by wealthy, high-profile Nigerians. They were in a position to use their privilege to meet people with money and get the items out of their country.

'The big thing is to find stones that are rare,' said Tracey, getting into full flight with her knowledge and surprising even herself. 'You never would have guessed that this is how some of the poor people of Nigeria can make big money. It's like a dream for them, like winning the lottery or the pools.'

I thought of the people at home who would spend their Saturday nights planning how to spend the rollover jackpot, certain in the knowledge that one day their dream would come true. The odds were as likely as being struck by lightning twice while eating a jar of piccalilli on a boat in the Lake District. But I don't recall anyone spending their evenings planning that.

She went on to say that some of the mining was legal but those prepared to get involved in criminal activity could get work where they use their local knowledge and sources to get the best stones.

'The jewels he found are what people are looking for,' said Tracey, 'so he'd been promised huge dosh. People are going crazy for diamonds, opals and aquamarine.'

The diamonds created particular interest, more so since there was a backlash against the Sierra Leone 'blood diamonds'.

'This lot give out some kind of certificate and people like that bit of paper. They pay more because they feel better knowing the stones aren't being mined by workers treated like dirt,' she added, slurping her beer straight from the bottle.

I thought back to Bill and wondered why he wanted me to find his stash. If they were worth what Tracey said they maybe could be, he made no official notes to say he was leaving them to me or what I was supposed to do with them.

I hoped the memory stick would eventually throw up some information once Tom had worked out the formats and looked through the files.

Tom had been distracted recently, since moving into Chinaza's spare room, so I wasn't hopeful of finding any answers soon. They'd discovered a joint love of a computer game, something to do with cars and stealing, in a big way, which I'm pleased to say explained why they were 'up all night at it'.

That didn't strike me as being the kind of thing Chinaza would participate in at all. She seemed more sophisticated than someone who would spend evenings placing themselves in an imaginary situation and thinking about how to kill people.

But then there were many people who'd been married too long to the wrong person, or one who turned out to be so, who probably did just that – but without the benefit of 'Grand Theft Auto' or whatever it was called.

'Blimey,' I said to Tracey, after she'd given me as much detail as she could about an industry that was clearly burgeoning in Nigeria on a number of levels.

'No wonder Baz was cross, he probably thought he was really onto something.'

Tracey screwed her nose up.

'He'd muck it up whatever. Anyway, those stones are yours, not his. Thieving little shit.'

I wasn't sure they were mine. Bill had only met us briefly for a very short time, so it was unlikely I'd be the only person he'd think of when leaving a legacy.

'So, what are you going to do about him?' I asked Tracey, fearful that the answer might mean her staying with Darius and me for the foreseeable future.

'Who knows, Cynth, after all I'm married to the little runt. He might not take that seriously, but I do.'

She looked sad and fiddled with her wedding ring, pulling it almost off her finger then ramming it back on.

'You don't have to stay with him. You could always go home.'

Tracey looked up at me with big, round eyes.

'I don't have a home,' she said. 'I came out here with everything I own. I let Posh Git and Donna have me house cos I didn't think I was ever going home.'

'You have a house?' I said far too loudly to be appropriate, realising that I shouldn't have sounded so surprised.

'Yeah, only off the council. Donna's name's never been off the register, so she's entitled to live there, like.'

'Well tell her you want to go back,' I said. 'Her husband can provide for her as he's so successful.'

'He's spent his money on his business interests,' Tracey said. 'He won't move out. He knows he's on to a good thing.'

We both drank our beers while in deep thought.

'I think I love him,' Tracey suddenly said out of the blue and I had a horrible feeling she'd lost her marbles.

'After everything he's done?' I said, hoping she wasn't going to go creeping back to Baz only to wait for the next disaster.

'No, Chiddy,' said Tracey and as if by divine timing her phone pinged with a text message. She looked at it and smiled. 'Guess what, he loves me too,' she added and got up from her chair to do a little dance. The men across the room looked startled but soon got back to their game of Scrabble which had restarted with the opening words 'Tywper' and 'Blerth', both of which I thought sounded like the names of some of the children from Bobbie's National Childbirth Trust classes. The 'bean bag and lentil' brigade as Colin would call them.

I wasn't sure what to think other than Tracey had fallen foul of Stockholm syndrome.

Freud came up with the idea, I think, to explain situations where hostages express empathy and sympathy, and have positive feelings towards their captors, sometimes to the point of defending them. These feelings are generally considered irrational in light of the danger or risk endured by the victims, who essentially mistake a lack of abuse from their captors for an act of kindness

I tested it out, knowing that Tracey was prone to bouts of being irrational.

'So, do you think what Chiddy did was OK, then? He kept us locked up for all that time,' I said.

'No, I don't think it was OK at all. In fact, I made him beg for mercy,' said Tracey. 'Which wasn't a pretty sight, I can tell you!'

Damn, I thought. It can't be anything to do with the Swedish capital then.

CHAPTER TWENTY-FIVE

'So, it turns out that our Mr Toyin Remy isn't the great guy we all thought he was,' said Darius.

Toyin Remy had promised so much in terms of supporting the Outreach Centre. He'd pledged a five-year donation of personal money to its development, with various authorities and businesses all pledging to match his input. He was key to what turned out to be a very elaborate PR stunt.

'Is he in prison?' I asked, looking over to Buke whose colour, despite her vibrant clothing, had drained to the point she looked like she'd been washed too many times.

'Yes,' said Buke. 'I tink he'll be there for a very long time.'

'He was involved with a huge fraud which he covered up with his import and export businesses. There aren't any details yet because he's still being investigated, along with many other powerful people in Nigeria and elsewhere. Whatever it is, it's big,' said Darius.

We were in his office and through the window I could see Tom and Chinaza hunched over a computer screen, talking animatedly about what they were doing, which in this case didn't look much like a game. I wasn't sure how to feel about their friendship, him being so much younger than her. Then I felt like a hypocrite.

'Is there no way we can get the money elsewhere?' I asked, knowing I was probably being overly optimistic. If there was anyone who could overcome adversity of any kind, it would be Buke.

'I've run out of ideas and now da centre has been tainted wit another kidnap and now this scandal, no-one will want to git involved. We will haf to close.'

I looked at Darius and he looked back with a slight shrug. She was right, the reputation of the centre was shot and even if Baz hadn't actually kidnapped anyone, the fact the place had been in the news so much, left it an unlikely recipient of anyone's good will.

'I don't know what to say,' I said, sad for Buke, the students and also Tracey and I who had forged such a good position. We both loved helping the girls and doing something that might have made a difference.

I knocked on the window to attract Tom's attention, but he turned very briefly to wave and went back to his conversation with Chinaza who touched him lightly on the shoulder, in what would pass for affection. I was pleased for him and hoped she wouldn't break his heart, however necessary that might be for his emotional growth.

The journey home was quiet with Darius and I unsure of what to say to each other. Words didn't convey the sense of disappointment after working so hard to get the centre off the ground.

As we walked in even Pussy picked up on the atmosphere as she made kissing noises, then saying 'sorry, poor Pussy. Pretty Pussy,' over and over again until we covered her up.

The door was open so we could see Alala struggling up our pathway with a large package – bigger than the one she brought with her to the police meeting after the reported kidnap.

Darius rushed out to help her, not realising who she was. That was him all the time, willing to help and always the gentleman. My tummy gave a little spin of appreciation.

'Alala,' I said. 'I wasn't expecting you.'

'I got a lift to the end of the road,' she said. 'I have your picture.'

'And what is this?' asked Darius, curious about my new 'friend'. I'd not mentioned her because the commission of the picture was meant as a surprise.

'Wait and see,' I said, gesturing to Alala she should come in and at least have a cup of tea. She was hesitant but soon persuaded by Darius's gentle nature and no doubt the fatigue that was etched over her face.

'I would like you to see it,' she said. 'It's a bit early but in case you don't like it and want something else instead.'

I looked at Darius and decided it didn't matter if he got his anniversary present early. I had no doubts I would like what this talented woman would have done for us.

With the same precision she used unwrapping the first picture of hers I saw, she gently and slowly revealed the artwork she'd produced at my request.

'It is absolutely beautiful,' I said, looking at the energy of the people, the fluidity of their bodies and the clearness of their intentions. An older white woman with a younger black man, wrapped together as if one person. The picture told a love story, not a sordid tale of advantage or opportunity. I wanted to cry.

'Can I look?' said Darius, who'd respectfully kept his distance.

'Please do, it is for you anyway,' I said and saw Alala shift with pride.

He looked at it for some time and I wasn't too sure how to read him. He was quiet, stepping back and then up close. I could feel my throat close and hoped I hadn't been vain and foolish thinking I could capture what I thought we had.

'That is just perfect,' he finally said. 'Really, really perfect.'

Darius stepped over to Alala and gave her a gentle kiss on the cheek.

'You are incredibly talented,' he added. 'Where do you normally sell your work? Do you have a gallery?'

She laughed and went to stand up to respond to Darius but couldn't quite manage it on the first go.

'Old bones,' she said, sitting back down again. 'No gallery, just a couple of dealers who take the pictures when I have them.'

'You should be selling these in your own right,' Darius said. 'This is just wonderful,' he added, looking appreciatively at the depiction of our relationship.

'I had it made for our anniversary,' I said. 'I'm so glad you like it.'

'Please, I would like to pay for this,' Darius said. 'We should buy this together because it is for both of us.'

I didn't argue as he went to pull out a large roll of cash from his wallet, which he passed over to Alala. She looked at it, took a few of the notes and handed it back.

'Your wife has already paid her half with the deposit,' she said.

Darius's mouth nearly fell open.

'You cannot allow your work to go for this price,' he said. 'It is worth very much more. The materials alone must cost you half what you charge.'

'It is all I can get from the dealers,' Alala said. 'It's what the market will pay,' she added.

'In that case you mustn't sell to them. We must find you another way,' he said and insisted she took the rest of the cash he'd offered.

'But first, some tea and then we'll make you some lunch,' I said. 'You look exhausted.'

Alala told us that she worked as hard as she could with her painting and anything else she could find to earn a crust, but she got very tired.

'Look at my hands,' she said, and we could see they were bent and twisted. She had the classic signs of arthritis. 'I'm in constant pain, which is why I can't sleep at night.'

'Can you not get any help, painkillers or anything?' I asked.

'They cost money. I need food first and there's never enough left over for anything else.'

'I'm not surprised with what you're being paid,' said Darius. 'Please, let me find you something to at least help for a short while.'

He went to our kitchen cupboard and found some ibuprofen we brought over from the UK. The pharmacies sold them for such a small amount of money it was worth stocking up.

'These are anti-inflammatories. They'll help a little,' I said as he handed them over. 'I take them for my back problems,' remembering back to the incident in my UK kitchen involving an unrealistic expectation of my flexibility and a desire to try out a more advanced position from the Kama Sutra.

Alala took them gratefully, opening up the blister pack and popping one in her mouth.

'I heard about the centre having to close,' she said once she'd swallowed the pill with some water Darius offered. 'That is very sad.'

'We are going to do everything we can to get it up and

running again,' I said, surprising myself with my comment – and Darius, too.

'Really?' he said, and then I could feel him warming to the idea. He was never one to be defeated. 'Yes, why not, we will find a way to keep it going. We can't let one bad apple ruin it for the rest of them.'

'I wish I could help,' said Alala, looking at her hands. 'But there isn't much I can do.'

'I disagree,' said Darius with a conviction I knew came from the fact he'd come up with an idea. 'Do you really want to help?'

'Yes, I do,' she said. 'If you can think of anyway that would be possible?'

'Let me give it some thought and if you don't mind, I'd like to come back to you when I have spoken to a few people.'

Alala looked at me as if to say she hadn't a clue what he was talking about but would go along with it for the time being.

'No problem,' she said, suddenly cheerful. 'Did you say something about lunch?'

Darius gave her a lift home despite protests she was OK by herself and when he returned, he told me of his idea, but only after thanking me – in his very special way – for the picture.

We were entwined together in bed, the warm dampness of his body like a comfort blanket, as he told me his plans and I had to admit they were very good.

'What about Buke?' I asked him, thinking she might not be pleased about someone stealing her thunder.

'The centre won't raise money from the traditional sources.' Darius said. 'She might even find there will be rumours about her own involvement with Toyin Remy and how she persuaded him to support her plans in the first place.'

It was true. Buke had put so much energy into the centre but the project had been tarnished by her association with a man being investigated for fraud, and a son who behaved totally inappropriately even if he wasn't doing anything particularly malicious.

We were just going in for round two when Pussy started jumping up and down and talking about 'dirty birds' so I knew

Tracey was on her way back up the path. I'd hoped she be out for longer as she'd said she was going to see Donna and Posh Git to 'let em have it'.

'Only me!' came the regular greeting from the front of the house, followed, as always, by the clip clop of ill-fitting shoes. 'Where are they?' she asked Pussy and was greeted with a tune from Glee which I assumed was a favourite of Bill's. He did come from Brighton, after all.

'Up here,' I shouted from the bedroom, disappointed that I felt I should get up. 'Be down in a minute.'

I came down the stairs, having hastily dressed.

'What's this?' she said, seeing the picture leaning up against the staircase. 'Wow, that a portrait of you two?'

I looked at it again and could see there was a vague resemblance to Darius and myself although that hadn't been the obvious intention. It was more about what the picture represented – love across cultures, ages and social norms. It wasn't supposed to be personal.

'Sort of,' I said while Tracey carried on admiring the picture.

'It's bloody brilliant,' she said. 'It's like it's been done by a proper artist.'

'My thoughts exactly,' said Darius, descending the stairs with an air of someone deep in thought.

'One who could change a lot of lives, including her own.'

CHAPTER TWENTY-SIX

'I really can't take this Buke,' said Tracey as she handed back the cheque. 'Whatever Baz has done it isn't your fault and I am sure you need the money for the school.'

Tracey looked over at me and smiled. We had been talking to Buke about where to go now the backing had disappeared along with Toyin Remy's freedom.

'My money is separate from any of my business or charity activities. I insist dat you take dis. My son has left you high and dry again even though you were so good not to press charges. Consider dis a divorce settlement,' said Buke, pressing the piece of paper hard into Tracey's hand.'

Tracey gasped.

'Divorce? I haven't asked for a divorce and don't I need to sign anything, even if I wanted one?'

Buke shifted in her seat and moved her colourful frame from one side to another. I could see she was thinking carefully about what to say next.

'My dear you were never married in da first place. I set it all up to frighten Baz after what he did to you. No man should ever get away with conning a woman for any reason. He might think he is wed but the law doesn't! You are free of him, if dat is what you wish.'

Tracey opened her mouth and closed it again. Then stood up from where we had been sitting around Buke's office table and started to pace up and down. Eventually she stopped, which relieved me somewhat as she reminded me of a trapped tiger.

'I don't know what to say,' she said, opening up the cheque to reveal its value.

'Jesus, Mary, Aunty Beryl and every cockney rhyming slang for bloody hell,' said Tracey. 'That's a huge amount!'

'It is only what I want you to haf. It isn't a lot, really it isn't. You could barely buy a decent car in your country.'

Tracey looked at it again, looked around the room and looked at me.

'Don't look a gift horse in the mouth,' I said to her, hoping that the ready cash might give her the opportunity to find somewhere else to live now that Baz and her seemed to have parted ways – if only through his obvious desertion.

Since being freed from jail he'd not been in touch with anyone and there were rumours he was last seen at Lagos airport trying to get on a flight without a ticket.

'I'll do something good with it,' she said. 'I promise'

At that point the door knocked gently and Buke responded with a loud: 'Come!'

She swept towards the door to greet the visitor, who turned out to be Darius.

'Well, a very good day to you my good sir,' said Buke, offering her left cheek for a kiss as she grabbed his hand in a warm welcome. 'And to what do I owe my pleasure?'

She was flirting a bit, but I didn't mind. Darius was very fond of Buke and had huge respect for her intelligence, commitment and integrity.

'Hello ladies. Ah Tracey, I'm glad you're here,' he said as he looked over to my dumbstruck friend. It was the first time I think I'd ever seen her truly humbled and was immensely grateful for Buke's kindness towards her, particularly in such difficult times.

'I've just been in the building to see a friend of mine in the Law faculty. He is a very good source of very sound legal advice having trained in the UK,' Darius said.

'He's been looking over those papers you have been asked to sign. Maybe I can catch up with you quickly about them once I have had a word with Buke?'

'Oh, those,' said Tracey. 'I'd more or less forgotten about em.'

Her phone rang and the name 'Posh Git' flashed up on the screen.

'Well, it seems your family haven't,' said Darius, looking over her shoulder as she pushed the 'ignore' button. 'I've got something to ask you, Buke, if you have five minutes?'

The conversation between Buke, Tracey and me had been going round in circles. The money from our sponsor had been stopped in its tracks as all of Toyin Romy's assets had been frozen subject to his trial – which could be months away. The complexities of his extra-curricular activities had been getting more tangled each day, with various people being implicated in what was turning into a massive fraud investigation. The facts had been few, but the interest of the police and other authorities suggested that whatever was going on was pretty serious.

'Please, go ahead,' said Buke. 'I haf all day.'

Tracey stood up and looked like she was going to leave but was actually just trying to find somewhere safe to put the folded cheque Buke had given her. She went to put it in her jacket pocket but missed and the cheque floated down in front of Darius. He scooped it up and gave it to her – pausing slightly to register the amount. He raised an eyebrow.

'Do you have any spare rooms or space near the art department of the university?' he said as he turned his attention back to Buke. 'It is just that I have an idea.'

I wasn't sure what was going on as he hadn't discussed the idea with me. I felt a bit miffed.

'I've only just thought of this,' he added as he leant against the edge of the large boardroom table and crossed his arms. I felt better knowing this wasn't something he was keeping secret. That would have been a first in our relationship and one that I wouldn't have liked very much. Colin was very good at keeping secrets, many of which I didn't find out about until after his funeral. Like his strange collection of antique irons that had been hidden in the loft for decades, a legacy of a fascination with heavy metal objects he shared with his father. A strange man, that was for sure.

'I do think we haf a room in the corridor leading up to the Adichie Centre,' said Buke. 'Why do you ask?'

'Well,' said Darius as he pulled up a chair and sat down in the middle of us. 'I think I have one way of bringing in some cash to the school so we can get it re-opened.'

I could tell that both Tracey and Buke were as keen as me to hear what Darius's idea was. We'd been talking all afternoon and trying to think of ways but 'Strip Karaoke' (Tracey's idea) and 'Charity Teas' (my idea) just didn't cut it. Buke felt she had used up all her political favours and didn't really want to risk another embarrassment by picking the wrong person to support the Outreach Centre.

'We open an art gallery and use the profits to sustain the school,' said Darius.

He looked around at all of us one by one and I had to admit that nothing was registering. The concept of an art gallery in Nigeria just didn't compute.

There were constant attempts to get various types of cultural centres started up back where I lived in Surrey and despite everyone's dinner party interest in painting, books and pretending to read *The Guardian*, even that didn't work. The inertia came from a snobbery suggesting that anything arty that wasn't situated in central London wasn't valid, coupled with the differing opinions of what was actually considered art.

Marty Jones didn't help by daubing most of our local shopping centre and bus stops with his cartoons of rabid foxes hunting out small mammals in a particularly bloodthirsty, if physically and anatomically correct, manner.

While some of the more liberal among the residents claimed the graffiti artist was expressing himself, there was a general public outcry demanding his arrest. That was, until a man from Manchester dressed in a Laura Ashley frock and wearing a monocle offered to buy all the pictures, complete with their 'canvasses' of various bits of brick work and plastic sheeting, for an undisclosed sum.

No-one quite knew exactly how much that sum was, other than it was sufficient to set up Marty and his family in a flat in a south London borough deemed sufficiently trendy to house such a talent. They never came back to Surrey and were often seen on late night television programmes about progressive art, the parents somehow thriving – despite years of obvious teenage neglect – in the reflected glow of their son's, quite frankly dubious, abilities.

Meanwhile some of my neighbours changed their view and said they really liked his work and weren't surprised he was 'discovered'. One even tried to suggest that his two weeks of volunteer work at a youth club Marty attended was all the motivation the boy needed to get painting.

'I told him to find something he enjoyed doing,' this neighbour would venture smugly, only to be completely ignored by everyone other than Mavis who would tell him: 'So we've you to blame for this whole sorry mess.' That would often be enough to shut him up, until the next time.

'We do haf a student's art gallery,' Buke said after a short silence. 'But how would that work?'

'I have an artist or two in mind,' said Darius as he looked towards me and winked. I panicked at the thought he could be including me in whatever idea he had up his sleeve. I'd only kept the life drawing of the bowl of apples because it reminded me of the first thing I did for myself when getting used to widowhood.

After Colin died, I was lost for a little while without my 'job' of being a wife. My days were longer than normal and filled with a constant internal dialogue about what I was doing with myself. So, I joined an art class and managed to complete one picture before realising I wasn't really cut out for creative pursuits. My daughter thought the apples were tennis balls and Tom asked if it had been painted by his younger sister – such was the childlike quality of the finished piece. In my wilder dreams I thought about going to see the man who discovered Marty in case he could find something astonishing about my perspective, but eventually hid the picture in my wardrobe as a reminder that not all occupations are necessarily valuable.

'Do you remember Mo's mother, Alala?'

I clicked and realised what Darius was thinking. She needed an outlet for her work and had also expressed an interest in helping the school get back up and running.

'I do, indeed,' said Buke.

'Ain't she the one that did that picture of you two – the sexy one?' said Tracey.

I blushed and said: 'It's not of us specifically.'

'Yeah right,' Tracey added, raising her eyebrows – which

thankfully were still in situ unlike the rest of her head's hair. 'But it is bloody brilliant.'

'I don't think I have seen dis picture,' said Buke with some enthusiasm. 'I think I need to though?'

Darius looked at me and I know what he was thinking. She would realise that Tracey's interpretation was fairly accurate. There was no doubt it was a sexy picture.

'Regardless, Alala has an amazing talent. She is being ripped off by the Lagos dealers who are no doubt taking her work, paying her a paltry sum, and selling the pictures for vast sums within the established markets of Europe and possibly the US. I see no reason why we can't get to the same markets but give her a much better fee for her work and take the rest for the school.'

Buke nodded sagely a few times.

'I think you could have a good idea, but it might take some time to get the money we need,' she said.

'It's a start, though?' said Darius. 'And even if we just get to help Alala, that would be something. I have a feeling her work is in big demand.'

'Let me look into it. I am sure dat we can try this,' said Buke as her office phone rang on the desk. 'Please excuse me.'

She went over to answer it and turned to the corner of the office and started to speak in hushed tones. I wondered if we should leave.

'So, what is this about the paperwork, big boy?' said Tracey to Darius. He pursed his lips at her nickname for him, but I knew he quite liked it.

'Let's just say I don't think your son-in-law knows what's coming to him. Particularly in light of very new information which I think will have particularly beneficial effects on your plans, shall we say?'

'You are talking in your riddles again, Darius. What does that all mean?' Tracey responded.

'Let's talk things through later. I just need to make a few calls before I can tell you what I have in mind.'

Tracey's phone rang again and this time she answered it. I could hear the screaming on the other end and knew it was Posh

Git. She held the phone away from her ear and moved her mouth up and down silently, mocking the son-in-law who was no doubt threatening her with all kinds of emotional abuse should she not comply with his requirements.

'Alright, alright,' said Tracey, finally bringing the phone to her ear. 'I've just got a few things to do and I'll get the papers sorted out tomorrow, OK?'

There was more screaming, but Tracey clicked off the phone.

'God, he gets on my nerves. I can't wait to get rid of him. I can't wait to sort those papers and hopefully that will be the end of him.'

Buke replaced her own receiver and looked glum as she came back and sat on her seat with a thud. For the first time ever, I thought she looked defeated.

'Things are getting worse,' she said quietly. 'It would seem that our sponsor had his finger in many pies, not just fraud. There is talk of smuggling, blackmail, bribery, human trafficking and global espionage – although I think the latter might be a little bit overstated. The head of criminal investigations here has a tendency to be a bit dramatic.'

'That's terrible,' said Darius. 'We knew his background was complicated, but it seems you are saying he is – or was – a very dangerous man.'

'The worst thing is, my dear friend, the police have let him go.'

CHAPTER TWENTY-SEVEN

Darius told me to be extra vigilant although I wasn't quite sure why. I had nothing to do with the politician and he was clearly involved with things far away from my life.

However, I was a little concerned to see the car driving past the house again – something that Ada pointed out as she was tidying around although the room didn't really need it. With Tom gone and Tracey spending plenty of time with Chiddy, everything stayed in good enough shape for my more relaxed standards.

Before the kidnap I might have worried about the windows, or the corners of the rooms where dust gathers, but now I was very aware that we were privileged in so many ways. We had a working bathroom – which was more than we experienced while holed up as hostages – and very little to worry about in terms of insect infestation.

But I wanted to give Ada as much work as we could afford. I knew she needed it but she would deny she had to work, so then I would insist I needed the help and then she would pretend to be reluctant about doing it. The arrangement worked perfectly.

'He's been around again, that man,' said Ada. 'He looks like he wants to stop, sees me and scarpers.'

I still thought if the man in the car represented anything sinister then something would have happened by now, so I again tried to dismiss it although it was a bit strange. I still didn't feel overly threatened and just kept myself aware if I was out and about, rarely going on my own and always telling Darius or Tom where I was going to be every day.

'He ain't black, the driver,' said Ada as Pussy piped up with a rendition of 'He ain't heavy, he's my butter' almost to the tune, if not the exact wording, of the Hollies' classic. It was another new one learned from the trainer although it could have come from the radio. Pussy sometimes copied tunes she heard but I wondered if her hearing wasn't up to scratch, particularly after her version of the Coldplay song *Paradise* she interpreted as 'parrot, parrot, parrot-dise'.

'Oh,' I said, not sure if I was surprised or not. 'Do you think that matters?'

'Not in the grand scheme of things. But seeing as you are the only white woman other than your frien for miles and he is t' only white man I have seen for some years, it might be of relevance. A long-lost friend or family member maybe?'

I detected a slight smugness in her response. I often got the feeling she thought along the same lines as my children – that I was a little bit dim, slightly demented and not really worthy of much attention unless it was to stop me tripping over a pavement or using my phone upside down.

'Anyway, I finished now,' said Ada. 'So, I be off.'

She put her hat on top of her glowing black hair, picked up her oversized handbag and walked purposefully out of the door. Before she closed it, she looked back and hesitated for a moment.

'Be careful, won't you?'

I was taken aback. Ada wasn't one to show her feelings and while she was always helpful, courteous and hardworking had never given any signs of affection. I felt she believed that any chink in her emotional armour could lead to total collapse, eternal weakness and an unwelcome need to rely on other people.

'Yes, of course Ada. Thank you,' I said, as she closed the door behind her.

'Humpty Dumpty ran up the clock,' sang Pussy and jumped so hard up and down in her cage that it fell to the floor, covering her in water and food until she looked like she had been crumbed ready for a deep fat fryer.

'Bollocks,' said Pussy. 'Show us yer tits.'

The fact she was reverting to her previously offensive self, told me that the parrot was a bit disturbed by the recent events so went to pick up the cage to sort her out. In doing so I noticed the bottom tray had bent. I went to push it back and noticed another tray beneath it. I pushed and pulled, and nothing would shift. I made a note to mention it to Darius when he got home as he could straighten it all out. He was good at things like that.

'Poor Pussy,' said the parrot. "Pussy had a great fall.'

For once the bird seemed to make some sense. I checked her out for any damage, brushed off the seed from her feathers, and went and got her a piece of cuttlefish. We kept it for her for special occasions – or to shut her up when she was being too vocal. She snatched it out of my hands and busied herself pecking at it with great enthusiasm.

'Ruby dazzler,' added Pussy and she wasn't making quite so much sense. I left her to it.

I was just about to think about getting something ready for dinner when the doorbell went, which was particularly unusual – mainly because it rarely worked, but also because we never had daytime visitors unless they were pre-arranged or were called Tracey.

I looked out of the window and could see the car that had been following me, parked outside.

My heart started to race and all the warnings I'd been given by everyone, even the cleaning lady, came back to haunt me. I ducked down and hid behind the sofa but the man had already seen me and started to knock on the door, before moving to the window and peering through.

'I can see you Cynthia. Please don't be scared,' said the man who looked around sixty years old with a kindly face and grey moustache. 'I'm here to help you.'

I could feel my heart pounding even faster, more so than even when I was at the crucial point with Darius, so I sank lower behind the settee hoping he would go away. He kept knocking on the door and I started to get cramp so had to move one leg out straight. As I did, I knocked over a lamp which hit me on the head. Pussy started to laugh raucously.

'Please don't be like that Cynthia. I am a friend of Bill's,' said the man outside. 'I have something I need to show you.'

I bet he does, I thought as I struggled to get comfortable on the floor.

'Just open the window so we can talk. I don't have to come inside if you are worried.'

I thought about this and looked around the lounge. There was a fairly heavy ornament made of marble. I think it was meant to be a dolphin but looked more like a pirate's hat and I had told Darius that many times. He always laughed and never told me where he got it from, but at that moment I was grateful it didn't get thrown out and pulled it over to me with a sense of foreboding.

I shuffled over to the windows holding the ornament closely to my chest and opened the top one very slightly, while hiding behind the curtain. I considered I was being very wise as that particular window was too small to allow entry by a man of any girth but particularly one the size of this person standing on my doorstep. I guessed he enjoyed a better diet than was generally on offer in Africa.

'What do you want?' I asked him abruptly. I wasn't going to get caught out by another scam. I considered my kidnap to be an unfortunate situation brought about by my trusting nature. That trust had dissipated quite rapidly since my release.

'I'm a friend of Bill's. There's something you need to know about him,' said the man. 'He might have mentioned me – we worked together in London for many years. Clive Ward.'

'Never heard of you,' I replied. 'Anyway, I didn't know Bill very well. We only met briefly.'

I sidled up towards the windowsill so I could see the man as he spoke, mostly to an empty room as I remained in hiding.

'I know. But you made a big impression. He spoke very highly of you, and very regularly, after you met.'

'Really?' I answered, wishing I hadn't sounded so enthused. I went to look round the curtain and came face to face with Clive, who was pushing his nose to the window so tightly it was squashed up into a flat heart shape, with lots of nostril hair poking out. If there were mammograms for noses, this is what it would look like, I thought.

'Oh, my goodness,' I shouted, shocked at the sudden closeness of Bill's friend. Without the glass our flesh would be touching.

Clive jumped backwards, equally as shocked by the encounter and stumbled back into the bush outside the front door. He went to get his balance by holding on to one of the branches, which I knew from bitter experience was quite spiky.

'Jesus, what on earth is that?' he shouted as I moved myself into a better position for viewing his antics. 'I think I've come into very close contact with some kind of porcupine?'

I edged towards the door and wondered about whether or not I should open it. Perhaps a few more questions about Bill would ascertain his exact relationship with this man.

After congratulating myself on what I thought was a sensible train of thought, it occurred to me that I didn't know enough about Bill to ask any questions. But I had to do something to prove I wasn't a total pushover.

'So, tell me something about Bill that will convince me you know him,' I asked through the letterbox.

Clive came forward and a little bit too close to the door for my liking when he replied. I could smell fresh garlic on his breath. I suspected he'd enjoyed a large lunch.

'Well, he's dead,' he said before holding up his hand so I could see that it was bleeding. 'Like I might be in a minute if I don't get something sorted for these cuts.'

I could see Clive's blood dripping onto the doorstep and as it had only recently been cleaned by Ada felt obliged to act quickly, so opened the door, still holding the hat-shaped dolphin.

'Oh. There you are. Thank you,' said Clive, seeming a little flustered. 'I don't suppose you have a plaster.'

I shuffled him into the kitchen and allowed him to sit down, all the while keeping an eye on him – and also the ornament – as I got some disinfectant, plasters and a bandage from the first aid kit. Pussy was very agitated and started reciting some very strange scientific information, or at least that's what I thought it was as she mentioned carbon twice and something about hybrids. Maybe Ada had been listening to chemistry programs to relieve the boredom of hoovering or something.

'Have you been following me?' I asked him as I gently

washed the cuts and picked out bits of thorn from his sausage-like fingers.

'Silly Patrick Stays Close,' said Pussy. 'Please Stop Clowning Around.'

'She's still at it, then,' said Clive. 'She always loved memorising the Periodic Table. It was the only way Bill could stop her expressing herself through obscenity.'

I didn't know what he was talking about but maybe some of Pussy's more bizarre statements could be explained by some strange desire to learn science. It also gave me the confidence to realise that this man must have known Bill well, as he knew about Pussy.

'I have been trying to talk to you, yes,' said Clive, wincing occasionally although hardly surprising considering the depth of his injuries. That bush could be quite savage when it wanted to be.

'I wanted to warn you about what was happening and tell you about Bill. He left you Pussy in his will for a reason.'

'Nothing on. Feeling nervous,' piped up Pussy. I quickly ran out to cover her up or she would just get herself into more of a state than usual.

'She knows more than you think, that parrot,' said Clive – so I glared at him. I didn't want to engage in small talk and really needed to get him out of the house before Darius came home. Not because he would think anything was going on, he just wouldn't believe I'd been silly enough to let him into the house while I was alone.

I looked at Clive as if he was slightly mad. People do usually leave things in their will for a reason, generally to pass on their wealth to a loved one. In this case I got a blasphemous parrot with an attitude problem from someone I hardly knew.

'There was more to him than you might know...'

Clive was just about to explain when the back door flew open followed swiftly by a very agitated Baz.

'Where is she?' he shouted brandishing his phone in the air as if it were a weapon. 'I know she's here.'

I'd got so used to Baz and his outbursts that I took no notice, but I could see that Clive was shaken. He was trying to hide his face behind his bandaged hands and looked uncomfortable.

'What the hell is he doing here?' shouted Baz. 'Come on, where is it?'

'I don't know what you mean,' replied Clive, jumping up from his chair and heading for the front door. 'I need to go. Sorry Cynthia.'

He made a dash for it, swiftly followed by Baz in hot pursuit. Clive raced as fast as he could, given his frame and lack of fitness, and bounced along the pathway to his car which he had left open allowing for a quick entry. It started immediately and he sped away at great speed – sufficient enough to knock Baz flying as he ran into the road to try and stop him.

I could hear crying and wasn't sure if it was me, Baz or Clive.

CHAPTER TWENTY-EIGHT

'What the bloody hell has happened here?' said Tracey as she walked up the road just in time to see Baz fly up in the air and land heavily in the road in front of Clive's car.

She ran up to Baz and we both reached him at the same time. Although he was in a strange position, as if he were praying for a miracle, he seemed relatively unhurt but was snivelling and snorting like a baby.

'Oh, do stop your whingeing,' said Tracey. 'You'll be OK other than a few bruises.'

'Is he dead?' Clive asked as he tentatively moved forward hardly daring to look at the scene. 'Have I killed him?'

'Unfortunately, no,' said Tracey as she bent down to have a clearer look. I tried to help Baz up, but he was still sobbing into his hands with a mixture of fear and self-pity.

'You get on the way before he decides to call any police or gets a timely call asking if he's been in an accident that wasn't his fault,' said Tracey as she helped me get Baz into an almost upright position.

'He could have wiped me out,' Baz coughed, as he checked himself all over for any signs of damage. 'I've broken all my bones.'

I nodded over to Clive to tell him to get going before things got messy, as they always tended to do if Baz was involved. He took the hint, jumped back in his car and sped off after promising to be back in touch very soon.

'I do need to speak to you, Cynthia. I need to do so soon. Before they get me,' he shouted out of the car window on his way past.

Whatever it was he thought he wanted to tell me could wait.

'I'll bloody get him,' said Baz limping up the driveway and no doubt assuming he could come into my house. Tracey hung back as I helped him and she stopped to look at something that had caught her eye where Baz had fallen.

'Just looking for evidence,' she said as I saw her pick something up and put it in her pocket. I made a note to ask what it was once we'd dealt with her now ex-husband, or in fact never-was-husband.

Tracey came into the kitchen and removed her headscarf which revealed a rather fuller head of hair than she'd had for a while. It was looking very dashing and showed off her rather fine cheekbones. She could look very good for her age when she wasn't trying to knock ten years off it.

'So, where have you been then?' she asked very calmly.

'Don't start on me now,' he said, crying again, but this time with less dramatic output. 'I could have died.'

'Humph,' muttered Tracey and turned her attention to me. 'So, who was that man? And how do you know him?'

I wasn't sure what to say as I didn't know Clive although he did seem to know who I was.

'I know who he is,' said Baz. 'And he's got something of mine.'

'Oh really,' said Tracey. 'And what might that be?'

'None of your business,' said Baz, hauling himself up and making a big drama of limping towards the kitchen door before pretending to lose his balance, requiring the need to grasp the door frame.

'Funny how you wanted to make it my business a short while ago,' she replied.

'That's when I thought I had a wife who would support me in my business ventures rather than running off with some low-life kidnapper turned music teacher,' Baz said.

'That, my dear Baz, was when you thought you had a wife, full stop. But then we both thought that for a while, didn't we?'

Tracey looked triumphant as Baz stared back at her quizzically. He genuinely seemed taken aback by her comments.

'What do you mean?' he asked.

'Well, oh loveliest of almost husbands, it would seem your mother was just teaching you a lesson for being a complete jerk and trying to rip me off for all my savings. We were never married in the first place. She set it all up in sisterly support and to make you pay for your sins. Talking of which, she has paid me off – let's call it compensation – and told me I don't have to have anything to do with you ever again.'

At this point Tracey marched to the front door and opened it wide, firstly surprising Darius as he had just come home and was about to let himself in and then secondly, surprising Baz by coming back for him. She grabbed hold tightly of his arm and threw him straight onto the bush that had so pointedly injured Clive.

Baz started squealing while Darius looked on in some kind of amused shock, dappled with the tiniest bit of concern as he could see that Baz was bruised, had some blood around his cheek and was visibly in further pain.

'Now, get lost!' shouted Tracey, slamming the door closed so all we could see was Baz limping down the driveway, picking bits of thorn from his arms. I was really rather impressed.

'Good evening, Tracey,' said Darius, placing down his briefcase. 'It is so lovely to come home to the warm welcome of a peaceful house,' he added before reaching down and opening up his case quickly to retrieve some papers, which he placed firmly under his arm.

Thankfully he had a twinkle in his eye, so I knew he wasn't very cross although probably a little bemused.

'So, is anyone going to tell me what is going on?'

I looked at Tracey and willed her not to say too much for fear of placing me in a difficult position, explanation wise, and she knew my 'look' well enough to keep things vague.

'Baz got run over,' she said, fiddling with whatever it was she put in her pocket from the road after the accident. She pulled it out to reveal a small key on a chain.

'And it seems this was pulled off his neck – quite interesting for a man who never wears jewellery.'

Darius took off his tie and unbuttoned his shirt as he looked at the item, before heading to the fridge for a beer. He didn't often have a drink straight in from work but on this occasion, I think it was justified. His expression suggested he was trying to work out what might have happened but had lost the will to do so.

'Have you any idea what it might be?' I asked, hoping to deflect the conversation entirely towards Baz and his mischief, rather than my encounter with an unknown man in my own kitchen.

'Nah. But I bet it has something to do with his so-called 'business' and is highly dodgy. Best we hang onto it, don't you think?'

I busied myself pretending I had been getting dinner ready and just needed to get back to it while Darius settled down at the kitchen table and pulled out the official looking papers from beneath his arm. I felt hypocritical keeping my secret, being so totally against them between people who should be honest, and vowed to tell him everything I knew about Clive, which wasn't much, at a more prudent time.

'Right,' Darius said to Tracey. 'I think you might be interested to hear what I have found out regarding your son-in-law's plans.'

'Probably not,' she said, kicking off her shoes and leaning back in the chair stretching her arms. 'But I guess it might make sense to find out.'

Darius laid out the papers on top of the kitchen table. As Tracey peered at them, he went to the fridge and opened a bottle of wine – some of the nicer stuff – and poured her and me a glass. He was a true gentleman, unlike Colin who would have made me get it myself, told me not to drink the good stuff and then later berate me for being a border-line alcoholic after a thimble sized class of cheap Chardonnay.

'I don't know what they mean,' said Tracey, swigging down half her glass of wine as quickly as she could get it into her mouth. Darius gazed at her, apparently humoured by her thirst.

'I've had a bad day,' she added as she more-or-less finished the glass and handed it back for a refill.

'Look,' said Darius, pointing to what looked like something very official. I certainly didn't know what it was. 'This is an offer to buy your house.'

'Who from?' said Tracey, taking on board Darius's expression as she was about to swig her second glass of wine as quickly as the first, so sipped noisily instead. 'It's not mine to sell.'

'The offer is to you, for you to buy your house — from the council,' said Darius.

'Eh? I don't get it,' she said, rummaging about in her handbag. 'I haven't lived in it for years,' she said, finding a pencil on the table to shove in her mouth and chew. I thought I'd better not tell her I'd used it that morning to dig out some rotting meat that was blocking the back of the fridge.

'The thing is,' said Darius, 'your son-in-law seemed to think if you signed everything over to your daughter one hundred per cent they could buy the property and then cash in on the fact you have been offered a massive discount.'

Tracey looked at Darius for what seemed like an age, which I can't blame her for as I was also struggling with the information he was passing on.

'Why would they offer me a discount? I still don't understand what you are saying.'

Darius took a small breath which I knew meant he was thinking how he could best explain matters without upsetting anyone.

He was very considerate like that, as I remember from the time he asked me to get rid of my 'comfortable' shoes. The fact they were flat and elasticated seemed to suggest to him that I was of an age way beyond my actual years and should only be seen dead in them. He didn't say that, of course, he just explained they weren't of a suitable quality for a woman of my 'great beauty' (his words) and that he would like to buy me a new pair. The fact the comfortable ones were placed straight in the bin by Darius after the conversation pretty much said it all.

'It would seem that in the UK if you have been a council or housing association tenant for a very long time you get the opportunity to buy your property at a vastly discounted rate,' said Darius – pausing to let the detail sink in. I wasn't sure it had got near Tracey's surface let alone any deeper.

Darius continued: 'It is my understanding that most people

were expected to do this to become homeowners and take pride in their own purchase for many years to come. However, there are many who take advantage by buying at a very low price, then selling on a couple of years later for much more.'

Tracey's eyes started to widen and a vague appearance of understanding swept over her face – now considerably less red than it had been for some time, almost glowing.

'But why would I want to buy a house I don't live in?' she said. 'And what's it got to do with Posh Git?'

Darius pulled out some other papers from the pile and showed her the top one.

'Is this what he sent you to sign a while back?' he asked.

'I don't know,' said Tracey. 'It might have been, but I didn't really take any notice.'

'Thank goodness as it would hand over the right to buy to Donna and then you would have lost out big time, while your son-in-law would no doubt profit considerably.'

Tracey laughed out loud. 'Thank goodness I don't do paperwork, eh Cynth?'

'The thing is,' Darius continued. 'If you were to sign the paper I first showed you, then you could teach him a lesson and help your daughter at the same time.'

Dinner was almost ready but I was starting to get captivated by what Darius was saying, so turned all the pots and pans off. I was full of pride at how he not only wanted to help people but was clever enough to do it without them even realising.

'I hope you don't mind me being a bit forward here, but I couldn't help see the value of the cheque you had the other day in Buke's office. That is more than enough to purchase your home in the UK.'

Tracey frowned and pursed her lips. With the curly wisps of hair and the new lush pink colour of her cheeks she reminded me of a baby lama I'd once seen somewhere near the New Forest.

'Do I want to buy a house in the UK? I might not even go back there,' she said.

'By doing so you'll stop your son-in-law getting his hands on it and you can pass it down to your daughter at any time you want in the future. It will be entirely yours,' Darius said.

'Or you could rent it out,' I added, hoping to offer some substance to what was a quite enlightening conversation.

'That could be a solution if you want to keep things simple,' said Darius. 'Rent it out to Donna and your son-in-law.'

At that point Tracey obviously realised her new found power and laughed until she was shaking – waking up Pussy who also started laughing and then shouting 'how's about that' in a Scottish accent. Goodness knows where she got that from.

'He couldn't afford the rent!' she said, looking down and reading the papers again. 'So, where do I sign?'

Tracey scribbled her signature and Darius promised to sort out the formalities for her, which he had already taken the liberty of getting in motion.

I could only hope to see Posh Git's face when he found out.

CHAPTER TWENTY-NINE

I was a little surprised to see that Buke had decided to employ Tony, the head teacher, to run the art gallery at the university.

'I haf to give him a job to do. He's on a year's contract so might as well use him,' she explained.

The opening event was something of a grand affair as Buke had pulled the few strings she had left to get some minor celebrities along, as well as a few of the limited number of government officials who so far hadn't been involved in any fraud.

I was busy talking to Alala about her work when I looked over and spotted an older man with a heavy grey beard, thick tortoiseshell glasses and an imposing hat – the type people wear when they want to look arty and interesting – in the corner, staring over in my direction.

He did seem familiar but I wasn't sure why. I looked around to Darius and was pleased to see him a few feet away, chatting to a group of students from the university and encouraging them to submit their work to help the cause. They were entirely engaged with his enthusiasm and I could see that any doubts about the project would easily be swept away once he used his charms to get people involved.

'You know that man?' said Alala, and I felt a shudder of déjà vu. 'He's been looking at you all night.'

I turned to have another look and as I did so he went to leave the room. There was something about him that made me question my memory. I couldn't really see much of him because of his outfit but there was something about his eyes. As he was about to leave the room I looked down and felt a shock of recognition flood through my veins. He was walking with a cane, encrusted with vibrant jewels – the cane I saw when I was pushed over in the market.

'This is going remarkably well,' said Buke, she said as she flowed over in our direction, distracting me from the man's exit. 'We have already had a few personal pledges and many sales, so I'd say the fundraising is at least on its way.'

I looked around again and the man with the cane was nowhere to be seen.

'Do you know who that man was in the corner, with the beard, glasses and walking stick?' I asked Buke who had been in charge of the invitation list.

'No, my dear – he said he was a friend of yours. Is dat right?'

Buke cocked her head to one side after I said I'd no idea who he was, taking her time to think, as she often does.

'Well, you are still something of a celebrity in these parts so maybe he is just an admirer.'

I wasn't so sure but let it go. I was a bit worried about Tracey. She was supposed to have arrived at the same time as us, but I hadn't been able to get hold of her. Darius had seen her earlier that day as he'd helped her sign all the necessary papers to purchase her council house.

'Do you know where Tracey is?' I asked him when he came round the room to make sure I was OK – and cheekily pinch my bum while no-one was looking. He looked spectacularly gorgeous in his lightweight suit, dark in colour but skimming his firm shoulders. His shirt was open to the second button and I wanted to open it further. His chest hair was teasing me with potential, particularly as my adrenaline was slightly high after seeing the man with the cane.

'Last I heard, she was off to see Donna,' he said while looking at his watch. 'But that was about five hours ago.'

As if conjured up from nowhere, Tracey came running through the door to the gallery, tipping forward in her high shoes and dragging along a very bedraggled looking Donna who was carrying a large bag, from which a variety of items of clothing were dangling precariously.

'Sorry we're late, we had to sort a few things out,' she puffed as they got within talking distance. I took the liberty of stuffing a pair of knickers back into Donna's bag and tightening up the zip to prevent anything else falling out.

A few of the guests turned to see what was going on but, for once, Tracey kept herself relatively quiet. Donna was seemingly stunned into some kind of silence and if I didn't know better, I'd have thought someone was holding a gun to her head to keep her from saying too much.

'What on earth has happened?' I asked quietly, keen to behave as if all this drama was actually very normal and nothing to write home about.

'Let's just say that Posh Git has learned a few lessons. It's OK if Donna stays with us for a bit isn't it – until we get sorted out?'

I wasn't quite sure what to say but felt it appropriate to discuss at a later stage rather than ask any details at this moment. There were people to thank, others to impress and also a couple of speeches. Now wasn't the time to find out what type of 'sorting out' Tracey had imparted on her daughter's husband.

Alala was shining in her moment of glory. The work she had brought along for the gallery was as good, if not better, than the picture she'd completed for Darius and me. She had kept the artwork small so she could produce more – and could also carry them more easily. The deal was she would get sixty per cent of any sale price and the school would get the rest. She did argue that her fee was too much but she was persuaded that she needed the money to keep herself well so she could paint for longer. I think she was happy to agree with that sentiment.

The speeches started and I was pleased they were short and to the point. Buke thanked everyone for coming and a few of the students stood up and said a few things about their art. Other than that, it was fairly low key.

Drinks were starting to flow again when there was a sudden boom of music coming from behind the make-shift stage, which had been backed with heavy curtains. Everyone looked around and Tracey started to jump up and down like an excited ferret.

'What's the matter with you?' I asked, slightly irritated that she was starting to act strangely having been so well behaved up to that point. I knew that it was too good to be true.

'He's here, he's here,' she said, and started wiggling around. Donna looked at me with an increased sense of animation which I took to be a good thing. She grabbed a glass of wine as the waitress made her way round the room, looked at it for one second then downed it in one. Like mother, like daughter, I thought.

The booming music continued and then the lights went out, quickly followed by a spectacular light show that seemed to be organised by some more students who came from behind the curtains – closely followed by Chiddy who started a rap which seemed to contain the words 'art for school, school is art, don't let the bastards take you apart' and then went on in that vein much to the delight of the younger members of the audience – and Tracey.

'Isn't he just great?' she said, beaming all over her face. 'He will do anything for anyone that man.'

Buke was standing in front of the stage with her mouth open so I guessed she hadn't been informed about the impromptu entertainment. Looking around, she could see many people enjoying the show so she shrugged and made her way over to us. Darius was still engaged in conversation with students and looking as impressed as they were with what was going on.

'I did not know anything about dis!' said Buke. 'Was dis anything to do with you?' she added, looking at me.

'I sorted it,' said Tracey. 'He's sick, isn't he?'

'Sick?' shouted Buke although she thankfully couldn't be heard over the music. 'Then he shouldn't be here. He might make us all ill!'

Tracey laughed and Donna almost smiled, even though she was still hanging on to her bag as if her life depended on it.

'I organised it,' said Tracey. 'Just asked for a special favour if you know what I mean.' She carried on dancing and it reminded me very much of how she got Chiddy to do special favours while we were incarcerated by our kidnappers.

I think Buke was about to reprimand Tracey until Darius came over with a man carrying a broadcast camera and a woman with a small microphone.

'Well, Chiddy has done us a huge favour,' he said, introducing the journalists from Nigeria's biggest TV station. 'He's better known than we have given him credit for – and as a result has got these lovely people involved to do a big piece on the school fundraising.'

Buke beamed and Tracey just smiled as if to say, 'I'm not as stupid as you might think' and it was a sentiment I entirely agreed with at that point.

CHAPTER THIRTY

Posh Git didn't take the news very kindly. He was obviously expecting a huge financial benefit from persuading Tracey to sign over her council house to Donna so they could buy with a view to profiteering.

'You did what?' he had shouted at Tracey when we went to meet him the next day and tell him his fortune.

He paced up and down like an angry chimpanzee about to throw his own poo at the audience.

'Do you know how much I have spent coming over here, trying to find you and to do the right thing by your daughter? You have ruined everything.'

Donna hadn't explained before she left for the evening, that she was going to leave him for good. She'd packed a bag on the basis she was going to the opening of the art gallery, telling her husband she would be staying over to help clear up in the morning. Apparently, he'd not twigged that she had packed everything she had brought over from the UK – and wasn't coming back.

'Where is she anyway?' he screamed again. 'I suppose you've manipulated her into thinking no good of me.'

'Oh, there was no manipulation necessary,' said Tracey, in an exceptionally calm manner. 'I think she worked it out all by herself.'

'Stupid little trollop,' said Posh Git under his breath, but not low enough so Tracey couldn't hear. He obviously didn't know her very well. One thing you didn't do was upset Tracey's family or friends.

I couldn't quite see how she managed to do it, but within seconds Posh Git was on the floor and holding on to his genitals, crying like a baby.

'I'll get you for this,' he shouted as Darius and I decided to start preparing to leave the room – hoping we had the strength to get Tracey out before she turned Posh Git's giblets into soup.

'I doubt there's much you can do,' said Tracey. 'And don't even think you'll be able to take it out on my daughter as she is staying with me until your divorce comes through.'

'She won't divorce me,' said Posh Git as he tried to stand up while still holding on to the middle of his trousers.

'I don't think you've much to offer her now have you?' added Tracey as she looked pointedly at his crotch area. 'That's if you ever did in the first place.'

Darius managed to grab hold of Tracey's arm and pull her out of the door, indicating that we should go ahead. As Posh Git tried to get out and follow us Darius used just one arm to push him back into the living quarters where he lost his balance and fell into some furniture. There was some cursing but he didn't come back, so Darius quietly closed the door behind him and walked calmly to catch us up.

'I quite enjoyed that,' he said as he escorted us both back to the car and I detected a slight smirk which was unusual. It was testament to the vileness of the man that my husband took such a dislike to him.

We were all in a cheerful mood as we made our way home. Judging by the smell of cooking, Donna had been busy and when we got back in, she worriedly looked at us all, one by one.

'So? How did it go?' she asked meekly, although not nearly as meekly as previous days.

'He kicked off of course,' said Tracey. 'But he calmed down after a while.'

'Really?' said Donna, clearly not believing that her husband had calmed down after being told that all his plans to make an easy fortune had been dashed by his mother in law. 'You sure he wasn't just pretending?'

Tracey shrieked with laughter.

'No, my darling, he is too worried about the state of his knackers and what might happen if he comes anywhere near us again.'

'Knackers, knackers, shining balls,' shouted out Pussy from the hall, where Darius had been on the phone.

'I wish that bird wouldn't scream obscenities when I'm calling work,' he said as he pushed his way into the kitchen only to be distracted by an amazing looking pie on the top of the cooker.

'Wow, what is that?' he asked Donna, whose cheeks blushed to almost the colour of the tomatoes she'd apparently been chopping for an equally impressive looking salad.

Feeling quite peeved that she was taking my role as the 'good cook' of the house, I pretended not to notice but there was no doubt our guest had put on an impressive display.

'It's a chicken, ham and leek pie in a goat's cheese sauce with sage pastry. I hope you didn't mind me going through your freezer?'

I did mind, but realised the girl was making a huge effort to earn her keep although I wondered how any daughter of Tracey's had ever worked out how to turn on an oven let alone produce a more than acceptable meal.

'It looks lovely,' I said and busied myself laying the table. I'd never thought of making sage pastry and was cross I hadn't got there first.

'Bleeding hell, Don – where did you learn to do all that?' said Tracey as she twisted a chain around her fingers absent-mindedly.

'The internet and daytime TV mainly,' said Donna, almost pumping with pride until her self-esteem self-deflated and left her looking a bit bemused by her own abilities.

'Well it looks good enough to eat,' said Darius as he placed his phone down to the side. 'And it will taste even better now you know that your husband has been escorted off the university premises and to the airport where a ticket has been bought for his return to the UK. He will be leaving on a flight very soon.'

There was something very exciting about having a man around who got things done. I liked the way he had 'cleared up' the issue of Posh Git and by doing so had liberated two women in one fell swoop.

'Now, did you say you wanted me to look at Pussy's cage?'

I had forgotten about the accident and how it had bent the bottom tray. Pussy had been quite quiet for the last few days, so I hoped there was no lasting damage from her fall.

'Pussy in the well, Hickory Dickory cock,' she piped up assuring me that her lifespan was likely to extend to the usual expectations. 'Diamonds are forever.'

The last phrase was a new one, but she'd not been making a lot of sense since Clive's visit. Various strange sentences were popping up from nowhere and were making her unusually content.

'Ah yes,' I said, leaving Donna to finish with getting the kitchen ready for people to eat. I wasn't sure I liked having someone take over all the domestic duties but was looking forward to the pie and salad. It's nice to not always be the cook.

I went out to the cage and Darius followed, weaving his arms over my shoulders to hold me tight as I explained how the tray in the bottom didn't seem to quite fit. He took Pussy out and placed her on his shoulder, where she happily stayed, pecking at the hair above his ears, while he looked at her living quarters.

He pulled and pushed and agreed that there was something not quite right but he didn't think the cage had been bent.

'There's something catching in the corner, I think,' he said. 'Oh, I've not seen that before.'

Pussy started jumping up and down on his shoulder as Darius tried to pull out the drawer. 'Diamonds are a girl's best friend' she shouted and got very animated.

'Oh, shush please Pussy,' he said, getting frustrated with the lack of movement at the bottom of the cage. 'I can't seem to move this.'

He took out a torch from one of the drawers in the cabinet in the hall and shone it onto the tray. Pussy got so excited she managed to poo down the back of Darius's neck although he didn't seem to notice. If he did, he did nothing about it, being every inch a gentleman.

Tracey came out to join us in the hall, still fiddling with the chain around her fingers. Darius looked up, deciding to check the back of his neck which he probably regretted as he then realised what the parrot had done.

'Good job I need a shower,' he said as he eyed what Tracey was doing. 'Can I have a look at that?'

She handed over the chain with the small key attached, the one she found on the road after Baz was run over.

Darius took it and grasped the key before tipping up the cage. He placed it in a small hole at the bottom and with some effort opened up what seemed to be some kind of secret compartment. Out fell a number of small gemstones and one, very large, diamond-looking stone – coupled with a computer dongle that merely said 'jigsaw' on it.

'Bloody hell, Cynth,' said Tracey. 'Our luck really is changing. What with all this money, now me own house and diamonds to boot!'

'I doubt they are real gems,' I said, keen not to get too carried away with our find. Everything was getting very complicated and quite confusing.

'Well, I'll be damned,' said Darius scratching his head and, by doing so, adding a considerable amount of bird shit to his hair. He looked at his hand then held it in the air for a bit not quite sure what to do, so he picked up the bird and put her back in the cage, locking her in and making good the bottom tray so she couldn't get out.

'Let me out!' shouted Pussy so I covered her up. She'd had enough excitement for the night.

'I'll give this to Tom as it might just add something to the other memory stick,' said Darius, looking puzzled at the items that had been hidden all that time in Pussy's cage. 'I'm sure we can get this analysed and see what it is made of, probably some kind of amalgam or even zirconia. That's often passed off as the real thing.'

Tracey was looking at the stone, picked it up and placed it on her engagement finger. I thought how she would just have loved to have been a footballer's wife. Not that she knew much about football – she thought a goal kick was when a woman managed to effectively kick a man in the nether regions.

'No good to me then,' she said as she handed it over to Darius as he picked up the evidence from Pussy's cage to put in a bag. 'Shame, although the blue one is pretty.'

'Maybe when they're finished looking at them, we can make some earrings or something.' I said, hoping to put a positive spin on our 'find'.

'I'll need to take them in to work as they are probably related to Bill's activities. It won't take long to put then through a few tests, then they're all yours,' said Darius as he sniffed his hand, reeling at the odour from Pussy's excretions.

'I think I'll go and get a shower while I think about what this might all mean,' Darius said and raced upstairs to clean up. I wanted to join him but remembered that he probably did need to wash on his own given the state of him.

CHAPTER THIRTY-ONE

A meeting with Buke had been called for the next day as there was no time to delay sorting out any possible prospect of Bill's involvement with Toyin and others.

I was sad there was a possibility he'd been mixing with such unpleasant people but had to accept I didn't know him at all well. Also, looks can always be very deceiving – as can so many human beings, of all types and backgrounds.

Tracey and I had decided to go into the market for a new teapot and some bedding. With Donna staying for what seemed to be the immediate future, if not longer, we needed more sheets and towels. The teapot was my idea as the cafetiere had been virtually worn out with Tracey's use so she could have her own.

'Let's have a livener before the meeting,' said Tracey and pointed to the café where we had previously been pushed over by the man with the cane. 'Let's see if Banjo is back'

I was a bit nervous. Having recognised a certain level of silliness in my own behaviour, I was wondering whether it was sensible to return to the scene of the crime. I couldn't live it down if I was attacked again.

Tracey knew me well. She slapped me on the shoulder then pushed me in the direction of the café which was situated at the back of a square behind a small concrete shed that was used for storing some of the market stalls and bunting overnight.

We were walking towards one of the empty tables when a small boy on a bicycle screeched to a halt next to us and nodded to a shadowy area the other side of the hut. I could see a hand attached to a large figure which I assumed was a man. He was waving us over but I couldn't see his face.

Having learned my lesson, I knew I shouldn't go over. Once bitten, or pushed, and twice shy. So I sent Tracey.

'Go over and ask him what he wants,' I said.

'Why me?' she said. She'd been fishing around in her bag so I suspected she thought sitting outside a café would be a good opportunity to top up her nicotine levels.

'Because you're so good at looking after yourself,' I said, totally believing what I said and also knowing it would be the right thing to say to Tracey.

She gave me her bag to hold as she marched over in great strides, her already solid frame made almost Amazonian by the size of the platforms on her shoes. I could hear her from my safe position, well out in the open air.

'What do you want?' she said forcefully. I was a little bit scared at that point.

'Please, come over here,' I heard loudly whispered as a crouching man popped his head out into the light. I could see then it was Banjo, so went over to join Tracey as the curiosity of what he was doing hiding in the shadows had got the better of me.

'Banjo!' I said far too loudly for his comfort, as he shushed and shoved Tracey and me into the darkest corner of where he had been standing.

'You mustn't tell anyone you've seen me. I'm so glad you came back to the market. I have been waiting and hoping for days, since I last saw you.'

Banjo's eyes darted around and into the light. The boy on the bicycle put his thumbs up in our direction.

'My son,' said Banjo proudly. 'A good boy.'

'I'm sure he is,' I said a bit impatiently as I wanted to know what he had to say to us. It all seemed very cloak and dagger.

'The man who pushed you over in the square that day,' he said to me with his eyes piercing mine. 'He is a bad man and you need to be very careful.'

Tracey pursed her lips at him and looked Banjo up and down thoughtfully.

'What exactly do you mean by bad?'

'He is very powerful and knows many people. He has money, lots of money and can do nasty things. He makes people disappear and no-one can do anything about it.'

Tracey looked at me and I wondered if we thought the same thing. That we should meet this man and tell him all about Baz and Posh Git and how we'd like them to both go away and never come back.

'There's loads of people like that in Nigeria,' I said, keen to look as if I wasn't as worried as I felt.

'Yeah,' said Tracey. 'Why would he be interested in us anyway?'

Banjo's eyes scanned the immediate vicinity. His son was resting on his bike looking bored, so we all assumed there was no-one listening.

'His business had to close because of you and all the publicity about your kidnap. He lost out on millions of pounds and isn't happy with you. He thinks you need to pay.'

'I can't see how that would be our fault,' I said. 'Why would our being kidnapped be a problem for him?'

'Because no-one paid out,' said Banjo.

'I'm not sure I understand,' I said. 'No-one paid out because we escaped.'

'Yes, and who helped you escape?' asked Banjo with his eyes widening as he spoke.

Tracey and I looked at each other. There were a few people who could have been mentioned for helping us out: Gowon, Chiddy, the one-armed taxi driver and then Bill, among others. Tracey shrugged.

'Bill maybe?' he said and looked at us both in turn with fear in his eyes. 'And look what happened to him.'

'He had a heart attack,' I said. 'There's nothing surprising about that given his diet and lack of exercise. I expect his cholesterol readings were higher than his shoe size.'

'That's what the coroner might have written,' said Banjo getting more and more animated. 'But I think others will tell you it was brought on by something quite sinister. Such as John.'

'John!' Tracey and I shouted at the same time. 'As in John the supposedly lovely British man who pretended he was going to help us and was in fact behind the whole Dear Beneficiary scam in the first place?' I asked. I started to shake.

'Yes, now do you know why I am warning you?'

Banjo went on to explain that John was not only behind a whole range of complex internet scams that had hooked women like myself all over the globe, but had been in cahoots with Toyin Remy and other politicians over various gemstone and money laundering schemes.

'He has his fingers in so many pies that he controls more in Nigeria than any Nigerian. It is because of him that Toyin was released from prison.'

'He paid people off?' Tracey asked, leaning against the wall and sighing with a real sense of shock.

'Amongst other things,' said Banjo, his lips blowing out with the release of so much information.

'He knows lots of people, their weaknesses and their loves. Blackmail is a terrible thing,' he said as he nodded over towards his son. 'I need to keep my eye out all day every day.'

'That's terrible,' I said. 'What has he got against you?'

Banjo's eyes filled with tears and he looked to the floor. 'He owns my café and when he found out I knew Bill and his friend, Clive, he wanted me to get them involved with his business. But they didn't want to know so he wanted me to do some very bad things. When I refused, he put my rent up tenfold and told me if I couldn't pay it I was to leave the village and take everything I cared about with me.'

Bill and Clive had tried to reason with John by all accounts – not realising what John was after – and so Banjo had gone without a fight, not wanting to get them any further involved.

'So, do you think Bill was involved with all of this fraud then?' I asked, thinking that I knew I was right about him. I might not have been a great judge of character over the last few months, but he definitely seemed like a nice chap. Not only that, he seemed far too fat to be a real villain. He'd never be able to run away.

'I don't think so. But he obviously had something of great interest to these powerful people and no-one knows if he was being offered big money or even being pressured somehow for his knowledge. History suggests they would pay well for it. They think money gets them everything they want and can't understand when people refuse.'

'Do you know what he might have had that was of so much interest?' I asked, wondering what on earth Bill had got into. I hadn't heard back from Clive, but he had said he wanted to tell me something.

'Bill was a clever man,' said Banjo. 'He was working on some incredible things at the university – things that would have been very useful to people with criminal minds. Clive knows what he was doing and is probably also in danger.'

'Do you know where Clive is?' I said as my mind raced for facts that might tell me a bit more about what was going on.

I started to wish I'd never taken on the bloody parrot. What started as a perfectly straightforward adoption process was turning into a murder mystery plot although this was much more real than the ones Mavis used to write for the church fundraisers. They nearly always ended up with me being murdered fairly early on in proceedings, usually by her in some kind of love tryst with the vicar. I could have complained but the main advantage of being dead is that you don't have to do much. That suited me perfectly.

'He's in hiding,' said Banjo. 'I think he was trying to contact you.'

A car raced past and the boy quickly cycled into the shadows alongside the three of us, before I had a chance to explain that Clive had already visited.

'It's him again,' the boy said, ducking down and pulling his bike out of sight.

'We need to get off before he sees us,' Banjo said, pulling his shirt up tight to his neck and looking around for the car. 'He'll be back I'm sure.'

'Can you get a message to Clive to get back to me?' I asked, as Tracey and I walked away, still wondering why I was yet again in the middle of chaos without any idea why. 'I need to know what is going on.'

'Of course,' said Banjo as he set off in the other direction, in whatever shadows he could find. 'I know people who will know where he is.'

'Can't you tell us anything else?' said Tracey. 'Nothing seems to add up.'

'I wish I could,' he replied and quickly walked away, not looking back. 'Just be careful,' he shouted back to us as he turned the corner, holding on to his son and his bicycle as they made their hurried way down the street.

The café was fairly busy with a few men playing Backgammon and others sitting around chewing the fat with friends, drinking thick black coffee and generally doing nothing. We weren't sure it was safe enough to go and get a drink as much as we both really wanted one.

'I could do with a large gin,' said Tracey as we looked around for any sign of danger. 'Come on, what's going to happen in broad daylight?'

It did concern me that if John was Banjo's landlord and had kicked him out, he might have taken over the café himself. But when we looked over to the bar area it was being run by a young African man with a very fluffy moustache. I suspected he was very proud of it, being the best he could manage given that his testosterone probably hadn't reached its peak.

'Well, blow me down with a feather duster,' said Tracey as she downed her gin and tonic in two mouthfuls. 'If it isn't one thing, it's another.'

The gin didn't taste like gin, more like something you'd light a barbecue with, but at least it was alcoholic. These days there are so many flavours of the spirit I'm surprised no-one has yet come up with a Nigerian version, just to add to the daunting and ever ridiculously flavoured array now available on the supermarket shelves. Insect-infused with a hint of burning rubber and an after taste of engine oil sprang to mind as I finished my drink.

I thought back to when Clive had visited. He was going to tell me about Bill when Baz flew through the door, disrupting everything – as usual.

'Just before Baz was run over, he was shouting that Clive had something of his. So, he must know who he is?' I said.

None of it was making sense and judging by the deepening frown on Tracey's now shiny face – the incident with the cream had left her with the sheen of someone who has had an exceptionally deep peel treatment – she didn't get it either.

'Why would he know Clive? He hardly knows anyone of any significance,' Tracey said. 'Maybe I need to pay him a visit.'

'Clive?' I asked.

'No silly. I need to find Baz.'

CHAPTER THIRTY-TWO

'It seems that Bill was an exceptional scientist,' said Buke. 'The head of department here said he was an alchemist, capable of great inventions and being able to convert matter from one thing to another.'

Darius and I were at the meeting Buke called at the university, where there had been a major investigation into Bill's activities. The fact he'd been undertaking research that could have had criminal implications had triggered an internal inquiry involving a range of authorities including Forensix.

Tom had been leading much of the research alongside Chinaza's sister, Paavai, who had been working at the company in recent weeks on work experience. She very much matched up to the meaning of her name, which is 'youthful woman' and I could see a strong familial resemblance, although Paavai had more of a twinkle in her eye than her older sibling. I was pleased he had someone of his own age to work with. The older woman theme didn't seem quite so right with my grandson.

Paavai and Tom had found they shared a lot of common interests and apparently had both been engrossed in Bill's case, taking personal pride in finding out as much as they could about my benefactor.

It would seem he'd spent a good deal of time in the labs, often on his own but also with classes of students. By all accounts he was a popular mentor and took time to help them with complicated chemical equations. I warmed to him as my own experience of teaching was a revelation; it is hard work and only the most dedicated, or creative, are successful. Tracey's popularity with the girls at the centre proved that.

He'd never mentioned an interest in science but then why would he in the short time we had spent together? I sort of assumed his spare time would have been taken up with food, alcohol and watching old films from the comfort of a worn out armchair. However, Tom and Paavai soon discovered he was working towards a degree at the university, all the time he'd been living in Nigeria.

'It was a shame he didn't talk to anyone else about what he was doing,' said Chinaza as she shuffled through some papers that Tom had passed over to her. She was still keen to hold pole position when it came to any investigation. 'Then we might know what he was up to and who else was involved. It seems he has left a conundrum we are going to find very difficult to unravel, even with our skills.'

Chinaza looked as if she wanted to bring the meeting to a close, but Tom blushed and fidgeted in his seat. He looked over at Paavai who nodded back shyly. Darius looked at them quizzically.

'You OK, Tom?' he asked.

Tom looked at Chinaza who wasn't paying him any attention, no doubt miffed that the object of adoration had shifted to her younger sister, and then to Buke.

'I think I have worked out what the formulas are on the memory sticks. The second one must be called 'jigsaw' because you need all three pieces to work out the puzzle ... the map being the first.'

Darius was looking at Tom with admiration and I was incredibly proud of them both. I would be delighted to tell Tom's mother when I next spoke to her how well they were getting on and how much Tom had progressed. It would probably make her spit because her plans for his university placement had been put on hold indefinitely. She'd have to find a different boast for her Zumba class friends, as her son being in-situ with her mother's black lover in Nigeria didn't quite cut it with the lycra-clad ladies who tried to avoid lunch.

'They are for making fake gemstones. The formulas convert otherwise inert compounds into materials that look like diamonds, emeralds, rubies and so on. They use a process that create colours or, in the case of the fake diamonds, remove them.'

Chinaza's lips were pursed and her eyes closing down slightly with a slightly stunned expression. She had been kind in so many ways but often ruined her good intentions with stronger desires to win at all costs. She definitely didn't like the youth of the team getting one up on her. She looked towards Tom as he continued to explain his findings, for the first time since I'd known her, I thought she looked a little shaken. She was always so confident. I couldn't help but feel a little sorry for her as I realised that everybody, even the beautiful people, have their moments of insecurity. It made me feel a whole lot better about a lot of things.

'Of course, this discovery doesn't look very good for Bill,' said Darius after a short pause, which I assumed he'd use to work out the implications of the latest discovery. 'One of Toyin's illegal activities was passing off fake jewels to international dealers. We are aware that Bill knew him and spent time with his shady contacts who were involved in various other money-making schemes – all of which go hand in hand with greed and sociopathic tendencies.'

Everyone in the room nodded as Darius made his conclusions, apart from me. I couldn't believe Bill was a crook. He didn't look or behave like someone who was after any more than he already had.

Buke looked over with a sympathetic smile.

'I'm sorry about ya friend,' she said as she came over to pat me on the shoulder. I thought it was a bit patronising. Not least because Bill wasn't a friend, he was just someone who helped at a very important time in my life. It was difficult to understand why he would do that if he was such an unpleasant character.

'There's no guarantee he was involved,' Darius said, adding more to his recent synopsis of events. 'Just because he knew how to make fake gemstones didn't mean he wanted to sell them to anyone.'

It was all quite puzzling and I hoped, at some point, we could get to the bottom of it.

I felt there was a need to clear Bill's name.

CHAPTER THIRTY-THREE

Tracey was singing loudly when she came back to the house, having been to collect the last of her things from the home she'd shared with Baz. She was amazingly sanguine about the end of her marriage dream. She'd also been cooking, which was particularly unusual. I noted she was wearing what she told me are called her 'fuck me' shoes after I'd once commented they didn't seem to have been designed for walking.

'They're for lying down in,' she'd explained at the time. To me it was a strange idea, having shoes to wear to bed. It was like a man who kept on his socks.

'I've invited Chiddy over tonight. I hope that is OK?' Tracey said as she emptied out a bag of various kitchen items, including a strange orange spoon for scooping out mangoes – which to my knowledge she never ate – and a selection of measuring cups usually reserved for the most professional of cooks. I couldn't work out why she had them, considering, but noticed they were in American measurements – so would be very useful for cooking lessons, given that they might be easier for the girls to understand than my apparently historic reference to pounds and ounces.

Darius looked over and raised his eyebrows suggesting that Tracey's new friend might be having a softening influence. I looked at the shoes and raised my own eyebrows, thinking that Tracey couldn't last long without male company. Her entire wardrobe seemed to be designed to lure men into her life.

'I've cooked for us all,' she added, lifting the lid on a pan that had been sitting on the hob since she'd gone out. I'd had a look and thought it was one of Tom's experiments. It resembled a very pale soup with lumps floating around. It also smelled of pet food, the type full of tripe and sawdust that gives dogs wind.

'Great,' I said not really wanting to contemplate what she'd put in it. 'Do you need any help?'

'This is Donna's recipe,' said Tracey as she stirred a large spoon around in the saucepan before taking a taste and then crinkling up her nose. 'I'm not sure I've got it quite right.'

I picked up a scrap of paper with a recipe scribbled on it for 'Hunter's Stew' and although I've never heard of it, was pretty sure it wasn't a Michelin star effort.

'Where is Donna anyway?' I asked as I scanned the scribbles for some clarity of what was cooking. It was worse than reading a doctor's prescription, so I gave up.

'She's going to get some of the last things she'd left behind, too, and just to check that dickhead has gone. Like mother like daughter. It's all very odd how things have turned out. '

She tried another taste of the stew and spluttered.

'Oh well, I'll add some wine. That should make it bearable,' said Tracey.

Darius took off his jacket, came over, kissed the back of my neck and indicated he was going upstairs; the cursory nod to my nether regions suggested, in an unusually coarse way that he wouldn't mind if I joined him. I forgave him on the grounds that sexual communication in a full house often had to be quick and unnoticed. Thankfully, if accepted, the next stage would be anything but.

'OK, I'm going to get a shower and get changed. Shout if you need me,' I said to Tracey as she alternately glugged in a small amount of wine to the stew and then tasted it. The amount of alcohol going in would at least kill any deadly diseases. I hoped she wouldn't shout if she needed me. I could always pretend to be deaf.

'I've got something to tell you, but it can wait until dinner,' Tracey said, opening another bottle of white wine and drinking a large swig straight down. 'If that's what you can call it. I think it might be best if we all get drunk.'

I remembered that I had a fish pie in the freezer, so we weren't going to starve. But thought it best to leave Tracey to make whatever adjustments she felt necessary to her cooking. At least it would keep her occupied for a while.

Darius took his time undressing me having locked our bedroom door and closed the curtains. We put on some music and danced naked together while the shower ran cold. I didn't care. I was lost in a rhapsody of flesh, moving against mine and bringing a tingle that expanded slowly from my toes, up my legs and through my internal organs like a creeping fire. So different from the occasional release of tension that interrupted my suburban marriage, like a power cut might interrupt a television programme.

'You are some woman, Cynthia,' said Darius, lying back with his arms above his head revealing his darkly haired armpits and glowing chest. His now flaccid penis was spent but still magnificent. I couldn't help but look at it in great wonder at its technical capabilities; down one minute and up the next. It reminded me of a trip to Newhaven to see the swing bridge in action.

The virility was certainly not something I had witnessed in my younger life and I was grateful for the opportunity in my later years.

We were just wallowing in post-coital satisfaction when a massive boom jerked us both out of our reverie.

'What the hell?' said Darius as he jumped from the bed and looked out of the window. 'Good grief, what on earth is that?'

I joined him to see a huge long base vehicle in our drive, down the side was a sign: 'Chiddy – More Bang Bang for your Buck'. The noise was the bass line of what I could only assume was one of his songs. Chiddy turned the engine off and jumped out of the driver's seat, thankfully putting an end to the noise.

Tracey ran out of the house as best as she could in her five-inch heeled shoes, skittering herself by some wild force of momentum down the drive to meet him, jumping up and aiming to be caught mid-air.

Unfortunately, Chiddy couldn't see, as he was wearing his trademark sunglasses, even though it was getting quite dark. She leapt forward and threw her arms round his neck, which took him by surprise so he stepped back then fell into the bonnet of his car – setting off the alarm – with Tracey falling on top of him; just as Donna was walking up the road with her bag.

'Oh, for God's sake, get a room,' said Donna. 'You're worse than the other two.'

Darius and I looked at each other assuming that she meant us. I thought we had been very subtle in our displays of affection, keeping them very much private.

Mind you, young people think they invented sex and we haven't got any idea about it so even a peck on the cheek is seen as overt flirtation in the eyes of anyone under thirty.

I could see Darius's swing bridge was on the move again so reluctantly pretended not to notice.

We had guests and they would probably all be repulsed at the thought of our physical activity – as most people are when they think of anyone, other than themselves or actors and porn stars, engaged in carnal gratification.

I couldn't help but pat the rising penis as it started to move northward, though, and if I knew who to write to, I would suggest its design was given an award of some kind.

Dinner wasn't any better than I thought it might have been. Tracey had found a mixture of ingredients that created a dish that could best be described as 'interesting' while she then fashioned some kind of salad using things that wouldn't normally be used in a salad.

Good job that I quite like bananas.

CHAPTER THIRTY-FOUR

Chiddy was being exceptionally attentive to Tracey and as a result of this she was in a very good mood, particularly as she told us her news. After our meeting with the investigation team she'd gone to finalise everything at her previous address, where she had come across Posh Git and Baz – both hiding themselves away as they plotted revenge on anyone they thought had wronged them.

They were surprised to see her, then claimed their lives had been ruined by her and her daughter and they were going to 'show them' what they'd given up.

'Cheeky bastards only asked for my help,' Tracey said. 'So, I've decided to do something that would definitely help' she said, holding a glass of wine in the air in an act of victory. 'It's so good to know there is justice coming in the world.'

I didn't get a chance to ask what she was planning because she was in mid-flow with her story, which was getting louder as she got more animated.

Tracey told us the two men ended up together because Posh Git had overhead conversations about Baz having valuable gemstones and had been trying, without luck, to get to London.

'Of course the arsehole wouldn't leave without trying to get something for nothing, so thought he would tap up Baz and suggest they run a business together back in the UK. Posh Git would be on a flight very soon and would have to remove his things from my house once he's evicted – you know, the one I've just bought but he doesn't know about the rest yet!' Tracey said as she tried to stifle laughter.

'But then the dishonest little shit tried to nick Baz's stash of gemstones so they got into a fight but Baz couldn't leave the house because he thinks the police are on his case and Posh Git had nowhere to go. Only those two could fuck it up quite so royally.'

I thought for a moment that Tracey looked sad, but she nodded slowly before jumping up from the kitchen chair in a grand gesture. I thought she was about to start singing a major opera or something.

'Make sure you all have a drink, people,' she said as Donna looked around for a glass so she could pour herself some wine. She was definitely improving in confidence. When she first arrived, she would wait to be asked and then apologise for having the audacity to even think she would be welcome to share anything.

'Anyway, your delightful ex-husband to be,' said Tracey to Donna, wiping tears of joy from her eyes with the sleeves of her oversized jumper 'seems to have been asked to leave the country.'

'Why is that funny?' asked Donna, drinking from a beaker she'd found on the mantelpiece. I didn't have the heart to tell her it had been there for weeks and last time I looked it had a spider making itself very much at home in the bottom. It was too big for me, or Ada, to deal with and I'd forgotten to ask Darius to take the creature outside.

'The thing is, Baz was stupid enough to tell him about his plans to run away with the gemstones and also said he was going to get the formula for making more, but was just waiting for a contact to come through with it.'

Donna's eyes lit up with signs of understanding.

'But they aren't worth anything,' she said.

'Exactly,' I said. 'But they aren't to know that – and neither are many of the unsuspecting customers that can be tricked into buying them, because the copies are so good.'

'Baz is such a con man, the fact they're worthless wouldn't stop the greedy little shit. He'd sell his own mother if she wasn't so canny at keeping one step ahead of him,' said Tracey.

'Better still,' said Tracey, 'Posh Git tried to run away with the stones but was caught at the airport trying to get an even earlier flight back to the UK with the fake gemstones. He was immediately detained before being listed for deportation – having had all his last cash taken from him in fines and a little bit of police bribery,' she added, laughing so physically that she was crying.

Having no money and no set date for his return to the UK – having missed his flight and not having enough money for another — Posh Git was forced to go back to Baz's and stay there – to wait until the authorities provided a flight as he couldn't afford one anymore.

'He's on a tag so can't go anywhere now, unless it's to get a flight outta here!' Tracey added, holding up her glass in victory. 'So, cheers everyone! The silly man will get back to what he thinks is his home to rent only to find his eviction notice waiting for him.'

'So that is the end of him, then?' I asked more hopefully than anything, forgetting to be sensitive in regard to Donna and any possible likelihood she still had any feelings for the man.

'I'm sure he'll pop up somewhere at some point,' said Donna, not looking in the slightest bit perturbed. 'He's not one to take no for an answer.'

Tracey looked at her daughter, scanning her face for any sign of distress but she seemed to be thoroughly enjoying her wine, despite the spider. Perhaps it gave an extra depth to that particular vintage.

'Anyway, that isn't my only news,' added Tracey while looking affectionately at Chiddy, who seemed to be listening to some music on his headphones and ignoring all the gossip. I had this horrible feeling she was going to announce her engagement or something equally as tacky.

'The good thing is that I know where we can find Clive,' said Tracey.

It turned out that Chiddy was still able to tap into the grapevine of his previous employers. Chiddy had found out that John had been in pursuit of Bill and Clive with a view to 'making them an offer they couldn't refuse' regarding the formula for the gemstones – and he was still in pursuit of Clive.

'Best we get to meet him then,' said Darius. 'I reckon he might just be the missing link in this story!'

CHAPTER THIRTY-FIVE

'He was never a bad man, Cynthia,' said Clive as he fell back into the armchair that still had pride of place in Bill's hut. 'He really just wanted to help people.'

Darius had found out the best days to find Clive and we had set off in good time. I nervously told him on the way that Clive had been to visit me previously and it was him who ran over Baz, but I'd not thought to say anything at the time because of all the drama. He seemed to accept my explanation, for which I was thankful. I played it down and didn't mention nearly using his ornament as a weapon.

When we got to the hut, Clive seemed to be waiting for us. It was difficult to know who knew what about whom in Nigeria. The grapevine was very active and had lots of branches. He welcomed us with open arms and seemed genuinely pleased by our visit.

Clive said he'd met Baz when he first went to the hut, after taking the map. Baz had been looking around and Clive came in and found him going through drawers and cupboards.

'He said he knew there was something going on and wanted to know what it was. So I told him. He got more and more excited which was hilarious as I knew he didn't have the brain power to put together all the information he thought he needed. It was quite good fun teasing him about how easy it was to make false jewellery and sell it for thousands,' Clive laughed.

'To be honest, even Bill hadn't quite finished his research. He was quite slow and methodical, which was why he was so good at what he was doing.'

It turned out that Baz got very animated and kept declaring that he wanted all the information available and that he would come back with Clive's share of any money for handing it over.

He told Clive he could be trusted and just wanted to make a decent living. I couldn't help admire his cheek.

'He started making all sorts of demands about formulas, so I showed him the memory stick which you found and said it contained everything he needed to know. Of course, that wasn't true and he'd never have worked out what to do anyway, but it was fun playing with him. I could see he was a complete jerk. Just as he went to grab the stick, I pulled a gun on him and he ran away like a terrified toddler,' Clive said.

The decision to go and find Clive was a good one. I was very grateful to Chiddy for telling us he'd found out Clive often went to Bill's after going to the local market when it was in town to pick up provisions. There was nothing left in the hut of any value, and Clive was particularly pleased to know that we'd eventually found the map in Pussy's cage and followed the trail to catch Baz in the office when he returned, after the coast was clear.

'Bill couldn't make the map too obvious because of the people who wanted that information. He knew you were intelligent and so trusted you to find the other clues eventually,' he said, nodding in my direction.

I felt a bit of a fraud because none of the conclusions were reached by me. Left to my own devices Pussy would still be shitting every day on top of a pile of jewels and the key to a highly valuable and desirable formula. I kept quiet and reflected in the glow of appreciation.

'Baz had been so fired up by the fact he thought I had what he wanted that he came back to the hut after seeing me go – I knew he would – and that is when you found him.'

'I didn't have you down as a gunman,' I said to him, a little concerned that I'd let this man into my home while alone. I was still slightly shaken by his comment that he'd pulled a gun, even if it had only been on Baz.

'I promise you I would never use it,' said Clive gently. 'After all the business with the politicians and John, then Bill's so-called heart attack, I knew my life was in danger. I bought it from a man in a bar in the village. I don't think it works, even if I did have any bullets for it.'

I breathed a sigh of relief. My ability to judge character had been under speculation over recent times but neither Bill nor Clive seemed like men I should be frightened of.

'Bill just loved science. It was something he wished he'd done at university but his mother got very ill when he was due to start his degree after he left school so he got a job and stayed at home to look after her until she died.'

I could feel a pang of sadness rising up to my throat. Bill's life was one of unfulfilled dreams and hopes for a future he never reached. A surge of gratitude for the many opportunities to finally live my own full life ran through my veins and I made a pledge to never forget how lucky I am.

'So where is John now, do you think?' asked Darius. 'He sounds like a very dangerous man.'

'That's why you need to get more involved and soon,' said Clive, looking towards Darius. 'He doesn't like it when he doesn't get what he wants. I believe he had Bill poisoned in a bar we used to go to. I heard he'd been asking the manager, Banjo, for months to slip something into his drink. When Banjo refused, he offered a young upstart the job of killing off Bill in return for the café business. By all accounts he was more than happy to oblige. It took a while, but John came good and now Banjo has lost his café and fears for his life while a mere boy has taken over his business.

As Darius and Clive discussed how best they could try and resolve the situation, I felt like I'd been transported from a safe and comfortable suburban life into the middle of an adventure film.

It was all rather exciting in a peculiar way.

CHAPTER THIRTY-SIX

The authorities agreed to protect Clive and, if necessary, repatriate him to the UK where he could set up home in safety. All he had to do was give as much information as he could to the police about the various scams being operated by politicians, John and others – and what they were all trying to get Bill involved with.

Forensix had agreed to host the interviews as the police, having a tendency towards fraudulent behaviour themselves, couldn't always be trusted to use information wisely or to produce an outcome with the most integrity. Once packaged up and witnessed by specialist investigators and the rest of the team – which I was pleased to note included Tom and Paavai – it would be too late for anyone to fire off any warnings.

Darius told me that in his preliminary interview, Clive had provided amazing detail for what Toyin Remy, John and others had been involved with. He'd explained that he was often seen as a 'nobody' in the proceedings, just a drinking friend of Bill's, so he'd often be privy to great secrets because no-one thought he was any threat. There were pages and pages of notes – all of which I was lucky to be able to read and digest.

Darius was kind and said he wanted me to look through them for anything I might be able to add with my knowledge of John from our kidnapping days. Of course, I didn't have any knowledge and was likely to be of no help whatsoever, but it was very kind of him to make me feel involved. Tracey was given the same opportunity – mainly as thanks to her and Chiddy for their help – but spent fifteen minutes mouthing some of the words from the pages, with her finger underlining each one as she read, and gave up.

'Reading's not for me,' she said. 'Just tell me all about it when they get to the end.'

According to Clive's accounts and memories, Toyin was a big part in negotiating the deals between gemstone suppliers and John's contacts from Africa to the UK, Europe and America. He used his position to make international deals with powerful people, picking out those who were most likely to be open to bribery and corruption. It's amazing how many there were.

'He was always throwing his weight about,' Clive told the Forensix team: 'He loved being in the limelight which is why he got involved in so many charitable and social projects. I laughed when I saw the pictures of him supporting the Outreach Centre. He couldn't look less interested but wanted to be seen to be good.'

The biggest difficulty at the start of the investigation into the major scandal was finding John. But Banjo's son, not even registering on the 'importance register', was just another kid on a bicycle. With full protection and the highest levels of guidance, the young lad was employed to help trace John by visiting and keeping an eye out at places Clive believed could be likely hideouts.

'We were often entertained by John, Toyin and others,' he'd reported. 'They were very hospitable and would provide us with vast quantities of wine and whisky in their attempts at getting us drunk. I often succumbed, not having quite the constitution of my friend Bill. It didn't matter what they got him to pour down his throat, he was never interested in joining them and never gave away any secrets. They offered money, women, power. All he wanted was to finish his degree and retire quietly without anyone bothering him. It was very frustrating for them.'

The investigation continued and it wasn't long before John was traced to a house a few miles from the town centre, believed to have been rented for government business. Banjo's son had spent some days on John's trail but independently came across Toyin driving through the town, and despite blacked out windows on the car, recognised his face from pictures on the TV.

'I just cycled in front of the car mainly because it looked important. I thought it might be someone famous and wanted to have a look,' the boy told the investigation team. 'He didn't even notice me, so I followed him to the house.'

As instructed, he didn't do anything but just mapped the journey home so the house could be accurately pinpointed. A further team were briefed to watch the property for comings and goings and when it was clear there were at least four adults inside, they sent in the police squad complete with dogs and guns.

The men were so stunned by the raid they all gave in almost immediately, after John realised that bribery wasn't going to work.

'That's a first, an African police officer not accepting a bribe,' he said to the leading investigator at the latest briefing. He was subsequently left in a room with someone who had a grudge and when officers went in a few hours later they found John covered in bruises and snivelling like a baby.

'I can't say I'd want to report the matter,' said Darius. 'There are plenty of people who would have done worse to him, including me.'

Darius had his own deeply hidden grudge against John for not only kidnapping me – and Tracey – but for setting up a scam that made Nigerian men look like they are all criminals.

'This country has a bad reputation and for good reason. It really doesn't help when some highly privileged narcissist with too much education and no empathy, turns that to their own advantage,' he said to me after I had commented that the police incident might have been a bit unprofessional.

'This is a man who has everything he needs to make a good life but wants to ruin others instead, just so he can look big and powerful.'

I'd not seen Darius properly angry before, but his blood was definitely bubbling away. I decided to take his mind off things for a while. Despite initial protests we tested out his swing bridge and it seemed to be working perfectly.

CHAPTER THIRTY-SEVEN

I felt for Bill as I listened to Darius and Tom tell Tracey, Clive and me what had been going on, over a dinner at ours. It must be difficult for him to know his close friend had been so wronged and not be able to speak up for himself, being long dead.

The fish pie came in very handy as Tracey had offered to cook again – Chiddy was on his way over for the third dinner of the week, amazing considering the variety of slops we'd been presented with. I was pleased for her that the adage 'the way to a man's heart is through his stomach' wasn't always true. Otherwise it could be a very disappointing relationship for both of them.

'We're testing all the gemstones now to make sure their composition matches the formulas we've extracted from the data on the memory sticks,' said Tom, speaking in a deeper voice than I'd heard from him before. He seemed to me to be so professional – a long way from the young boy I'd left behind before my travels. The transition was 'lost teenager' to mature adult in just a few months. His mother would hardly recognise him – something else to encourage her disapproval.

'So, the gems, they will definitely be worthless?' said Tracey and I couldn't help but notice a slight air of disappointment.

'I'd think so,' said Darius.' All the evidence suggests that Bill was focused on making fake stones, mainly as an exercise in alchemy and not for any fraudulent purpose.'

'Unfortunately, people thought he was fraudulent and that is the shame of it,' said Clive. 'But at least, thanks to you lot, his name can be cleared, and we can celebrate him for the incredible man he was.'

'Yes indeed,' said Darius. 'Also, I've had a thought and hope it might be appropriate, once all this is cleared up?'

I wondered what he'd conjured up now. His ideas were usually good and often came as a surprise. A fact I knew well and would be repeatedly grateful for.

'We seem to be doing well in terms of raising funds for the Outreach Centre through the art gallery. It's early days, but there have been more and more substantial donations coming through, mainly thanks to Alala's art gaining worldwide recognition. Also, Buke has been determined to overcome the problems caused by John and Toyin and also quite vociferous in her campaign to get the girls their education back.'

He added that there would be a meeting very shortly to discuss all the opportunities for a staged re-opening of the centre and that part of the capital fundraising would be for a science room.

'The thought is that we should dedicate it to Bill and also use some of his lesson plans to help girls understand chemistry in a practical way,' Darius said, and again I was mesmerised by his ability to pour comfort and pleasure on the feelings of all those he came across. He was practically perfect in every way. I wondered if he could be cloned for the good of womankind. Then I decided I didn't want to share him and forgot any desire to be charitable to those less fortunate.

'That's an amazing idea, really, truly amazing,' said Clive as he wiped a tear from his eye. 'Honestly, that would be so special and I know Bill would have been thrilled at such an honour. He loved teaching and everything about education.'

It was agreed that the suggestion would be rubber-stamped and moved quickly to fruition.

When it came to the meeting about the centre, Buke organised it to be held after an exhibition in the art gallery – not least to display Alala's paintings to a number of significant local people. The guests were chosen from more reliable backgrounds than those associated with Toyin and friends – and the crowd gathered cheerfully to partake in canapes, drinks and pleasant conversation.

'Those pills you gave me,' Alala said to Darius, running over from talking to a man with a very expensive looking suit, which made him look like he might be important, 'are a miracle!'

She added that since taking the ibuprofen, and getting a regular supply from a number of supporters and a local doctor, her arthritis had abated and allowed her to work every day.

'I won't say the pain has gone completely,' she said, 'but it stays in the background rather than coming up to bite me in the arse every five minutes.'

Darius laughed and I couldn't help but smile. There was another transformation thanks to my amazing lover. He'd turned my grandson into a man and this weak and pained woman into a vibrant and successful artist. He was my own alchemist, equally deserving of recognition. Not that he would take it.

Buke flowed up to us as we were talking to Alala, beaming with enthusiasm as she pointed out the artwork on the walls.

'Look at dat?' she said. 'Such beauty, such colour – we are so blessed to have found you.'

Alala blushed. 'I am blessed to have found you,' she said quietly. 'Without you, my life would be over.'

I thought she was being a bit dramatic but didn't have time to respond as Tom, Paavai and Chinaza came into the gallery, closely followed by Tony the headmaster, chattering with excitement and making their way quickly over to us.

'We need to talk to you,' said Chinaza, to Darius, uncharacteristically flustered. 'We've got something really interesting to tell you.'

'Can it not wait until the guests have gone?' I said, looking at the number of people animatedly talking to each other and participating exactly as we'd hoped. We were still waiting for Tracey and Chiddy and felt it only reasonable they should be part of any news.

'This really is very important,' said Tony. 'As you know we have been doing a lot of work on the gemstones'

'Tony's knowledge of this area of science is fantastic,' said Chinaza as she beamed a smile in his direction. I'd never seen her look so warmly towards anyone.

'Well, it's not so much my knowledge of science as the weekend job I had in a jeweller's shop. You learn a lot about what is real and what isn't,' Tony said as he flashed an equally warm look back at Chinaza.

I'd be pleased if she had a man in her life. It might remove my concerns about her apparent availability. I don't care what people say, there is something very unsettling about a single, attractive and intelligent woman when she spends a lot of time with your partner.

There was a loud noise from a staged area behind us and when we turned we could see Alala in front of a microphone with a large, white, well-dressed man holding up one her paintings.

'Um, excuse me,' she said almost unheard, so the crowd continued to chatter.

The man took hold of the microphone and boomed his voice, at which point everyone could work out he was American.

'Hey you guys, listen up. This young lady beside me is one heck of a talent. She is working her butt off to help raise money for a local school so now's your turn to support her. What am I bid for this amazing picture?'

Alala blushed as the American opened an auction and cajoled the guests into offering sums that left her aghast, holding her hands up to her mouth in shock.

'In dollars that would forty thousand, I believe,' said the American, closing the deal and handing over the painting to the wife of one of Nigeria's eminent politicians. The cynic in me wanted to know how she had that much money, but I was quickly told by Darius that her father was a very well-known businessman who left her significant funds and a private income.

'I've just agreed a deal with Alala and will be acting as her agent in the US. I've halved my usual commission fees to ensure that she, and the school, will still get a good share to help them continue. So please buy everything on sale here and tell your friends to visit our new website to buy more.'

He jumped down from the stage area to a round of applause and a grand entrance from Tracey and Chiddy who seemed to have been 'hiding' behind the stage. Chiddy swiftly helped Alala down, before she was surrounded by a group of newly-acquired fans, all keen to speak with her.

'Fabulous deal,' said Tracey as she came to join us, leaving Chiddy to sign autographs and talk to the American who claimed to have recognised him from a You Tube rapping clip. He didn't look the type to be into all the gang-style music. He looked too much like he enjoyed ironed shirts, expensive cufflinks and a few rounds of golf to be into anything heavier than a few choruses of John Denver or The Carpenters – and then only on special occasions.

'This really is great,' I said. 'At this rate Tracey and I will be back working in a few months.'

'Oh, I doubt you'll need to work,' said Chinaza. 'Not unless you want to, anyway. There's even more good news.'

I could hardly take in breath when Tony told us that the large diamond gem found in Pussy's cage was genuine.

Tracey looked at me, then I looked at her, we both let our mouths drop and then we looked at Chinaza, willing an explanation.

'Having looked at all the lists of fake gemstones the diamond doesn't exist, so we believe it was from a private collection. Maybe it belonged to his wife but wherever it came from the law states it is now yours, Cynthia,' she said.

It took me a couple of seconds to take in what I was being told.

'But it is huge, it can't possibly be real,' I said.

'It's real alright,' added Chinaza. 'It's all been checked out properly. You're a rich woman.'

Tom looked thrilled and I saw Tony and Chinaza gently link hands. Darius threw his arm round my shoulder and asked if he could be a kept man from now on.

'We are talking hundreds of thousands of dollars,' added Chinaza to emphasise again what I'd inherited.

I thought back to all the strange circumstances of my kidnap, escape, finding Darius and then my life just getting better and better.

Maybe there was a God?

CHAPTER THIRTY-EIGHT

Everyone wanted to go out and celebrate and it seemed like a good idea, but I was stunned. Tracey was jumping about truly pleased for me and it was only then I realised if it hadn't been for her, we might never have found the jewel in the first place. In fact, I might not even be here at all.

'We need to share it,' I said to Tracey, between her shrieks of joy and determination to suck the rather large lips off Chiddy. 'You helped find it and it's finders' keepers where I come from.'

'Hey, keep some for later,' Chiddy said, as Tracey lunged in for another kiss. 'These boys got plenty of that to do yet!' He laughed his deep laugh and Tracey looked like a child who had been told they can't have their presents until Christmas – in July.

'Nah, it's yours Cynth. Bill wanted you to have it. I got my house now and my daughter back. I don't need anything else.'

I was humbled by her generosity. It would be easy to think she was the type of woman who would happily take anything if it was free, but I knew Tracey better than that. She could be starving in a corner and share her last crust of bread with you.

'Well, how about we do something really good with it?' I said to Tracey. 'Like get the Outreach Centre up and running again, using some of the money from selling the diamond.'

'Now that sounds like an idea,' said Tracey. 'But with one condition.'

I wondered what her stipulation was going to be. I just hoped it didn't involve anything that might aggravate my back or cause my grandson to turn away from me in shame.

'You need to spend some of it on yourself, a bit more on your man, and then some on your family. You can't just plough it all into the centre. That will soon run itself with local support.'

Darius nodded his agreement.

'It's true. Once local organisations realise the success of educating our girls, they will want to be involved. It is all good PR. Good thinking, Tracey.'

They did that 'fist bump' thing between them and it seemed like it was a deal. Wishing to retain some control I countered that Tracey also needed to do something for herself and her family.

'Well I do need to find a bloody good hairdresser,' she said. Her hair had grown back but it was a variety of shades of brown, yellow and white and was far curlier than I'd ever seen it. 'And I'd like to set Donna up in business somehow.'

Part of the celebrations was a girls' trip to the market, firstly to find Tracey a hairdresser and also to visit Banjo who, since John's arrest, had managed to get his café back.

Donna was excited about the opportunity of running a business and had suggested hair and beauty until she took a look at her mother and realised it could be fraught with danger.

'Maybe I should run a café or something,' she said as we took our seats in Banjo's. He overheard and came rushing over to our table.

'You thinking of going into competition with me?' he said, half joking but also with a furrowed brow. 'It's so good to see you ladies and thank you so much for getting me the café back.'

We explained that it was more to do with his son and very little to do with us, that we were just doing our best to stop John and his cronies in their tracks.

'We never thought it would all be so complicated,' I said to him, noting how more relaxed he was without gangsters trying to take every penny off him or threaten the lives of his children.

Banjo explained that the soft moustached barman had been arrested for the suspected murder of Bill and, although I'd heard this might have been a possibility, it was painful to think of such a nice man ending his life in such a nasty way. I just hoped it wasn't too awful and he slipped away thinking he'd drunk too much.

'Now, what can I get you ladies?' he asked. We went through a list of things we'd like starting at a cold beer and because that wasn't available, ending up with a warm wine. There was little food either, just some type of fried snack which I suspected could be insect-based and a few almost-sweet biscuits. The type they used to give you in hospital if you felt sick after being put to sleep with gas.

'Not much of a menu,' said Tracey. 'You'd better watch out or Donna will be taking all your business!'

Banjo explained that the young barman had fallen out with all the suppliers, stolen the fridges and oven and trashed everything else.

'I still don't have the money to replace what I need but I hope to get there soon, and we will be the greatest café again.'

Donna had been looking at her feet and avoiding eye contact with the café owner then she suddenly jolted her head up, her eyes sparkling and colour coming to her nearly-always white cheeks.

'I hope you won't be offended or anything,' she said quietly. 'But do you think you might like a business partner. One who could replace all these things and help you back on your feet?'

Banjo looked at Donna for a few moments not taking anything in. I willed him to respond as I didn't think she would have the courage to offer again.

'But how?' he asked. 'I can't afford to give too much away as I have so little. Any partner would take a share and there isn't enough for one, let alone two.'

'I would only take profits on what I bring into the business,' said Donna. 'I will make sure it has so much more revenue that you will benefit. I don't want anything other than what I can earn for myself. But I'll buy all the equipment and we can both use it.'

I'd never seen her so animated. Life away from Posh Git certainly suited her.

'Anyway,' I said. 'If it hadn't been for you and your son, we'd never have found John and his cronies so we'd all still be worried about what our future held. It's the least you deserve.'

Tracey added one of her conditions, and that was that Banjo found us some cold beers – even if it meant going into the one and only hotel to buy them at a premium rate. She handed over a wedge of cash and we agreed to look after the café until he came back.

'I think we have had rather a good week,' she added, leaning back on her chair and taking a cigarette out to smoke.

On this occasion I took no notice.

CHAPTER THIRTY-NINE

The court case started the same day the school re-opened and there was a real sense of justice floating in the air.

Chiddy hosted the music and Tracey danced around him, offering drinks and canapes and being effusive in her enthusiasm for the school. Chiddy's new single had done really well and he had set up a stage, bought lots of different music instruments and a sound system and promised to bring lots of musicians to the centre to teach. He would be donating a percentage of his royalties for that specific purpose.

Darius was at his best, relaxed, hospitable and proud. He chatted easily to everyone. The girls, their mothers and guests were all there, as well as a few new sponsors who were keen to come on board now Toyin and his cronies were out of the way.

Alala's paintings adorned the walls of the classrooms and gave a vibrancy and colour suggesting a whole new life for the centre, while she seemed relaxed and comfortable talking to the guests.

'Hey, guess what?' said Tracey as she came up to me with a mouthful of pastry that crumbled and sprayed in my direction as she spoke.

'What?' I replied, as I wiped off pieces of food from my rather sophisticated, even if I say so myself, little black dress.

'Got a call from Posh Git, he couldn't understand why he couldn't get back into his house!'

Tracey told me she'd arranged to have all the locks changed and installed a tenant through an old school friend who had become an estate agent.

'He was bloody furious!' she said, laughing and spraying a bit more pastry. 'Particularly when he found out that the storage room where all his stuff was moved to had a leak, and rats!'

I was pleased she'd got the better of the nasty little man, not just for her sake but also for Donna, who, with Banjo as her new partner, had taken on the catering for the event with such gusto and enthusiasm it was a joy to witness. The food was excellent, and they were fusing their ideas well. Not only that, I overheard one of the sponsors asking for a price list for the various business events they hosted – so it would seem they were on their way. When I spotted Banjo giving Donna a kiss on the cheek in a quiet moment, I'm sure I saw her blush.

'Hopefully you won't hear from him again,' I said, wondering if the same could be said of Baz. The police didn't seem that interested in him, as Buke's son, he was likely to be given some dispensation – even though she would never ask for it.

Buke looked like a different woman. The weight of shame and embarrassment at her links with Toyin were lifted and her rightful place as a highly respected member of the community was regained.

I was basking in a sense of deep satisfaction when I realised Tom hadn't arrived yet. He said he and Paavai would be late to the party as they would be giving most of the evidence to the court against John and his gang. Darius had delegated the job to them, under Chinaza's guidance.

Just as the music was getting louder and voices more animated, the three of them turned up and rushed immediately over to Chiddy, who turned down the volume and handed Chinaza a microphone.

'If everybody wouldn't mind stopping the celebrations for just one moment, I think you will all want to hear what we have to say,' she said, looking at Tom and Paavai and smiling.

Darius came over to me and slipped his hand round my waist. I felt warm and safe and incredibly lucky as I looked around at what had been achieved.

'The court has just reached its verdict and we can be confident in saying that we are highly unlikely to ever see John, Toyin or any of their sidekicks for a very long time,' she continued. 'Not unless you're into prison visiting.'

A huge cheer went up and Banjo popped a bottle of

something fizzy, sending the cork flying through the air and landing straight between the eyes of one of the new sponsors. He was a large man in every sense with a booming voice and a big personality. Quite frightening if angered I suspected. He froze for a moment and looked directly over at Banjo.

The silence in the room was almost deafening and I thought I might pass out from holding my breath.

Then the man let out a burst of laughter, pointed at Banjo and went over to shake his hand.

'Good hit, my man! I should take you out hunting, you're a better shot than me,' he said, rubbing his forehead where a small lump was starting to form.

'Let's get on with the party,' he added, indicating to Chiddy that he wanted the music back up and then to Banjo that he'd like another drink.

I let out my breath and allowed my stomach to relax. I'd been holding it in for most of the day as little black dresses don't suit a belly that's anything other than flat. Even my Spanx couldn't contain the evidence of four babies and a penchant for salted peanuts on their own.

Darius pulled me to him.

'I think we can say that all turned out rather well,' he said, as he kissed me very lightly on the neck, I thought I might faint.

'What shall we do with the money from the diamond, then?' I asked him as we sipped more sparkling wine, having been kept very well topped up by Donna on her rounds.

'It's yours to do with as you wish, but if I'm allowed an opinion maybe it's time we took a trip to England?'

He cocked his head to one side waiting for an answer.

'We?' I said, my tummy starting to turn in a mix of excitement, nerves and possibly too many salmon-topped blinis.

'I think it's about time you introduced me to your family,' he said. 'Seeing as we're an item.'

'Oh God,' I thought. '*Mavis is going to have a bleedin' field day.*'

ACKNOWLEDGEMENTS

With thanks to:

There are always so many people to thank on the journey to publication, not least my very supportive husband,family, friends and followers who have encouraged me to write this book.

However, particular thanks to my 'old mucker' from journalism days, Kathy Lewis, for her invaluable help in reading through the first draft. I would also like to thank the ever-patient and highly professional Paul Swallow for completing a full edit and finding lots of faults, many of which I hope have been eradicated.

Then there is the lovely Rachel De Cock who has produced the fabulous illustration for the cover – giving Pussy exactly the glamour she deserves.

There have been many others offering their good wishes, expressing their anticipation and generally wondering if I'll ever get the bloody thing written. It's taken four years so I just hope it's worth it.

Thank you all.

Cynthia is a sixty-year-old widow who takes up with a 38-year-old black lover. When she receives a 'Dear Beneficiary' email she believes it to be from Darius who has gone back to Nigeria – and decides to follow him out there. The hilarious tale takes her through a journey involving kidnap, rescue, car chases and life with Tracey, her cell mate and eventual friend in need.

Price £7.99
Available from www.bobaloobooks.co.uk
or Amazon.co.uk

ALSO BY JANET KELLY

Doris Morris is an illustrated children's book aimed at four to six year olds and tells the story of Doris the cat who lives with the Morris family. In the first of the series, The Invasion of the Neighbours, Doris has to deal with Gangsta and Lizzie, local cats who come in and trash the house – getting Doris into trouble. Thankfully Amy and Ted are to hand to put things right.

Price £12.99
Available from www.bobaloobooks.co.uk
or Amazon.co.uk